Unfixed

Amy L. Sauder

Cover design by My Lan Khuc Valle (LaolanArt)

Edited by Kate Yelland

Author photograph by Nan Doud (www.nandoud.com)

Fonts: Briaroak Shire, Chunk Five, EB Garamond, Elzevier Caps, Kramer, & Newscast

Readers on *Unfixed*:

"Ladies and Gentlemen, it is my joy to prepare you for the whimsical whirlwind that swept me up when I first followed the characters along the twisted tracks of their hidden histories; watching often in excitement, other times in horror, and most commonly in a mixture of both as the quirky cast of *Unfixed* struggle to unravel the mysteries of the past in order to establish a safer, happier future. This book kept me riveted to the pages and to the twisted fates of each broken, beloved character I met."

~ Jennifer Esther Wieland, writer, artist, videographer, and all-around creative

"Virginia Woolf meets Edgar Allan Poe in Amy L. Sauder's stories. Her writing is layered and makes me think about life, love, family, and goals. As I read, I think, *there's more to this story…*"

~ Kim Kouski, author of *Hidden Secrets* and *The Last Maúl*

"*Unfixed* is indeed 'somewhere circus' from beginning to end. The effortless balance between past and present greatly resembles the balance between the three rings of a circus. With a winding narrative that often hangs somewhere between twisted fairytales like *Pinnochio* and dark whimsy such as Tim Burton, *Unfixed* is sure to not only delight you, but keep you on the edge of your seat."

~ Megan Fatheree, author of *Codex, The Half-Shape Child*, and the *For Such a Time* series

*For the stories that don't end
when you fall apart.*

Prologue

RAND STORIES OFTEN BEGIN with the most inconsequential of circumstances. For instance, a silly exchange with a stranger in a doctor's office can propel a tale that doesn't quite fit that intro; even fantastical tales can start with the mundane.

Mrs. Trencher approached the receptionist while Mr. Trencher found a seat comfortably away from a jittery young man waiting his turn. The doe-eyed girl—a burgeoning adult, really, with too naive a look about her to go by the descriptor—slowly made her way to the seat next to Mr. Trencher.

"Trencher here," Mrs. Trencher told the receptionist. "For checking over after...a complication...last time we were here."

"Yes ma'am, I recall," the lady said with robotic cheerfulness. "The doctor will be ready for you shortly."

Mrs. Trencher went and sat by the girl, taking great care to keep the fingerprint-free glass coffee table between her and the nervous youth. He sat hunched over in the waiting room—eyes darting about, noting every inconsistency, every blemish of the room. His demeanor suggested that he had arrived in hostile territory rather than a costly doctor's office, yet here he was.

"What are you here for?" His voice projected more confidence than his form.

Mrs. Trencher clutched her handbag tightly, resisting the urge to fidget in response to his energy. She was positive he had spoken to her, and she glanced in his direction to assess him more adequately.

"My daughter," she responded with an air of indifference—not at the content of the exchange, but at the idea of conversation at all. He looked toward the girl, who pretended to be unaware of the conversation, focusing intently on the portrait of a man above instead.

With a jerk of the head toward the girl, he turned toward Mrs. Trencher and asked, "What is she here for?"

"To be fixed, of course. Dr. Wise will determine what is wrong with her and fix her."

"I see."

Mrs. Trencher averted her eyes to the door, then leaned back around the girl to see Mr. Trencher. She gave him an emotionless smile and exhaled.

"My name is Sylas."

Mrs. Trencher looked across the table towards the young man—Sylas apparently—and replied, "Sylas, I hope you will find everything well with yourself today when you see the doctor."

"I don't know," Sylas scanned the room, rather than looking at the family he spoke with. "He requested to run some tests, see if he can figure me out. Why not let him try, ya' know? We'll see."

Mrs. Trencher nodded.

"So the doctor hasn't figured out your daughter yet."

"Don't you worry, I'm sure the doctor can fix you fine."

"Oh, well that's not what I meant. I don't need fixin'. I mean, I have this, uh, this ability I guess you'd call it. To see how things work."

Sylas caught a quizzical look from the girl before she returned to her study of the framed waterfall on the wall.

"I see," Mrs. Trencher said doubtfully. She had no idea what Sylas was trying to convey.

"See how things work?" Mr. Trencher interjected. "What do you mean?"

"I just do," Sylas replied. "Don't know how. Just the way I am."

"And you could look at our girl? See how she works?"

The girl looked at Mr. Trencher, then at Sylas. This time she kept her eyes on him, awaiting his response.

"Well, yeah, sure I could—I mean, I am. I don't turn it off."

"What?" Mrs. Trencher said as she eyed the men disapprovingly. "No offense, Mr. Sylas, but we don't need a circus trick. Dr. Wise is studying her just fine."

"I am sure he is."

"It wouldn't hurt to try," Mr. Trencher muttered.

It didn't take long for Mrs. Trencher to imagine her husband at a dinner party recounting a tale of magic that could heal her daughter that she had been too superstitious to refuse. Being neither superstitious nor eager to be the joke of a dinner party, Mrs. Trencher decided there would be no harm in showing him how silly a notion this Sylas trick was. "Mr. Sylas, what do you think?"

"Just Sylas, not Mr. Sylas. It's my first name." Sylas glanced over to Mrs. Trencher, then scanned the rest of the room. "What do you mean, 'what do I think'?"

Mrs. Trencher resisted an eye roll and said, "Work your magic. Here is my daughter." She motioned toward the girl. "Look at her and explain her inner workings."

Sylas glanced at the girl in the midst of his cycle of glancing at everything else in the room. "Well, there's a lot there."

"Obviously. How is she broken?"

"I never said I could tell that. There are too many layers. I can see that layers work and layers don't, but it's too many to keep up with in most people, most objects even. And sure, she doesn't work good in some ways just as she works fine in others."

Mrs. Trencher twitched her lips towards a frown. "What?"

"Look, that chair works good, in fact, every chair here works good besides a couple layers somewhere. That artwork works pretty good, too. But the pen by the receptionist, that doesn't work good. The magazine rack don't work good. I don't work good. You or any other human doesn't work all the way good; because of all the layers something is gonna not work. And so, your girl, she doesn't work good either. That's how it is."

"Well you certainly *don't* work good at all. I knew you couldn't help. Good luck getting better, Mr. Sylas." Mrs. Trencher nodded his direction without ever looking and stepped outside, indifferent to the door shutting behind her without her family following.

"Well there's something else I'm not," the girl said. "Working good. I'm not working good."

"Whatever that means." Mr. Trencher stood, shook his head, and followed Mrs. Trencher. As the door closed behind him, Mrs. Trencher cast a disapproving glance through the opening. "I knew there was no point to it."

Meanwhile, inside the girl was still curious to know more. "You're a circus man."

"Not with the circus," Sylas corrected. "Just...different."

"What do different people do, other than join the circus?" the girl retorted.

"Apparently visit Dr. Wise." Sylas let out a cautious laugh as he observed the nurses' station.

"Hmm," the girl looked at the ceiling in denial.

Mrs. Trencher, tired of waiting outdoors and realizing that her daughter had no intention of following, entered the building again and approached the nurses' station. Mr. Trencher entered sullenly as well, but remained by the door.

Sylas followed them with his gaze, then returned to watching the girl, while Mrs. Trencher began speaking to the receptionist. "We need to reschedule. Now isn't a good time..."

"What brings you here instead of the circus then?" Sylas slumped back in his chair and leaned his head back.

"Death, actually," the girl retorted. "I recently resurrected from my second death, thank you very much for your concern."

Sylas ignored her miffed reaction and instead responded to the content of her words with a laugh. "Second death. And you wanna be fixed? Seems to me everybody else needs a fixing." When the girl didn't respond or react, Sylas asked, "What's your name?"

The girl jerked her head down and furrowed her brows. "Julia. Why?"

"An exchange of names is common amongst acquaintances," Sylas replied.

"I thought we're different," Julia faked a laugh. "Why act on what is common?" Sylas shrugged and tapped his foot, returning his attention to every occurrence in the room.

Julia decided that the conversation was finished, then wondered if Sylas had already come to that conclusion. To affirm the dialogue's end, Julia said, "I should leave," and exited quickly with one last glance at Sylas—the not-circus man—on the way out. Mr. Trencher nodded his goodbye to Sylas, who looked over only to see that Julia had already left. Mrs. Trencher exited the room not long after without acknowledgement of Sylas's presence.

And so, Julia—the girl that now has a name—with a passing word from a boy who was as different as she, had an idea planted in her head of where people like her might belong. Not a doctor's office to be fixed. But somewhere else. Somewhere circus.

But the characters in this story don't know this beginning that you and I do. In fact, who you'll meet next doesn't know much at all. Bear with him as he tries to put the pieces together, and watch the story unfold from a different place than the beginning. It's up to the characters in the tale to determine if this story starts at the end, or the middle.

CIRCUS OF STRANGE MARVELS VANISHES IN FLAMES

After a vast fire in the barley fields last night, "The Great Geppetto's Circus of Strange Marvels" leaves little left to see. Several prominent circus acts have vanished, leaving behind only a few historic circus wagons. The investigation into these events is still underway.

The circus that once had small attendance attracted vast crowds on its final night with rumors of a new act like never seen before. Thankfully, with the prompt attention of those on scene and our community's emergency response team, only minor injuries were sustained.

We have reached out to numerous hired hands at the circus for comment. None have responded at this time. There is speculation that the new rumored act would be performed by the daughter of Mr. And Mrs. Philip and Tabitha Trencher. They were not available at their home for comment.

Dr. Viel, who owns the property, thanks the town for their careful response measures. "The historic circus wagons will remain as they are, as a reminder to the community that not all is lost. That beneath all this 'magic' hype, the true magic exists in historic preservation, in scientific inquiries, and in an ordinary life."

Is this a magical enchantment, or a circus trick gone awry? Officials assure that all is "normal."

"Our emergency response team provides great service to this community as always," Chief Rodgers states. "This was a typical fire response, nothing more. The community will carry on with this fresh reminder that fire safety practices are critical for each and every one of us."

1

In Case You Forget

Clue 1: The rise and fall of a legendary magical circus, linked to the abandoning of a haunted mansion. All of this happened at the time of the darkness.

 M...UHM...MAX."

It still doesn't feel right. Slipping from my lips and traveling to the back of my mouth 'til I swallow the lie. I don't want to lie. I just don't know how to say the truth. And the truth wouldn't get me into the mansion.

The lady blocking the doorway has frumpy clothes, a misshapen bun piled atop her head, and an index finger jabbing the air. I don't think she'd appreciate any story I tell, let alone my own.

So I try another lie. "I'm an aspiring journalist, doing simple upkeep here while investigating the vanishing Trenchers."

"Uh huh." It's clear she's not convinced.

Maybe I should try the offensive. "What are you, a squatter?"

"Don't you even," she barks. "I won't have it. You do your thing, I'll do mine. And steer clear." She begrudgingly stands aside to let me enter.

I'm not one to up and believe squatters, but she acts like she owns the place. That mystery could wait. For now, I need to explore the house. On second thought, *house* is too simple a term for what this is. I walk the halls, the grand sweeping staircase, the empty dining hall, master suite and ballroom. What remains of the furniture and decor is stiff, lifeless. The absence of keepsakes, portraits, or art—evidence of a life lived here—make the place eerie and forlorn. I'd almost agree it's haunted. Little dust has collected; it's all too recent. It doesn't take long for everything to change—small events escalate to big ones until you can't even recognize yourself.

I try jotting notes—meaningless notes, hoping I'll find the key to break the story wide open. But there is really nothing to write until...

I approach a small bedroom. I creak open the door and would you believe it. After rooms right and left meticulously cleared of all property, this one is completely furnished, but more than that. Someone had lived here. A girl, teenager perhaps, though a doll glaring at my intrusion makes me wonder. This room must be the key. The answers have to be here.

2

Clue 2: Fully furnished lived-in room, in the abandoned mansion. Check it out!

 WALK TO THE LACE-COVERED BED—simple yet elegant— and turn the doll face-down. I know it's stupid, but those eyes—considering all I remembered, the gaze somehow seems too real. The curls still protrude from the bed, but I can search in peace now. I walk to the desk and open the drawers. Though the absent girl seems organized, right on top lays a crumpled piece of paper. Crumpled, yet saved. That should mean something—strong negative emotions, yet valued. Maybe? I open the simple paper, an artificially aged yellow color with warm bold red wording—*The Great Geppetto's Circus of Strange Marvels*. It had to be connected. A small sticky note covers the smaller lettering, with handwritten scribbles that read *she needs you*.

Who needed her?

"'Something, isn't it?" The frumpy woman barges in.

"I thought the circus might be related."

She sniffs. "'Course ya did. Doesn't everybody. Thought she belonged there, ya know. Thought it was the answer to everything."

"Why would someone need a child, let alone this one?"

The frump barks a laugh. "The place is frozen in time, I admit.

She may have been naïve, sheltered, quick to trust like a kid being offered candy. But despite all that, she was grown, ready to be off on her own, if anyone would accept it and release their clutches."

I squirm at the familiarity. "How would you know?"

"That circus, though"—she ignores my question—"really was 'strange.' Even Julia Trencher's abnormalities weren't enough to prepare her for her first visit."

I want to knock some sense into her. "The mysticism is hype. Masterful illusion at best, likely just rumor mill exaggerations." I pause, tossing the paper back in the drawer before plopping on the bed as far from that creepy doll as possible. The frump clambers onto the desk, her hair bobbling precariously with the strain.

"No matter. Investigators listen to all sides, even the rumor mill ones. Zip up and listen."

One

THE STORY STARTS WHERE there were no spectators, only speculation. Perhaps after Julia threw together her haphazard pack of belongings and ran from her posh yet haunted life, she sat at a coffee shop to see many customers enter and exit, many drinks purchased and emptied, many messied tables cleaned multiple times. She'd sit there wondering if she had left one space she didn't fit only to find there were no other spaces to belong either. She'd wonder if she'd turn back to where she had been; but she'd stubbornly sit, immovable as stone, refusing to accept that fate.

And maybe fate or destiny or some god did guide one's actions, for eventually she would notice a bulletin board of advertisements along the wall. You can envision her perusing each and every ad in hopes of one being worth her while, reading each word thoroughly, taking each grand claim to heart. But none stirred her spirit until...one did.

Julia, not removing her eyes from the page for more than an instant, moved to a seat. She stroked the paper, admired the bold colors and enchanting design.

Now understand that Julia did not have to read more than a word to know that this advertisement was the one she had been looking for. She knew in a moment where she would be headed when she left the coffee shop. Yet she could hardly believe it and took in every portion of the design quite readily. *The Great*

Geppetto's Circus of Strange Marvels stood out in brilliant red print against the artificially yellowed paper. Underneath, and offset by a simple gold design, was a vague description meant to pique a reader's interest: *Come One, Come All, To Behold the Eerie Marvels, the Mystery of the Peculiar, the Unfathomable Unknown.* At the very bottom of the page was the poor equivalent of an address. *At the outskirts of town, amongst fields of barley.*

It was a simple advertisement, perhaps even more catching for its failed attempt at grandeur. Still the word "circus" was all that Julia needed to read to know that she would be finding this location.

Meanwhile, the Trencher household—no longer containing one Julia Trencher—discovered their daughter's disappearance. Uncertain if worry was necessary or expected, Mr. and Mrs. Trencher found ways of occupying themselves. Mr. Trencher contented himself with looking at every book on his shelves, certain there was some book that could captivate his eyes if not his mind. Mrs. Trencher chose to retrieve the doll from the dinner table and place it on her daughter's bed. She then sat waiting, staring at the doll's eyes. Mrs. Trencher couldn't help but wonder if the doll knew where Julia had run off to—what secrets could such a curious doll hold?

When Julia Trencher had not returned once night had come and gone, Mr. and Mrs. Trencher still sat in their respective locations, neither willing to admit that this daughter may have abandoned them like the law of sowing and reaping.

3

 DON'T BELIEVE HER. "How do you know this?"

"Technically that part I don't," she reiterates. "No spectators to how she came upon the circus, but I can imagine."

I wave the flyer at her, doubtless the exact flyer she'd referenced in her tall coffee shop tale. "You're just making up stories from a piece of paper. And not even accurately; clearly there's a message that brought her there."

"Sure, it's circumstantial at best." She shrugs. "You probably don't believe this place is haunted neither."

"Why would I?"

She smiles. "They say the ghost of a soul travels with the Trenchers, strikes deep into their bones like a curse."

I groan. "Fairy tales... You're just trying to scare me out of here. It's not working."

She sighs.

"Besides, how would you know?"

She claims she was a housekeeper for the Trenchers, Julia's one confidant that could share snippets of the circus tale. And of course I don't buy it; but I'll take what answers I can get, credible or otherwise.

I go out on a limb, thinking of the note on the flyer. "Who needed her at the circus?"

She shakes her head. "My story to tell."

Then, just to irk me I'm sure, she refuses to tell it. After much persistence on my part, she demands, "What are you really doing here? Don't throw out that investigative journalist crap idea again."

I'm not falling for it. "You won't even tell me who you are.""

"As if Max is your real name," she scoffs.

"And what do I call you?"

She harrumphs. "Whatever you fancy."

"Fancy" it is then. I don't know what this Fancy wants or where she came up with the story, but I'll have to keep her on my radar in case.

4

Clue 3: "The Great Geppetto's Circus of Strange Marvels" crumpled flyer with note saying "She needs you"—found in Julia Trencher's room.

OTHING ELSE IN THE ROOM catches my eye. I can't get Fancy's story out of my head though, that frump of a woman who thinks she owns the place. How would she know the tale? Lies, so many lies. But I would uncover the truth.

I chuck a pack on my shoulders—notebook, pen, a meager lunch of berries and crackers (the only portable food in the grand kitchen). Fancy seems to have the kitchen in use though. Even now a pot of water boils and the scent of a hunk of meat wafts through the air. I'll have to snag some of that later. That probably makes her the world's best roommate and me the worst.

I look at the directions on the circus flyer. "By fields of barley." So precise.

Fancy it is. "Fancyyyy!" I yell through the haunt.

"Uhm, Maaax," she yells back. What a pal. She approaches from around the corner.

"What ya doin'?" I try to be nonchalant.

"Minding my own business." She grimaces at the pot of boiling water. "You messing with my food?"

"How 'bout you take me to the scene of the crime?" I wave the flyer at her. "Fields of barley, what the heck is that supposed to mean? That's no sort of directions. No wonder it's a flop of a circus."

Fancy shakes a crooked finger at me. "Anyone 'round here knows there's only one place with fields of barley. Matter of fact, out-of-towners see the barley on their way into town, too. What are you, some kind of nitwit?"

"Just...take me."

Fancy gets off her high horse I guess. She tromps out the front door with a grumble after turning off the boiling pot. Drives a-ways east, 'til there is no more town left, and sure enough, only a barley field. A scorched barley field. Nothing to see here, folks. The smell of ashes and smoke still hangs in the air. Further over some barley remains intact, waving toward the circus that is no more.

In the midst of the scorched earth and the waving grass, there is a clearing atop a small slope. The circus. Or all that is left of it. I race ahead of Fancy to get a look.

A firm bed of dirt packed in from all the crowds it hosted sits artificially higher than the soft plowed field next to it. It's the opposite of a ditch, an incline to climb from sustenance to something...more. At least, that's probably how people were supposed to read the situation. I just see it as a waste of dirt.

"It's magic ground, they say," she either forewarns or scoffs, I can't quite tell.

"It's empty." That's an exaggeration, because it's clearly not empty. Before me in the distance are five wagons, unscathed, untouched by the destruction around it. But somehow it's underwhelming. Not a lick of evidence of anyone traipsing around here, performing here...or vanishing here. No tents or sign of course, but not even the occasional fallen popcorn, cigarette butt, footprint. As if nothing happened. As if it had been erased.

"Forgotten as it should be." Her wording feels eerie. Forgotten.

"No," I say. "There has to be more." I walk up to the wagons.

I regret referring to the wagons as underwhelming. Up close they have a commanding presence, a towering presence. Fairy tale tableaus on the side introduce whimsy. The first hint of "strange marvels." I hesitate, then approach the first. I feel as if I am being watched, scrutinized; as if I am trespassing, and I'm not sure if that is from the character on the side of the wagon, from Fancy's penetrating gaze, or from general paranoia. Either way, I suck it up and knock on the first wagon. Of course, no response. I try to open the door, but it's locked. Nothing to see here, folks.

"Soooo eager," she frowns. "Julia, you'd do well to be more like her. Skittish. Still somehow rushed into things too fast, but hey, it was 'destiny' or 'fate' I suppose."

It was my turn to scoff. I don't believe in hauntings or magic, and I'm not too sold on fate either. Life is what it is. But Fancy isn't finished. She has to tell her side.

Two

HIS ISN'T MAX'S STORY. Max has entered the middle of a story and is trying to find the beginning.

You and I both know this isn't Fancy's story. Even Max suspects it.

But this isn't Julia's story, either. Julia entered the middle of a story, too.

(And really, what is the beginning of a story but the middle of another? We are all mid-story, entering into the middle of other stories, and leaving stories hanging with no end...but that gets into the question of if there is an end to a story, which is a different discussion for a different story I suppose.)

And so, we're going to zoom out, beyond Max's tale alone, beyond only Julia's tale, beyond Fancy's retelling. We'll follow Max and Julia of course, but we'll see pieces of the story that not Max, not Fancy, not Julia, or any one person could know. We'll sneak into moments we have no business in to see glimpses of stories beyond the page.

But here, we start with Julia and her piece of this story, because that's where we left off...

Julia found the fields of barley that the flyer had referred to quite easily. Really, crops were only kept on one side of town, and then the red and gold tents stood out against the natural landscape to the few passersby. The space was rather smaller than expected—a midsized tent that could hold no more than a dozen benches for an audience, surrounded by a spatter of smaller tents. The small tents alternated between red and gold, while the middle tent was striped with both colors. A row of dilapidated circus wagons peeked out from behind the main event as if to say "Here I am."

Julia sighed as she approached the entrance, a mixture of relief and nerves.

Large banners of each act welcomed the crowds—or, in this case, the few stragglers—as you walked the path toward the entrance. *Geppetto's marvelous puppets*, each proclaimed in bold print.

The first one promised a peek into your future or past, with a closeup of a bright blue ball and deep eyes gazing into it. The second depicted breathtaking acrobatics as a young beauty hung precariously from a trapeze. And the last, a haunting shadow of a man spitting flames from his mouth. Julia wondered what her banner would be. Nothing as bright as the acrobat, nor as beckoning as the fortune. Perhaps it best fit alongside the flames, an eerie pile of bones peeking out from the gloom.

She was so enraptured by the cast of characters displayed above that she hardly noticed the ticket booth. A bright red and gold circus sign greeted her as she approached, assuring the big top show would begin at 6pm and the individual acts would open soon.

Home, she thought, uncertainty still hovering like a mist around her. Still she pulled a crisp bill from her pack and paid for entry, studying the man a little too long as he handed her a ticket. Was he a freak like her? To her eyes, he seemed as typical as any person she encountered anywhere else. She moved along, staring back at his glum figure a moment longer before facing forward.

The circus wasn't quite abandoned at this point in the story, but there were few gawking spectators. Julia didn't notice, though. She was too busy studying the woman selling popcorn, the man pointing the way to a small tent to some group asking questions, the bumbling fellow with a large name tag that said *Sullivan* who was picking up a bit of trash that had fallen to the side, and the general hum of meager circus activity from seemingly ordinary folks who found their way here. Were they like her, too? While the acts hadn't begun, each tent was open for exploring. Julia ducked into the closest tent to see the circus life, stroking the silky material with her fingers for the briefest moment.

No other patrons occupied this tent. Julia's face went pale at the sight before her, realizing the advertisement of "strange marvelous puppets" was quite an apt description. A lady sat slumped over, head and arms resting on the wooden desk before her, long dark curls covering half her face. Strings tied at her wrists rose up and disappeared through the roof of the tent. A painted foam ball rested in one hand, and her eyes stared unblinking at the wonders within.

Uncertain what protocol would dictate in such a situation, Julia began to back out of the tent, then paused, and stepped forward again. Finally, after seconds passing without incident, Julia turned and exited the tent. She wasn't certain if she was prepared to enter another tent right away.

The people out here seemed so different from the acts, and she wondered if they were, or if it was some magic trick. And if it was some magic trick, was it the magic of looking ordinary or the magic of looking extraordinary? The woman continued selling her popcorn, the man was chatting with another group of customers, and "Sullivan" was picking up that same piece of trash still as if no time had passed at all. As if the world outside these tents carries on oblivious to the uncanny within.

She wandered to the other end of the circus and saw a mother with a couple of children entering a red tent. That tent must allow safe and uneventful entry. Following the small group, Julia entered the tent to find a similar phenomenon. Sure, in this tent there was neither desk nor chair, and instead lanterns surrounded the borders of the tent. Yet in the middle of the tent lay a grotesquely gangly man, strings tied to the wrists at the end of arms that were much too long. Strings were also tied to his ankles and rising to the ceiling, his legs as eerily long as his arms and extending to the end of the tent, next to a lantern; Julia wondered if the girl she'd seen had also had strings on ankles hidden behind the desk. The man was motionless, eyes open and staring up to the ceiling, unblinking. Julia diverted her attention to the children, watching their reaction for a cue of how to respond herself. To her surprise, they were awed and excited.

"This is my favorite puppet, Mother," the boy said, tugging on her sleeve for attention.

"We'll have to come here and see his performance later," the mother replied calmly.

Neither children nor parent seemed to have concern or panic. It was as if once you step into the confines of a circus, all the boundaries of convention cease to be. No thought to what should or shouldn't be, simply what is. Magic or curses, extraordinary and haunting, the world welcomes it when limited to just the right setting.

Julia stood motionless until she was alone with the body. At first Julia tried to avoid looking at his eyes, then imagined him staring at her curiously while she unbeknownst pondered his oddities; this thought caused her to watch his eyes closely despite the fear it placed in her. Tentatively approaching, Julia crouched at his side and put her hand on his chest. A heartbeat. He was most definitely alive, more alive than she had been. And now she was relatively fine, so maybe this man was not in danger of imminent—or at least not permanent—death. Maybe this was an odd part of the act.

Daring to break eye contact enough to study the top of the tent, Julia wondered if this man could even stand in the space without ducking his head. Perhaps his act required no standing. Abandoning that fruitless line of thought which would bring her to no conclusion until she saw his act, Julia put her hand in front of his mouth and felt his relaxed breath brushing against her gently. Yes, the man was definitely alive. Could a drug do this to someone? She was not certain.

Julia scooted away from the man and sat on the ground, legs up close to her chest, arms fiercely clutching them. She could not convince herself to leave this man in such a state. Yet every other tent likely held the same terror—certainly the lady she had encountered earlier at the very least. Julia was beginning to understand the Trenchers' reactions to her; even Dr. Wise's response. Julia had never encountered someone as odd as herself, and now she found an oddity not unlike her own and equally cowered and pondered with fascination. *Here I would be normal*, she thought, and wondered if she liked that reasoning anymore, if she could bear being considered comparable to this man.

5

Clue 4: Circus wagons in the barley field at the edge of town, but they're locked up.

 M WITH JULIA. A bunch of smoke and mirrors, that's all this circus was."

Fancy shrugs. "You'd like to think so."

"You told the cops this? This is why they think the whole investigation is a joke?"

"Don't be silly; I'd be locked away with the rest of them if I told those stories."

My eyes widen. "Rest of them? They're what, in jail?"

"No, no. I can't say about them all, couldn't keep track of that group worth nothin'. Always knew how to scurry, especially after the fiasco." She gets this far-off look in her eyes and sighs. "Geppetto, RaeChaeline, Analiese—history, no one will find those old coots. Phoebe and Nick, that's who I placed my money on finding. Phoebe, if I were a betting person, wouldn't have got far; wouldn't make much of herself neither. I'd bet my life on it she can't keep a job, a house, a life worth nothing."

Just as I resign myself to her stories being no help at all, she smiles and offers up the tantalizing morsel that reels me in.

"Now Nick, he's the easy one. Surprised you don't know; it was all over the news, his antics. Went all a-crazed after the incident. Locked up. 'Nicholas Cirque' they call him, ha! What a hoot. Outlandish stories, unstable fellow, scared of the dark, obsessed with fire, nearly burned himself to pieces I hear. Shame."

I can't believe it. She knew one of them. And not a missing one. 'Nicholas Cirque.' But he's in a mental ward, I can't go there. Not with my past or whatever. "Fancy, you gotta get the story from him. Go ask him what happened. Take notes. "

Fancy throws her head back and laughs, all melodramatic like. "What am I?" she spits. "Your errand girl?"

I shake my head. "You can get the story. For me." She isn't buying it, I know. Have to throw in something extra for her. "Sooner I have the story, the sooner I'm out of your hair...you can have that mansion all to yourself, yeah?"

"Waaait a second," she shakes her finger with great enthusiasm like she's the cleverest of crones. "What's so you can't go yourself? You're not telling something, and I say it's time you 'fess up."

"Oh, mind your own!" She is much too suspicious for my good.

"Not if I'm visiting the pyscho," she says. "Max, Max, Max, I'm Max, you say. Maybe you're the psycho, can't even give out your real name worth a thing."

"Oh right, Fancy, since we're all for honesty here."

"Oh hush, I have no reason to give you my name. I want nothing from you. Bribery at its finest—I see Nicholas for you if you only say what in the world of cirque you're doing with all this meddling."

"I told you," I feed her the line again. What's so wrong with my line?

"Right right, an investigative reporter. Barely of age, you think I believe that? You think anyone believes that?"

"It's true." But I can't even convince myself.

"Then you report on the psych ward yourself." Fancy trudges away.

"Don't," I plead. I'm aware I'm getting pathetic. "Please." But I need this. "I have to—you have to—" but she continues ignoring my pleas. "Ignatius!" I yell. "I'm Ignatius, now help me."

Fancy turns. "Ignatius. Is that supposed to be more believable than Max?"

"Who would make up that name?" I say, hoping she won't realize that me, I would make up that name. First thing to pop into my head.

Fancy tilts her head and eyes me up and down. "Ignatius. Has a certain ignorant ring to it I suppose. Fitting."

"Thanks," I mutter.

"Ignatius," she emphasizes again, "let's us go check out this psych ward now."

I can't. I just can't. My fists clench and I feel heat racing up my face. "Don't push me, Fancy. I won't go."

"And why not?" she prods.

"Cause I—I—" How could I respond? "Those places are the heebie-jeebies, right? You been there, no big deal. Me, I steer clear of the weirdies."

Fancy laughs. "Steer clear of the weirdies, huh? And you're investigating a haunted mansion and a magical circus? You're a pack of lies alright."

I swallow loudly. I'm too close to this investigation; she sees it. She'll find me out. Asks too many questions, has too many answers I'm too invested in getting. My cheeks swell with heat. She couldn't know. Not with us going to a glorified asylum.

"This Nicholas guy," I try to stay calm, breathe, "he could have answers for you, too. Like where Julia and the Trenchers went.

I'm sure you're not getting paid for your housekeeping 'til they're located. Gotta be something you'd want."

The good guy routine didn't seem to be working, so I add in a mild threat to try on for size. "If your story actually checks out and you in fact are a housekeeper."

Fancy isn't ruffled. "You need me too much to try turning me into police. 'Sides, they'd not kick me out. I do more housekeeping than you have as of yet. But," she wags her finger, "but couldn't miss a chance to see Nicholas for myself, what he knows, what of his mind is gone...couldn't leave well enough alone..." She pauses. "Bah, follow me. Ignatius," she cackles at the name again. "Ignorant Ignatius."

What a joke. Max, Ignatius; she sees right through this facade. Fancy is dangerous. I can't predict her, can't figure her out. What's her angle? And here she's got me pegged, squirming under her gaze. If she'd leave me alone long enough to find it— find...it...somewhere is the answer.

Anyhow, hopefully this Nicholas guy will have some answers. Fancy seems all tickled, almost giddy, about seeing him. Don't know why the switch, but it's almost hilarious if it weren't so nerve wracking, her personality switch. She seems, dare I say it, hopeful. About what? Who knows.

My paranoid self is slightly worried she's about to have me locked up next to this Cirque guy. That'd give her hope, right? Be rid of me for good. But I have to remember she knows as little about me as I know of her—nothing to lock me up for.

Anyhow, off we go. Here's to staying sane awhile longer.

Clue 5: Nicholas Cirque in mental hospital, supposedly former circus performer

Three

JULIA SAT IN THE MAN'S TENT for some time, watching the dead eyes connected to the apparently living body. Over and over again, Julia thought it must be near time for the act, that she would see this man awaken from his motionless state to confirm that yes, he was in fact alive and well and this was all a silly game. He would then perform some great feat to mesmerize the crowds with marvel instead of macabre, a grand showman's trick to dance across the spectrum of audience emotions from one end to the other.

Yet time is deceitful, and he did not wake. It taunted her with moving the sun across the horizon much slower than expected.

Eventually a rustle of the tent alerted her to another's presence. Julia swiveled her head to get a view of the intruder.

The lady looked forlornly upon the bound man. Though she wore simple jeans and T-shirt, nothing quite glamorous enough to be circus attire, she still appeared to be of this particular circus.

How, you ask? She was nearly half the size of the lanky guy—though with his height that's not saying much—with chin-length dark curls formed perfectly around her masked face. The mask was not of artificial means, but rather appeared natural; her eyes were larger than they should be, covering over half of her face, contrasted freakishly by her freckle-sized nose. The mouth seemed to be of normal proportions, but shaped into a sharp horizontal line. Her chin naturally jutted out without a single move of her face, and her ears were hidden beneath the curls as if they did not exist. Due to the size of her eyes perhaps, there was no forehead. Julia concluded this lady must be a part of the circus, to gawk at her appearance if nothing else.

"Careful, your eyes are rivaling mine in size," the Mask said without removing her gaze from the motionless form.

Julia realized she had been staring, and considered the irony since she was the one accustomed to being gawked at. She glanced at her scars encircling her wrists, arms, legs, fingers, and recalled many more hidden from her view at present— encircling so many joints and intersections, enveloping her like a patchwork human. This Mask human had plenty to stare at herself, like one grotesque figure looking in a mirror at an equal and opposite grotesqueness.

Julia returned to looking at the man, something uncanny in a more palatable fashion. "Is he all right?" Julia asked.

The Mask let out a dry laugh. "Every tent is similar. The puppets awake when the acts begin."

Julia recalled hearing the young boy refer to the man as a puppet as well. "But he would be...he is..." Julia shuddered at asking if he was alive and decided to change her line of questioning. "...human. Right?"

"Of course. A puppet human."

Julia and the Mask continued to watch the man in silence. Julia followed his blank eyes to the up-and-down breathing motion of his chest, then up his arms to the strings that bound him to the ceiling.

Julia glanced cautiously at the Mask. "Where do the strings lead?"

The Mask rolled her eyes at the question. "The puppet master controls all the strings in every tent, without the spectators needing to be aware of the other end."

Julia considered responding with an eye-roll of her own for the cryptic answers. Instead she stood up, brushed the dirt and grass from her dress, nodded at the Mask in farewell, and exited the tent.

The Mask followed her out of the tent, though, and folded her arms across her chest as if to scold her. "The circus is glamorous not because of the tricks, but because of the mystery. Enjoy it."

"It's eerie," Julia replied.

"It's no haunted house," the Mask argued. "Children enjoy it because they are smart enough to see magic where adults see it as illogical."

"No magic dooms a human to such a fate," Julia said.

"Not human. Puppet," the Mask corrected.

Julia shrugged. "Puppet human."

The Mask laughed, this time with sincerity. "I'm Analiese. Simple stagehand here."

"Analiese. I'm Julia. Simple spectator here."

"I gathered," Analiese said.

"You aren't a part of the act?" Julia said incredulously.

"Don't be so shocked. My looks aren't a performance; spectators spectate, but that doesn't mean I have something to showcase, nor that I want to *become* a showcase."

Julia shrugged, and decided to give her line of questioning one more shot, so she walked back into the tent and the Mask—Analiese—followed.

"Do you get reactions often?" Julia asked, wondering if it was socially taboo to ask such questions, even at a circus.

"Depends on the day," was Analiese's answer.

"Besides, uh, lengthiness," Julia ventured, "What is this man's show?"

"Each puppet is neither clown, juggler, trapeze artist, or contortionist—though some may mimic such tricks in their act," Analiese explained. "This circus is abnormal, entirely unique, as you may have noticed. So without the ability to categorize this puppet with complete accuracy using typical circus lingo, he is referred to as a Shadow."

"Do you have a unique name for every act then?"

"Half the act is the hype, no name is required." Analiese pointed at the Shadow then flicked her wrist down to her side again. "You are intrigued, perhaps repulsed by his being already. The audience will behold the oddity quite on its own without a title for the actions. The act names are only for those who inquire and those who participate."

A group of teenagers, hardly younger than Julia, entered and made their way to the far side of the tent. The girls squealed as they clung to the guys, who were putting up a brave front.

Analiese added, "It is nearing showtime. I will leave you to...enjoy." Julia nodded, and Analiese exited, tugging the tent flap as if gravity could not close it on its own. Julia's brow twitched realizing she was once again alone. With others yes, but on her own.

Julia inched closer to the entrance, but remained in the tent, unable to avert her eyes nor abandon the Shadow before her. She did not have much time to ponder the show she was about to observe before...

"He moved," one of the girls pointed toward the Shadow and ran into the midst of the group.

"Did not," another said adamantly.

"His hand," the first girl insisted.

Some in the group rolled their eyes, but smiles proved the exasperation was all in jest.

Julia did not watch the teenagers, only listened as she observed the Shadow, and for this reason she was certain that the claim of movement was either a dramatic point of connection with her friends—one small part of the theatrical performance of belonging to the group and maintaining their norms—or perhaps an imaginative vision caused by the fear and hype.

A bell alerted the audience that four o'clock had struck. The circus was too far from town for church bells to be heard, so instead of a majestic gong, it was a few meager drawn-out clangs of a dinner bell wishing to join in the heavenly chorus of the hour. As the last clang fizzled out, every lantern in the tent was instantly extinguished, save one just behind the Shadow, illuminating his silhouette to the crowd. The Shadow did not move, but remained in his motionless near-dead state.

"What now?" whispered one of the teenage crowd, but no one responded as all eyes remained fixed on the body. Perhaps seconds passed, or minutes, but time once again was unknown as they all watched the Shadow, so appropriately named as that was nearly all that could be seen of him. Enough time passed that they assumed some awakening or movement should have occurred, but still the audience awaited the awestruck moment promised.

Julia's worry that the puppet may not awaken increased with each breath, that some mistake would rip the promise of this space from her, that the magic ends in death.

The last lantern flickered, threatening to leave the audience sightless; then threat became reality for a brief moment as the lantern blinked out before immediately alighting again. In the mere second of darkness the gangly puppet had switched to sitting upright, arms and legs hanging limply at his side as if he knew not what to do with them, strings attached but hanging uselessly. The Shadow, still only a silhouette in the poorly lit room, watched the crowd, as curious to their reaction as they were to his show. After what must have only been a few seconds, but seemed like a gaping eternity, the lantern flickered out again and when it alit, the Shadow was in his prior position, a deathly silhouette unmoving.

Julia blinked and shook her head. Was it all a dream, a hope, a hallucination in this darkness that the man had moved? She pinched the bridge of her nose and breathed deeply, not knowing if she could trust her eyes any longer. No one could actually move quick enough to be sitting once the lantern came back on, but perhaps it was a trick of time rather than a trick of her eyes. Perhaps in another moment she could assess the situation more accurately to see if the whole thing was a delusion, a silly magic trick, or some nature of true magic.

She waited for another dark give-out of the lantern, but nothing seemed to be changing. The other group was shuffling, growing bored perhaps with the waiting. One of the boys, presumably the brave leader, approached carefully the silhouette and squatted to get a good look. "His eyes aren't moving again," he proclaimed. "Guess the show is already over. Pathetic."

Before the boy could stand back up though, the lantern was extinguished again. A yelp and a stumbling crash was heard, but then quiet as the lantern did not light up the tent again as expected. Julia looked around, but it was of no use—not a hint of light emanated from the tent opening, the bottom crease, nor from the rest of the audience.

"Charles, you there?" a girl's voice squeaked.

"Yeah," said the once brave leader from the middle of the tent area. "Tryin' to make me wet my pants," and he let out an unconvincing laugh.

Julia considered finding her way to the Shadow to see what was happening, but figured she would stumble into or over a body at some point with the other group present. She began to feel lightheaded in the dark, though, and tried to maintain her balance. She brought herself to a seated position, hands fumbling in the total absence of sight simply to touch the ground.

"Uhh," Charles voice was heard as he mumbled his nerves out, escalating from confusion to masked fear. Eventually he switched to more descriptive language. "He's not there, guys. I can't find him."

None of Charles' friends had an immediate response to his realization, so Julia had some silence to think, and she assumed the others in the room were pondering the situation as well.

Julia had expected the Shadow to be in his same position, but upon hearing of his seeming absence she smiled at her gullibility; of course the lights were meant to go out and the Shadow reposition himself yet again, so he could not be in the same location. She wondered if the lantern would light again shortly or if there was an unanticipated glitch leaving the tent indefinitely black. She doubted this seeming malfunction was unplanned, yet thought that a circus would have more buildup to a great blackout in the act. *Then again*, she thought, *what would you know about a circus to decide how an act's blackout should occur? Mere story and hearsay, none of the reality that you experience here.*

"This is crazy. The light is obviously broken." Charles' exasperation with the distance from his friends—mere yards, but the darkness stretched out each yard to an impassable expanse—brought about a tangible eyeroll that required no sight to be known. "Someone open the tent so we can leave this shoddy shambles of a show."

Julia reached her hand behind her and felt the opening of the tent, but she was not ready to allow light an entrance quite yet. Perhaps these moments were building tension, leading to a climactic finale that her interference could devastate. And yet, if she did not open the tent, Charles would likely stumble towards her and the opening, perhaps trample her in his barging, frantic haste. With that thought, instinct kicked in, and Julia watched her hand push the flap aside, allowing a crack of the dim light of sunset to penetrate their enclosure.

A girl's scream caused Julia to jump and face the inside of the tent again. As her hand released the tent flap, Julia saw a face, inches from hers—the Shadow. Then the tent returned to total darkness. Only one thought had time to enter Julia's mind in the instant: *His eyes blink now*. Julia put her hand out, not sure if her intent was to push away the too-close stranger or to ascertain his presence, but the inches became feet as her reach revealed no presence. Her furrowed brows and the teenagers' whispers compelled her to slip out of the tent and puzzle over a different exhibit. Another shriek—from the same girl?—was heard, but Julia felt no need to respond as she walked away.

The Mask—Analiese—stood with ankles and arms crossed opposite the Shadow's tent, a slight smirk towards Julia hinted on her firmly horizontal mouth. Analiese's large eyes caught Julia off guard for a moment, and she hoped she hid it well as she rolled her eyes and turned her steps toward Analiese.

"Are all exhibits so bizarre?" Julia asked.

"See for yourself," Analiese offered another vague answer and shrugged, indifferent to the criticism.

Analiese began to saunter towards the next tent, and Julia followed. "Wait, but...the man in there. Is he all right?"

"Of course, we've been over this." Analiese waved her hand in the air, dismissing the concern. "It's all a show. I told you before, he is very much alive the entire time."

"As a matter of fact, you were very cryptic earlier, like now. And...th-the Shadow. He was not all right," Julia insisted.

Analiese stopped walking and faced Julia, who had seemed content to match pace with Analiese and remain a few steps behind.

"What do you presume to know about this act to make such a claim?" Analiese's lips stretched to emphasize the word "act," a great feat for the immovable straight line.

"Nothing about the act, nothing about the show," Julia agreed. "But I saw his eyes."

Analiese's eyebrows had been mostly hidden beneath her hair, but were finally noticeable as they furrowed, scrunching her face until her eyes nearly threatened to cover her nose and mouth.

Julia spoke quietly, hoping to soften what could be seen as an accusation. "Some portion of this performance was no scripted show. That man was terrified."

The eyebrows returned under their cover, and Analiese watched Julia silently for moments—studying, it seemed. Then Analiese giggled; Julia almost missed it, because the firm lips hardly moved, but a few seconds of quick breaths and brief sound escaping ascertained it. "You clearly are no *mere* spectator, you're the keenest spectator yet," Analiese claimed. "No one has mentioned that before. Do me a favor and don't tell Nick if you see him later; he doesn't like discussing his fear."

"Why can't I tell? Why shouldn't I tell?" Julia asked.

"You should not speak of it because it's embarrassing, of course." Analiese explained. "This is a circus. I am sure that lion tamers and sword swallowers and trapeze artists feel fear with their daring acts, and just the same there is fear in some of our acts. Every performer works to conquer their fear, and more importantly works to assure themselves that no audience member will notice their fear."

Julia nodded, uncertain if it meant acknowledgement of the reasoning or agreement to the request.

"Why don't you observe a less absurd act?" Analiese suggested, pointing to the first tent Julia had entered. "This tent here, well she is almost comparable to one of your fortune teller or psychic shows. She may know your name or your past, your deepest regret or triumph, sometimes even your future."

Julia stared at the tent, then glanced at the other tents and back to Analiese's formed face. "I don't know how ordinary of a spectacle that will be once I am in there…"

Analiese's tight lips curved upward ever so slightly in a smile. "Oh, everyone assumes their secrets will undo one who sees deeply, but let me disappoint you right now—which we are not supposed to do as performers, I might add—and assure you that it will all be boring same-old to her."

Julia doubted Analiese's words, but then again this lady probably knew The Shadow—Nick, Analiese had said—so a breakable girl would not be terribly shocking, would it?

"Come along," Analiese said with a wave of her hand. Still unsure, Julia's feet followed Analiese, dragging her in the direction of the first tent that her eyes had seen the contents of.

6

Former clues: Vanishing circus. Julia Trencher, supposed abnormality, abandoned mansion. Flyer & note in Julia's old room. Cirque folk, namely Nicholas Cirque (asylum). Circus wagons in the barley field at the edge of town. Trust Fancy?

OU STILL HAVEN'T GIVEN any indication of magical properties at this circus," I challenge Fancy. "I told you it's all over-the-top outlandish claims."

"Just you wait," Fancy says. "I'm saving the good stuff for later."

Entering the asylum isn't hard. Something tells me exiting is the difficult part. How many people like me walk in here innocently enough only to never leave?

Of course, they wouldn't actually call this place an asylum. It's "The Institute of Long-Term Psychiatric Treatment." Fancy says it's known on the street as Psych Institute though.

The reception area is bland, stiff, sterile. Brochures detail in-patient and out-patient care and specialized treatment for "unique and complex physical, mental, and psychological disorders." Scratchy chairs line the lobby. Nurses in bleached uniforms stand at attention at the front desk.

A slick, framed portrait of some doctor is prominently displayed next to out-patient care. Not our section. We need the in-patient prison—I mean, treatment facility care place. You know what I mean.

Fancy isn't looking around, though. She barges right up to the front desk. "Here to see Nicholas Cirque." She jabs the air in my direction. "He's with me."

The two nurses exchange looks, either on Fancy's entitled diatribe or her contrasting flimsy appearance. Maybe both. I shrug at them, not sure how much I want to side with Fancy on this one.

"I'm not sure Nicholas Cirque is approved for visitors," the younger nurse hazards. "We'll contact family to visit once he no longer poses a threat."

"Oh, we're not family," laughs Fancy. "No no, we're here to investigate. This here boy is an investigative journalist, right boy?"

"There's nothing to investigate," the older nurse clips. She pushes her glasses up her nose and sniffs.

"Oh nooo," Fancy bobs her head. "It's all very hush-hush, but there is an investigation, and I'm afraid we need to speak with Nicholas Cirque. If we must, we can return with a warrant and search the files and interrogate the staff and it's all a mess, but we'd rather not go through that process when we can just ask the crazy himself some questions to clear this all up."

I could swear Fancy winks at me. "Talking about the hassle of a warrant always works in the shows, don't ya know," she later tells me.

The nurses exchange glances again. "Well, I suppose he's not specialized..." one says under her breath. "But the paperwork..." the other. "Doctor Wise would throw a fit if this crosses into specialized."

"What's specialized?" I ask.

That is all the pressure they need. The nurses look at me, deer in headlights.

"Nothing your current lack of warrant would cover." The old bossy one again. "There's simply more—complex—patients that prefer privacy." She gestures with her head at the timid nurse. "Follow her. She'll escort you to the crisis room for your interrogation."

Fancy bounces on the balls of her feet, overly eager.

"Ease up a bit," I whisper. I reach for her shoulder to calm her, but she dodges away.

"Don't get grabby, you overzealous ignoramus!" Touchy.

It isn't to be that easy, though. Darned doctor, has to barge in. "What's this?" The leering doctor from the portrait, alive and in person.

The nurses babble—attempting an excuse. I roll my eyes. "Sorry for the inconvenience, Doctor. We are here to speak with your patient, Nicholas Cirque."

The doctor cocks his head and plasters a smile. "I don't believe I caught your name. I'm Dr. Wise."

"Dr. Wise. Appropriate." I try not to stumble. "I am—"

Fancy jumps in. "Excuse me, doctor, it's all a ploy. This here fellow claims he's a journalist to interview the mental patients. A lovely ruse I came up with to bring him here. Been driving me crazy—not literally—at the Trencher mansion, he has."

(I should have seen where this was going. Instead) I copy the plastered smile of Dr. Wise.

"Up and shows one day, says he's investigating, but he's a loon." Fancy bobs her head affirmatively. "You best escort him to a room for evaluation as quick as can be."

Here I'm catching on. "Now wait a—" But I have no time for defense.

Dr. Wise apologizes. "We can't book an alleged patient without documentation, orders, abnormal study findings, something. You will have to schedule an appointment."

I don't know what Fancy is doing, but I'm glad it isn't working.

"Doctor, understand." Fancy gets desperate, clutches his shirt sleeve. "It's not normal, the things he does. Plum crazy, brings a darkness with him. I swear he's accursed with some power, the power to take a soul I imagine. Please."

Now Fancy is acting crazy, and I'm right about to decide she would be locked up instead of me, but Dr. Wise's brow furrows. "Accursed, you say? What problem does he have? Exactly."

Fancy is fumbling now, but I've heard enough. "Hello, talking as if I'm not right here. This here Fancy gal's the psychotic one."

"Now calm down," the old nurse pipes in. "We can resolve this without any trouble." She pats my arm as if I'm some child to appease. I recoil and bump into Fancy.

"Stay away from me, you devil!" Fancy says. "Watch him...he's got no power now, but lights go out and he's gonna take us all."

"You seem upset," the nurse continues, but she is looking to me and not to Fancy. Why isn't she looking at Fancy? "Why don't we discuss this calmly in the back?" She's talking to me.

I am done with this madness. "I won't calm down and I'm not going back there. I don't need any interview, and I'm certainly not psycho." I jab at Fancy. "This was your plan, wasn't it? Make me chicken out. Well it worked, I'm outta here. I'm not goin' after this Nicholas, and I'm certainly not being locked—"

I must be too distracted, too befuddled to even notice. But Fancy's plan is set into motion in the blink of an eye. Not a plan for me to chicken out. But a plan for me to be escorted into the most brightly lit room in this building—Nicholas Cirque's cell.

The younger nurse that isn't trying the whole "calm down" routine has her own calm down routine that involves a syringe. I should have known the quiet one is the one to watch out for. A single prick, and I go limp.

"Hold on," Fancy places her hand on my face as if she cares, as if she hadn't gotten me into this mess. "I'll get ya out of here, just don't let go of the big picture. The darkness is too strong." I can hear them, feel them move me; in fact, I think I move some of the way myself. But the blur is too strong, the light scalding. I glimpse a figure in the center, darkness amidst the white: Nicholas Cirque. And then sleep comes as whiteness instead of black.

Four

PHOEBE'S FLAIR FOR THE DRAMATIC should have taken over her act, but telling a shy kid his name or revealing some idiotic moment in a scoffing teen's near future was getting old. While she stuck to the stereotype with flowing skirts and simple gold jewelry, overall her presentation left something to be desired. This gig was not supposed to be like this, but even seers of the future are bound to the laws of time that involve waiting. So Phoebe feigned looking into the future—not with a crystal ball, but one made of foam and paint spatters to add dimension. No need to add showmanship when you've got undeniable talent.

Julia would neither be disappointed by Phoebe's indifference nor delighted by her costume, because Julia had never seen a fortune teller before. If they were a fake, why waste the money? and if they were real, well, Mrs. Trencher wouldn't allow that thought any attention, due to the concern it would raise that any psychic idly walking past the area Julia inhabited could foresee some instant of Julia's abnormality and raise a ruckus.

As Julia slipped into Phoebe's tent behind Analiese, she noted that everything was as she had left it, except that Phoebe was awake of course. The family that Julia had seen earlier was present, as well—the young girl wide-eyed and the boy hopping in place, either antsy to move on or in dire need of an outhouse.

While Phoebe's attention had been solely on the girl, she glanced up to politely acknowledge Analiese and Julia. The glance quickly turned into a fixed stare when Phoebe's eyes met Julia, the latter attempting not to squirm under the scrutiny. Phoebe bit the left side of her lip and tilted her head, still refusing to take her eyes off of Julia.

The mother grabbed the girl's hand and the boy's shoulder—in an attempt to contain his energy—and scooted them out of the tent, assuming their time was finished though Phoebe had stopped mid-sentence. Analiese nodded at the family on their way out, her silent attempt at an apology.

The tent made a rustling noise as the family exited that caused Phoebe to start. Her hands gripped the table as she collected herself. "You need to leave now, Julia," Phoebe said.

Julia leaned towards the tent entrance, but her feet froze in uncertainty at Phoebe's piercing gaze. Anyone caught in that gaze knew beyond a shadow that Phoebe saw things she had no business seeing. For what reason—destiny or calamity or happenstance—that was yet to be determined. Julia wrapped her arms around herself protectively.

Phoebe leaned forward and whispered, "Go," dismissing her with a wave of her hand that jingled the gold bracelets adorning her wrists.

"Phoebe, what are you talking about?" Analiese interjected.

Phoebe ignored Analiese and kept her eyes on Julia. Julia willed herself not to move, only return the inquisitive stare Phoebe had originally given. Analiese, not one to be ignored, said, "Phoebe, you're in show mode. Come on. What's gotten into you?"

Phoebe's face hardened. Julia inwardly pleaded to be released from the scrutiny of those all-seeing eyes, wondering, hoping Phoebe could hear her thoughts and acquiesce. Phoebe finally faced Analiese, giving Julia the opportunity to slip out of the tent while Phoebe said, "Get her out of here. I have nothing to say to her."

Julia hurried around the tent for a reprieve. From the other side of the cloth she could hear Analiese's anger. "You can't do that, Phoebe. She's a paying client. Give the 'You have a hurt in your past' or 'You have a bright future' or whatever it is speech, like always."

There was a small pause before Phoebe's response was heard. "Too late."

Analiese left the tent soon after Julia, but not seeing her anywhere, stormed off.

Phoebe took advantage of the moment alone to exhale all of the expletives that she could come up with. Her eyes darted around the tent, begging for some escape. She racked her brain for a memory that could help, mentally flipping through decision after decision like dusty music records on a long-neglected shelf.

And perhaps if Phoebe had found nothing, if the memories she held had been fruitless, we'd have a different tale altogether. Perhaps the circus wouldn't have vanished along with its cast, perhaps Julia wouldn't be lost, perhaps Max would continue living his oblivious life, and the Trencher mansion would predictably hold two Trenchers. But I'm not sure that's a story worth telling, at least not at this moment. (A great reader and storyteller could one day prove me wrong, and I'll be blissful to hear it!) So, of course, there's a moment that Phoebe's mind recalls that propels the tale in this particular direction that leads us eventually full circle to Max's investigation...

Finally, a distant hope entered her thoughts, a fond nostalgic melody to play over and over again. "You can always come back here if you need a way out," the lady had said. How little the chances of that helping. She didn't need a way out, she needed a way through. She needed a guarantee that the truth about Julia wouldn't be found out, and she couldn't trust herself with the knowledge she now carried.

Still, it was her only hope. She pushed herself out of the seat and rushed to the tent entrance, listening to be sure that Analiese and Julia had left the area, hoping her pounding heart could not be heard, and wishing for the show to end before it was too late.

Five

HOEBE HAD KNOWN JULIA'S NAME, but demanded she exit the tent—one cannot be banned from an act as a spectator unless causing a ruckus, right?

Perhaps this lady truly had a power and had seen something. Perhaps Julia's atrocious first death or gruesome second death. That would be enough to strike fear, right? Of course the realization of such a reality was too painful for anyone to face. No one should be exposed to Julia's fate, the inevitability of a perpetual dysfunctional existence in the world.

Perhaps a return to the Trenchers was a necessity. All of the victory of escaping her old life overshadowed by the inescapable presence of her abnormality.

And Julia was still pondering the Shadow's performance—what had happened? His eyes of fear—if he were a toddler with a night mare, she'd almost certainly cradle him in her arms and let his sobs pulse, hot tears dripping on her arms and neck, reassuring him it was only a dream, that the real world held only rainbows and kittens. Only he wasn't a kid, and the world held more than rainbows and kittens. He was a grown man with more terror than a child's imagination, and that must mean reality was far worse than what children dream up.

Julia stood behind Phoebe's tent, considering leaving the circus altogether. Perhaps the only reason she did not exit the area immediately was that she wasn't sure where else she would go. She refused to return to the Trenchers, the veritable evidence of defeat. And her original hope upon seeing the flyer, the tents, the uncanny performers, had been that this was her true home. She wasn't ready to give that up.

Finally, Julia compromised and plopped down in the grass at the edge of the barley field. The barley blew in the nice breeze, a soft golden hue highlighted by the peeking sun. The definition of rooted and free. If the barley had been uprooted, well then the breeze would drag it every which way it pleased, and how free would that be?

While the soft barley and gentle winds slowly lulled Julia from deep pondering and worry into a restless sleep, Phoebe yanked at the puppet strings holding her firm. The barely visible thread held tight though, permitting no exit of the tent. Gnawing with her teeth, pulling with all of her weight, even climbing on her desk and attempting to untie the knots at the center of the tent—all was futile; the strings had a relentless grasp.

Six

JULIA WAS ROUSED FROM HER SLEEP by a soft buzzing, followed by the tentative tickling of a junebug exploring her face. Brushing the insect away with a shudder, she pushed herself to a sitting position, propped up by her hands. Multiple insects flitted and roamed the barley fields where she had assumed insect varieties did not interact. She was beginning to realize that the actuality of life was so different from a textbook, where every fact had its own tidy compartment to form an intricate but inaccurately exact schema in the student's mind.

She'd slept through the night on hard ground, missing the big show. With what she'd seen so far, she wasn't sure she minded.

Turning her head to view the gold tent behind her, Julia debated entering the circus world while no act or performance awaited. She tilted her head and rubbed her brow, then shoved herself quickly to her feet before she could change her mind. After relieving herself in the barley field—stumbling over her bundle in her hurry to finish the humbling business—she began to walk through the silent circus.

Julia heard a few light cracks as she began to walk, muscles aching and demanding relief from the firm bed of dirt it wasn't accustomed to. She ignored the pain and stumbled on, listening for a sound of circus folk—would it be a raucous group or groggy from a late night? Perhaps there would be no noise at all as the puppets would be in their dead-but-not state.

Julia heard murmurings from the big top and circled to the entrance on the other side. She stopped abruptly as she approached the entrance, not certain she was ready to be seen. She considered walking back into town instead. Her stomach would complain of hunger soon, her body would likely break, the circus illusions would prove disappointing, and the grumpy, insistent psychic would let all know how unwelcome Julia was in the area.

So many less-than-pleasant possibilities presented themselves. None could convince her to leave though, for there was no more desirable or promising alternative.

Julia peered in the tent. Three people sat in the dirt chatting — one woman she didn't recognize, but the other she knew as the glamorous acrobat from the banner in the entrance to the circus. And she sighed in relief to see the Shadow. He was much shorter with legs and arms of natural length, but she was certain it was him because he held the same hunched posture, the same instinctive head tilt, and the same shaggy hair hiding his wide, searching eyes.

"Julia!" It was the woman she didn't recognize who waved her forward. Julia studied her face more closely as she approached — she had dark, stringy hair to her shoulders and strikingly blue eyes—contacts? Julia was certain she had not seen her before, so saw no reason for them to have exchanged names; the psychic or Analiese must have mentioned her, but why?

Julia shuffled toward the group. The acrobat eyed her warily. Julia watched the Shadow's reaction—did he recognize her? He seemed to think she was a stranger, though he had the opportunity last night to study her face from two inches away.

Blue Eyes waved her hand towards Julia, then back to the group. "Everyone, Julia. Julia, everyone."

"Hello," Julia murmured.

The Shadow stood and reached his hand out, clutching Julia's timid grasp as they shook hands. "I'm Nick," he said, "This's RaeChae, and you know Analiese."

Julia looked at the two seated. Analiese? Was Blue Eyes actually Analiese? There was no natural mask now, though the eyes stood out.

"Hello," Julia murmured again.

Blue Eyes-Analiese piped in, "Did you see their shows?"

"Only, uh, Nicholas's show."

"Just Nick," The Shadow interjected.

"Nick," Julia tested, forming the syllable with great effort, as if she required all her brain power to cut off speech before instinctively adding more syllables.

"You'll have to see RaeChaeline's sometime," Analiese said.

"Sit." The Shadow—Nick—offered a spot of dirt with a wave of his hand. Julia squatted and Nick sprawled out, hands propping up his body next to hers.

Julia turned to face Analiese—the blue-eyed, straight-haired, comparatively average face Analiese—"You had a mask before?" Julia pointed at her face.

Analiese laughed, RaeChae and Nick joining in with a sputter and a smirk. "My face changes often. If someone you don't recognize knows you more than you'd expect, go ahead and assume it's yours truly." Analiese laughed again.

Julia shrugged. How else could she react to that vague explanation when she had her own inexplicable anomalies?

"Hungry?" Nick asked.

Julia shrugged, uncertain what circus life protocol for hunger was.

"Good, 'cause we got nothin'. Phebes was in charge of morning food. Did she get mornin' food?" Nick paused, leaned forward, and stared at Julia.

"I don't know," Julia defended.

"Well, neither do we!" Nick shrugged and waved his hands, then leaned back again. "She's nowhere around, so who knows? We starve, 'n she...well...she who knows?"

Julia smiled, a dimple forming in the corner of her mouth.

Analiese smiled back. "Forget it. She would have a good reason, I'm sure."

"Sooo," Nick leaned to the side towards Julia, nudging her shoulder with his. Julia scooted a couple inches away, but Nick appeared unaffected. "Y'saw my show and no one else's." He winked, then nodded dramatically with a sly grin. "That sick a show, couldn't take more?"

Julia said, "I saw the psychic show, too. Well, I saw a little. She knows my name."

"Ahh, so snubbin' RaeChae here?"

"You were scared," Julia proclaimed.

Nick's smile froze and he tilted his head away from Julia. "Why'd ya think that?"

"You would deny it otherwise," Julia responded.

"Like I said, that sick a show." This time Nick had no smile, no wink, only painful sincerity as his eyes stared at the tent entrance and a forceful swallow bobbed his throat.

Seven

Phoebe is a fortune teller. At least, she let everyone believe that, and she played the part well.

But look deeper. Phoebe is not a fortune teller either, regardless of her job description. Sure, she reads your future like you may read a dictionary. She may know complete strangers' names on sight; and yet she will never hold a memory of most of her daily interactions. She cannot read minds, the stars, or a foam ball.

She is actually a gifted one, or a broken one, or simply different depending on your perspective. And perhaps her worst fear was coming true, that she was losing her ability forever. Night terrors became more expected than a familiar face—dreams of awaking with no memory, of being hospitalized, of never recognizing anyone's face ever again.

So Phoebe disappeared to the one memory that held a glimmer of hope for her. A rundown diner where the woman behind the counter said, "You're welcome here any time," but not in some normal polite waitress way. More genuine. She'd pat her hand, look her deep in the eye, and that was a big enough decision for Phoebe to see that one out of all the other possibilities. So she'd return there, again, in hopes of a haven—each time not sure if it panned out, if she'd been there before, because she couldn't see those other moments. She'd been there before many times of course, as recently as the other night.

Hope. It was hope that kept drawing her back.

She worried that she was losing her memories, and she wondered if her memory was improving or declining since she didn't have enough memory to remember. She wondered if she'd been worried for years or months or minutes. She wondered who the curious Julia was, the mysterious stranger that would cause such a break in her already volatile memory. And she headed back to the circus after awhile, because what else could she do.

Only days later, the diner would hold that mysterious stranger, who herself was looking for a haven she had yet to find. But, we haven't got to that part of the story yet...

Phoebe returned to her tent with a sigh. No luck. No bad luck, good luck, or any form of clue.

Brushing the tent open to enter, Phoebe started at the sight of someone sitting in her seat, fingers tapping the desk, eyes gazing into the blue expanse of the ball. Phoebe exhaled and placed a hand on her chest, feeling her heartbeat settle to near normalcy.

"We missed breakfast," the man said. "Rather I should say, *you* missed breakfast, so *we* missed breakfast."

Phoebe brushed her hair back from her face, resetting the part as it fell back gently around her shoulders. "I have news."

"I assumed there was a reason." A sparkle in his eye reassured Phoebe that she was in the clear. She had no memories of Geppetto's anger—wasn't even sure it was possible—but she was certain that she did not want to be the first to incite his wrath.

"I saw the girl," Phoebe explained.

"The biggest decision of my life," Geppetto clarified. "She the one Analiese told me about? You dismissing her from your room without a show, potentially ruining any chance of her sticking around?"

"She will stick around. She is for certain your biggest decision, remember?" Phoebe audibly inhaled. "But I could imagine I may have kicked her out. There were complications."

"Come, sit, explain." Geppetto motioned across the desk, where no chair was present.

Phoebe walked over and propped herself on the desk, turning slightly to eye him.

"Is everything well?"

"I don't know," Phoebe took a few breaths and swallowed. "She came here, to this tent. I saw...the vision... It was so abrupt, so empty."

"What did you see?" Geppetto coaxed.

"She entered my tent. I said, 'Wait, Julia, this is the most important decision you will make in life—for your good or for your destruction. Think it through some more.' She shook her head, determined, self-assured. She said, 'I know. I need your help.'"

Phoebe's eyes glimmered, and she brought her fingers up to scratch her nose.

"What happened then?"

"Then...then nothing happened. Everything went dark. Not the tent, but everything. That can't be the entire vision; I should see more than that."

"Are you sure there is nothing else in the vision?" Geppetto asked.

Phoebe brushed away a tear that had escaped down her cheek. "I can tell you what she was wearing, or that my tent was the same as it is now, or I can tell you that I left this morning and roamed the streets and every stranger's vision was complete. Only hers is cut short."

"Let me tell you a secret." Geppetto leaned towards Phoebe and glanced around the small tent. "When I was a mere boy, I loved the circus, yes? You know this." Phoebe nodded, but Geppetto had already continued "But I never attended a circus. 'A pile of falsehoods and lowlifes,' my parents would say. I would see the bright tents, the eager patrons, sometimes even an exotic animal—but never attend a show." Geppetto spread his arms wide, motioning around the tent. "But did I need to behold the show to create my own circus? Of course not."

Phoebe looked past Geppetto, nearly hypnotized by the puppet strings dangling, brushing against Geppetto's hair with seemingly great fondness. Geppetto did not notice her distraction and continued with his baffling anecdote. "I simply knew that crowds were drawn to a proper circus and thought to myself, 'What would draw a crowd?' And there you have it, now I have a superior circus that no hogwash show can dream of duplicating."

Phoebe sighed—another one of Geppetto's life lessons that could not connect for her.

"What I mean is this." Geppetto had decided to elaborate, and Phoebe nodded her head, all too familiar with this script. "Maybe you do not need to see anything more than what you have. Instead, consider it a clue. Concern yourself with what would cause your vision to be cut short, and what the ramifications could mean. In the meantime, let me know if there are any new developments, in vision or thought." Geppetto abruptly stood— briefly colliding with the puppet strings and causing them to whirl—and walked around the desk.

"There's something wrong with me," Phoebe said. "Tell me it's not true."

"We will know later." Geppetto waved his hand in dismissal and exited the tent without so much as a backward glance.

7

"NO GOOD."

The first words I hear. I feel goosebumps spread across my arms—whether from the eerie declaration or the cold temperature, I couldn't say. My forehead pounds. My eyes flutter, then squeeze tight. I cover my eyes and groan. Too bright, why so bright? I cup my hands tight over my eyelids and open, blink, then slowly move the hands away to grip my head instead. Still so bright.

"You're no good." It comes from a corner of the room, a growl. A figure in black, a welcome relief from the white light in every other direction. He crouches as far from me as possible.

My thoughts are clearing the more I stare at the darkness. "Nicholas," I breathe. "Nicholas, do you know me? I'm here to ask about the circus."

"Monster," he says.

Him or me? Or the circus? "What happened to the circus?"

We aren't getting anywhere fast, and the light is killing my focus. So much light. I squint, looking around. White everywhere. I see a hint of a doorline in one corner—only noticeable by the brief shadow under the doorway crack. Of course it's darker in a well-lit hospital than in this torture chamber.

I crawl toward the door, barely looking as I try to protect my eyes. When I hit wall, I dare to glance. A crack. Definitely a door, the way I'd come to entrapment here. But no doorknob. I pry, but to no avail. The door is, of course, latched.

"Nick, here."

I stumble to my feet and walk slowly toward him.

It occurs to me that I am some jerk, scared of him because he got locked up for being unstable, and here he is probably scared of me because I was locked up for being unstable. I decide to stop approaching to be a bit less threatening.

"Is there a way out of this bright room?"

He leaps up, like my words were a gunshot threat. "Don't go to darkness, it's too strong."

The darkness is too strong, Fancy had said. What's with these people being so scared of the dark?

I put my hands up, reassuring. "No darkness. Just out. A friend trapped me here. How do I get out?"

"A friend trapped me, too." He raises his hands in front of his face, and I realize they're bandaged. "All tricks, circus tricks." How would he help me when he hadn't escaped himself? I am on my own.

Or maybe I'm not. Fancy said she'd get me out, and maybe, just maybe, the lady wasn't mocking. In some hypothetical, outlandish psych ward way, if she actually meant she wanted to help and was on my side, then she'd also said something about the dark, something I dream of seeing (or not seeing) after all this bright. Funny how darkness is such a theme in this place of so much light.

Don't let go of the big picture. The darkness is too strong.

"Nick, why is it so bright?" I have to word this carefully. I can't freak him out with talk of darkness.

"Without light, the darkness spreads. Everyone knows this. But it stretches and stretches, and we don't want to stretch. The light must stay or the shadows will go on and on until the light."

I can't make one word out of his rambles. The dark is strong, they say. I like that right now. If the darkness is strong, maybe it could put out this godforsaken light. My head is pounding, and I think it's from the brightness, not whatever meds they jacked me up with.

"Nicholas, help. Do you know a way out?"

"There's no escape. You can't back out of the contract."

Contract. The most clear thing he'd said. What contract?

I look around again for some means of escape. If I could even dim the noise—the lights aren't making noise, but it sure feels like it—maybe I could think.

I can't look straight up without major squinting, so I can't even tell how high the ceiling is, how far the lights. There are no objects around. Nothing. Just the room, the lights, me and Nicholas loon du Cirque.

"Hey Nick. Buddy," To someone who's been locked up against their will, do I sound friendly or like some total douche in a suit? At least I'm not in some cop uniform or nurse uniform or anything, but anyone in this situation would be paranoid, worried that everyone is undercover out to get them, right? Of course, I'm not paranoid about people tricking me, at least not yet. Well, except for Fancy. She's totally suspect.

"I need to get up. High. Can you help?" I motion like he can't hear my words or doesn't speak my language, raising my hands up above my head, then down low cupped as if to hoist; then I realize I'm a patronizing jerk.

It's probably pointless. I might not even be able to reach the lights.

But he races over and before I can even think, he grips me around my waist and lifts. My eyes are wide with fear, but force a flinch. My arms are pinned to my side, and I feel so off-balance as my feet leave the ground. But to give him credit, he holds tight and we stay aright.

"No! No, Nick," I struggle against his grip, but the man's got gains. "Nick," I try to calm down—sure, I have a nice position to kick him where it hurts, but I prefer to stay on the good side of anyone I happen to be trapped with. Still, I'm not used to being restrained. "Nick, I need my arms. I can't reach."

I wriggle, and he corrects his grasp, bending his knees for support as he loosens his grip and lowers it to my butt. Awkward. Even in a world where I'm stuck with an ex-circus guy and no escape, still so not my type. But I have a chance to wriggle my arms from his grip at least, so I grasp his shoulders for balance and once he has steadied I reach upward. Toward that light I know is there but I can't look because Ow!

First I find only plain ol' white ceiling with the texture like styrofoam crumbles. I brush it until my fingers hit searing hot pain. "Found it," I say. "The blasted burning light." I wonder how he hasn't gotten a sunburn. The thing has to be a slow cooker. "If we could set some turkey and potaters here, we'd have a right fine feast in an hour, champ."

Nick says some sort of gibberish I can't hear over the brightness.

I creep my fingers around the edge, singeing the tips, making me wonder if I'd ever licked the too-hot peach pie straight from the oven off my eager stubby kid fingers. I ascertain the light is a square shape with no noticeable hinges. Must be in the middle. I brace myself for the heat—can't be helped— and slam my hand to the center. I know my hand is blood red, but the surface of the ceiling is flat as could be, no protrusions of screw-heads to be found. My hand sizzles; it's actually cooking. I bang on the glass, "Stupid—oven—just—break—" and it's like the oven heard. Only it's like all the lights in the building heard me.

This is how it looks when a second whirs by: First the lights flicker. Nick loses his bearings, I'm sure from the sudden dark after how many ages of light, and he tumbles. The lights go out. Nick catches himself, but I have already braced myself for the fall. I grasp his hair—probably yank it, the poor guy—then reach for something more sturdy and find his neck—the really poor guy. I swear I'm not trying to kill him, but suddenly he vanishes from my grip, from everything. And then, I vanish too, from everything.

No, not quite everything.

It is dark, no, I am the dark and it is terrifying. I have become my memories—darkest black. I stretch and stretch, like a tarry blackness spilling across the endless ocean. I am not alone, either. There is a presence in the tarry blackness with me. No, that's not right, I can feel it—we are both the tarry blackness, not two separate entities in tarry blackness together. We are the endless dark, the cold, the nothingness that is something, the limitless, and it isn't freeing; it's the terror of losing oneself and losing the world, the absence of light but a much stronger presence of power—power that chills. The presence, the darkness, and I, we are one and we are scared.

And just like that, it is over. I am crumpled on the ground, my face wet with—tears? sweat? snot? please don't be vomit... I swipe at my face. It's clear anyhow. I'll take that as semi-good news.

I stand shakily, then stumble. Swallow. The hallway spins for a moment. Don't vomit. I grab for the wall.

I get my footing and take in my surroundings. My shoes are

missing. I am under a light—a glorious, non-blinding, fluorescent light. Based on the doors with room numbers, I would say I'm still in the hospital, but I'm certainly not in my white cage. How did I get here?

The lights flicker, then steady. They must be as discombobulated as I. Then, footsteps. Someone is coming. Nick or doctor? I don't want to take my chances with either of them, so I walk away from the noise towards the flashing Exit sign.

Notebook, I think. I have to get my notes. They must have confiscated them after they knocked me out. I go through the door marked Exit, down the stairs. When did I get upstairs? I could try the element of surprise on the front desk clerk, see if there's some Lost and Found my notebook was dumped in. Maybe behind the reception desk, or worse, in a new patient file of mine behind locked doors.

But I can't think of that now. I am down a few flights when a door bursts open and there stands some guy in scrubs.

I smile. Force myself not to curse. Appear normal. Then the door down another flight bursts open. Too many people. But no! It's Fancy!

"Maximus!" she barked. "What ya waiting for? Get down here."

Mr. Scrubs furrows his brow; he's figuring it out. Before he can, I dodge past him with a little nudge, but he grabs my sleeve. Pretty sure it's the tears-sweat-snot-somethin' sleeve. Ew.

I yank, and we stumble a few steps. I slam into the railing, ending the possibility of us toppling down an entire flight of stairs. I guess you could call it "lucky", except for the fact that I'll get a pretty sick bruise. But I'll live with a bruising if I can just not be in an insane asylum.

Anyhow, where were we? Ahh, yes…he grabs, we stumble, I slam. Fancy huffs up the flight of stairs while I wrestle my sleeve out of Scrubs' grip. He isn't security, so at that point he backs off a bit. Isn't up for a fight, I guess.

"Come on!" Fancy glowers at Scrubs, but he doesn't move.

"Lotta help you were." I race past her down the stairs, and she follows once again.

Once we've cleared the building, I'm ready to race back in for my notebook. I head toward the front entrance, I suppose, planning on demanding the notebook from the receptionist… I don't know, I haven't got much thinking done at this point, I just go. Fancy must have thought I'm rushing for her beat-up, hunk of trash car. "Hold your fine horses," she says. "It's 'round back. But first, where did ya lose Nick off to?"

I pause in my tracks, realizing Fancy might know something. "Who gives two licks about Nick?" I say. "I need my notes. Where'd they take 'em off to?"

"Don't you dare, Maximus Prime!" Fancy is not one to argue with. "I ain't comin' here for nothing. You say we need Nick, I get you Nick in a master escape, and YOU—" she jabs her fingers at me like I stole her handbag "—YOU ditch him, ya good-for-nothin'."

"First off, I'm not Maximus. Just Max."

"You're not either." She grins, and for the first time I think I see a human underneath the facade. A timid reaction to a riotous joke. A sparkle to her face that says, Here I am. Do you see?

But she is getting me off track, always a step ahead for whatever end game she's playing. If she is gonna be all dramatic, I figure a freshly escaped convict like me can be dramatic, too. I count on my fingers. "Secondly, I want you to hear this loud and clear: you got me locked up. You don't get any credit for my escape. Lastly, and most important, I prefer to not be locked up, so if you'll excuse me but that takes priority over finding some cirque escape artist."

She reaches for me, like the man in the scrubs all over again 'bout to grab the gross sleeve. Only, she hesitates. Withdraws her hand again. "Your notes are more gone than Nick. We stay for your notes, we get locked up. We stay for Nick, we get what we want and might escape."

A gruff man bursts through the door. He wears scrubs, too. Much like Scrubs One, he's likely not security; unlike Scrubs One, the size of Scrubs Two ensures we're in for it.

He has nothing to detain us with, only himself, but that seems enough to capture at least one of us. Luckily, he reaches for Fancy first. His grip ensures she would go nowhere.

I feel a sting of regret, but then again Fancy got us in this mess, so I brush it aside as I trot away. He has his hands full.

Then I hear a gasp, a muffled pop, a moan. Instinctive curiosity has me turn around, stop in my tracks. The linebacker of a guy clutches his arm to his gut, hunched, face agape with terror. Fancy lightly holds his neck, not a drop of force to it, yet he stands frozen as if a mere flinch would be his demise. "Please," he whispers.

"We're here for Nick," she says.

"Yes," he responds. Is she seriously negotiating with him?

"Bring Nick, and we'll be out of your hair."

"And my notes," I interrupt. "I need my notes."

Fancy gives me the side-eye, surely unappreciative of my running when she got in his clutches. Like a denying disciple once the risk was too great. "We ain't getting the notes," she says yet again.

But we have leverage this time. I need those notes.

Security officers turn the corner and are heading our way.

"Give me Nick," she says to Scrubs Two again.

I hate it more than any decision I ever remember making, more than my decision to let Fancy take me here. But I know she's right. The notes are long gone; didn't stand a chance of finding them now. I'm not about to get locked up again.

"You can't make me stay," I tell Fancy. I continue to the car mere yards away, prepared for a retort. "Let's get outta here before we're put in white pantsuits."

Fancy purses her lips. A moment of stare-down before she turns back to her moaning captive.

"To the car," she says. "We get away, or your neck goes kablooey."

"Stop!" Scrubs Two yells to the security. They slow. "Don't come closer."

Security lifts their weapons, though I assume they hold some sort of tranquilizer; this isn't a prison, at least not quite.

"Don't shoot!" he yells again. "If she goes down, I'm a goner."

A couple lower their weapons, while others keep their guns aimed. One speaks into his walkie, but it's too garbled for me. We may not make it out yet.

Scrubs Two and Fancy waltz to the car in a precarious "One-wrong-step-and-I-die" and "One-wrong-step-and-you-die" sorta way. Fancy sidles into the dumpy car. She clambers into the driver's seat with extra effort, holding her super-loose grip on him the whole while, so I am in no hurry to catch up. She adjusts her touch to his neck through the window as she settles in. I don't know if she'd hoped to leave without me. I figure she knew there was no hope of racing away when the dumpy car tromped along like a circus elephant.

"Hey, were there any elephants in this vanishing circus? Did elephants disappear too, like a Dumbo feather trick thing?"

Fancy gives me her signature side-eye while firing the ignition. "No elephants were harmed in the making of this mystery."

"Ya know, Fancy, I gotta admit, sometimes you..." How do I say it? She makes me want to laugh again (again? Had I laughed before? Surely at some point in life) and simultaneously makes me want to strangle a pillow 'til the feathers burst out. How do you describe that to someone? "...sometimes you're downright interesting."

"Hold tight, boy." She pulls her arm into the car, no longer touching Scrubs Two as he stumbles toward the security guards. Fancy stomps on the gas, and the car chirrups and groans, then starts moving. We churn away from the crime scene—wait, is it a crime to break out of a psych ward? I wave adieu to my captors who are too focused on the prattling story from Scrubs Two to chase after our turtle-crawl car. I'm not sorry to leave them behind. But I am sorry to leave behind all my notes.

Clue 5? Let's say clue 5: Is there a contract related to the circus? To the asylum? Or just a crazed man's gibberish?

Eight

RAECHAE WAS ALOOF AND UNRESPONSIVE, but Analiese and Nick carried the conversation easily—Analiese cautious, but Nick charging through every sentence with reckless abandon. Julia, having hardly spoken to anyone at length other than her parents, doctors, and a doll, added input but wondered how often her words were wrong. With less than twenty minutes of conversation, she found herself weary. Her eyes strayed from her companions to the tent opening behind her, where hired hands were arriving to set up for the day. Her body wriggled in the discomfort of yet more ground contact, and her mind longed to return to the automatic pilot mode of aloneness.

"We not interesting enough company for you or something?" Analiese interrupted Julia's straying thoughts.

Julia stood, running her hands through her tangled hair, then down her wrinkled dress. "I—I would love to stay, but I should tidy up."

She wondered how she had not considered her appearance earlier. How she hadn't thought to take her comb out of her pack and tame the waves, or to freshen up so that she would not smell of earth and sweat.

RaeChaeline perused her appearance and nodded approvingly. "See ya later then."

As Julia exited the tent, a man was waiting for her. He was a grand man, but not in a businessman way. She noted that he tried much too hard to add flair for any professional setting. His suit flowed down his stout frame in the circus's bright colors of red and yellow. The clothes were not necessarily too large, nor baggy, but seemed to float in any gentle breeze that should pass. His mustache was very precise, perhaps even forcing the curled tips with some determined hair gel. And the man's hat—well, his hat matched his shoes, bulky and brightest gold to catch the eye of any within a great distance.

"You are the girl who is causing such a sensation in my group," the man bellowed. "Such a pleasure to finally behold you for myself, Julia."

Julia did not know how to reply, so she paused long enough to take a step back from the man, but he managed to edge a half-step forward in response. Finally her words began to escape. "I don't know what sensation I have caused or how you would know my name."

"Well, my dear Phoebe, mostly," the man responded. "Although Analiese said most all of the group has made your acquaintance."

Julia frowned. "Phoebe the least of all."

"Oh, she knows more than you think." He beamed and bobbed his head. "On that note, do tell me, Julia, what your gifting is that would cause me to invite you to join our group."

Julia rubbed her forehead and pursed her lips. "You would not invite me."

"Oh, but I would. Not here, not now, but Phoebe is certain of it. And when she is certain," the man folded his arms and rocked back and forth on his golden shoes. "Well, when she knows something, she knows it. And she knows that you will be invited to join."

"And do I?" Julia asked. "Join?"

"That I have not asked her for a long while now. Last I heard she did not know."

Julia took another step back and tried to peer around the man to find a reason to walk away.

"Oh, do forgive my rudeness. I have yet to introduce myself, Julia." The man took a small step backward, but right into Julia's line of vision again. "My name is Geppetto. I am the circus master."

"Pleasure." Julia ducked her head in a quick bow, then edged away. "Forgive me, I must leave to—"

"Oh, we do not have to be coy with one another, dear," Geppetto interrupted. "I know very well it was not a pleasure, you are not sorry, and you must not leave; you simply want to."

Julia stopped mid-step and took a deep breath.

"Go, be on your way," Geppetto continued. "We will see each other again once you sort out the inevitability of your future." Geppetto shooed her off with an unnecessary wave of his hand.

Julia was already halfway behind Phoebe's tent with newfound determination to retreat to tidy up, yes; but more importantly, to process the oddities she had recently encountered.

Nine

JULIA HADN'T DECIDED if she was on her way home or simply clearing her head with a walk, and when sufficient time had passed and she still hadn't reached a conclusion, she found herself back in the barley fields behind Phoebe's tent.

This moment alone was her chance to breathe, to recuperate, to analyze her next move. What had overcome her since leaving her parents? The stoic, direct, practical girl she had once been was replaced with this emotional wreckage of the past 24 hours. And Julia wasn't sure she liked the change. *You have always been alone, with people trying to fix you*, she thought. *Same way here, so pull yourself together*. Then she added, *Figuratively. And literally, I suppose.*

She crouched on the ground, looking back into town. She didn't quite belong there anymore (or ever) but she didn't quite belong here yet either.

Phoebe, likely in her dead puppet state on the other side of the silky cloth, had claimed that Julia was special—special enough to join this crazy show. Did Phoebe really know about Julia's abnormality? Is that what she had seen? And if so, why had she not shared the details of Julia's broken body with Geppetto?

Julia shivered and wished she had thought to bring a jacket. Phoebe could not know her secret, not already. And yet, if she did, if the secret was already out... Julia wondered what the point of this forced unbelonging would be. If she was already known, and the circus folk weren't frantically scurrying or sending her away, then perhaps she could be accepted with this one small step of opening her arms to them.

Julia found her way to an outhouse, relieved herself, changed into her one other dress, and combed away the knots to pull her hair into a twist atop her head. The sink water was murky, yet she still scrubbed her arms, neck, and face with the soap and paper towels available. Cleaning her teeth and dabbing some perfume were really the only other options for her current morning routine. "Next time you run away from home, bring a suitcase," she muttered to herself. "Roughing it" now seemed more repulsive than romantic.

"This is your lot," she reminded herself while rinsing away the suds. "You choose filthy water for a new life. A new life."

There was no escaping the inevitable. Julia tied up her pack again and marched back to the big top, right past the smiling "Sullivan" who still wore his silly name tag as if people might forget, or as if he walked through life as a greeter though he didn't actually say much to anyone. The circus crew sat in a circle, each in various stages of downing a late and meager breakfast of apples and oats. Phoebe had been staring into space while Nick attempted conversation with RaeChae. The ringmaster—Geppetto—listened with a tilted head. Analiese was nowhere around—not even as an extra unrecognizable body with extreme features.

"I will join your circus," she proclaimed.

Upon hearing Julia's words, Phoebe squinted at Julia with mild recognition, and RaeChae's nose flared. Julia briefly worried that she was no longer invited to join the circus, no longer wanted, and wished she could melt into a puddle to avoid the stares.

"Uhh..." Nick started to speak, but the sentiment was interrupted by Geppetto.

"Dear, that is all well; but I want you to be informed, so I must caution you."

"No caution is necessary," Julia jumped in, ready to seal the deal. "What is my act?"

Geppetto sighed. "Julia, you may believe you have made your choice, but there is a lot of cost in this endeavor."

A chill swept into the tent, and Julia turned, bumping into a strange girl presumed to be Analiese.

"I'm so sorry, Julia." The girl briefly massaged her shoulder in apology. Her face was oblong now, as if squished until her eyes nearly touched each other and her lips were taller than they were wide. Her curls flopped against her face, full and thick to replace the space her face should have covered.

"No harm is done..." Julia paused. "Analiese?"

The girl laughed and nodded, then brushed past to sit in the circle. Julia tentatively followed and sat beside her.

"Julia wants to join our circus." Nick announced with a smile.

"Oh." Analiese tilted her head in thought. "Oh!"

Geppetto fumbled to his feet. "She will be spending time with us before making her decision. Learning the trade, the conditions and whatnot."

"Of course," Analiese barely responded before Geppetto clasped his hat and left the tent. She hardly noticed his exit though. "What's your act?"

Julia crossed her arms with a shiver and stared into Analiese's too-close-together eyes. Turning to the rest of the group in hopes she had not looked so long upon the abnormality as to come off rude, Julia saw all other eyes focused on her. Perhaps staring was not uncalled for here. She shuddered and shook her head. "I have yet to discuss those details."

"Shivering maybe?" Analiese laughed.

"Apparently," Julia said in unison with RaeChae, the latter adding an eye-roll.

"Well you'll have to 'fess up to more than the chills eventually," Analiese said. Julia forced herself not to look at Analiese again, keeping her eyes on RaeChae instead. "You can either tell us or have fun letting us be surprised when it finally happens."

"Stop staring, you freak," RaeChae grabbed an apple and left the tent.

"I'm all for a lil' fun," Nick said.

"My apologies," Julia called after RaeChae.

"Forget her," Nick said. "We're all freaks here 'nd she knows it."

A nervous giggle escaped Julia's mouth. "Yeah?"

Nick looked across the group at Phoebe. "Of course," he replied.

As the late breakfast fell into silence, Julia was relieved to be able to hear her own thoughts again. Sure, she worried what she was trying to sign up for. Wouldn't anybody? But she didn't think to worry about the foreboding that surrounded this macabre circus, nor did she worry of the stern warnings from the circus folks. Her cheeks grew red and her stomach performed its own acrobats, but she didn't notice.

Instead, she worried what the group was about to find out about her. Following that of course, she mostly worried she would find out that she was in fact quite different than the silly, false tricks of this circus fit for children.

She was so worried at her own abnormalities to sufficiently see any warning sign of what was to come, that the circus would devour all in its path like an inferno. Oh, but we didn't get to that part yet. You'll have to wait to find out with Julia I suppose.

"Wanna help?" Nick interrupted her thoughts with a nudge. Julia had no idea what he was referring to. Had they been discussing some predicament that might require her assistance? "Setup," Nick said, catching on to her cluelessness. "Exhibits don't wait; we'll be dragged there in a jiff'," he laughed.

And just like that, Julia found herself tagging along with Analiese to learn about circus prep work. But, this is no ordinary circus, remember.

Sure, RaeChae's tent was predictably of an acrobatic nature, with aerial equipment Julia tried to decipher. A rope at a steep incline could be a unique tightrope, or perhaps some other sort of rigging. Julia was leaning towards the latter because a slab of wood ran parallel to it mere inches away; perhaps the wood was the act equipment. A wooden ladder gave access from the ground to the lower end of the board. Puppet strings dangled from the center of this tent, too, only a gold ribbon hung with them and flashed for attention.

"Tie me up." RaeChae approached with a smirk, wheeling a small unicycle and propping it against the ladder. Julia watched as Analiese tied the puppet strings to RaeChae's wrists and legs. She did not have time to wonder as to RaeChae's act though, because Analiese was fast—perhaps from years of tying such knots—and ready to move to the next tent right away.

Next was Nick's tent. "Nick and Phoebe have the longest prep, so I save them for last," Analiese explained.

"So many lanterns to ignite," Julia agreed.

But the lanterns were already lit, Nick having had ample time to spare while they were at RaeChae's tent. At first Julia thought it was quite considerate of Geppetto to hire Analiese to simply tie some strings. Then again, there was probably a lot more work to do in setup and teardown when the circus moved. Plus, Julia remembered Analiese saying something about advertising strategy when she first met the full group.

"What do we want this time?" Analiese grabbed Nick's wrist and twisted.

"Uhh," Nick stuttered. "Not that."

Analiese's lip pouted, then she shrugged and patted his arm with reassurance. "Whatevs."

"I'm thinkin'..." Nick glanced at Julia. "She know?"

Analiese raised her eyebrows. "Surprise." Shoving him to the ground, she straddled him and twisted his nose. A drawn-out cracking caused Julia to gasp.

"Ahh!" Nick covered his face with his hand.

"Remember not to fight, buddy," Analiese crooned, grabbing for his ears next. Julia considered stepping in, only dissuading herself because she still could not determine what was occurring.

"Gimme a mo-" Nick's muffled words only put a smile on Analiese's face as she yanked his ears out, stretching to follow her fists. "Mmmgh."

Nick used one hand to cover his nose, laid back to dodge another painful grasp, and pursed his lips. His ears, now of abnormal size, flopped to touch the ground. Raising his other hand to Analiese's face, he said, "Jus' gimme... a moment... t'brace myself."

"I couldn't decide between a real Pinocchio look or Dumbo,"

Analiese said. "Also, I kinda wanna throw in some surrealism if ya don't mind." Analiese reached for his arm next, the one in front of her face. Without hesitation, she twisted, causing another cracking sound.

Nick yelled out, and Julia could not stand by any longer. Approaching Analiese slowly, she said, "Analiese, I think that's enough. You're hurting—" Analiese shoved Nick to the ground and whipped her arm around latching onto Julia's wrist. With a gasp, she released her grip.

"I'm so sorry, Julia. I'll fix it, I promise." Analiese's thick lips moved like a fish as she babbled her apology. Julia kept her gaze on Analiese while stooping to check on Nick. When she finally realized Analiese was finished with her forceful tirade and insistent on stumbling over her worrisome phrases, Julia finally looked at Nick. He bent around his injured arm and continued to cup his nose, but seemed disinterested in his own injuries, instead staring at Julia's wrist with wide eyes.

Julia followed his gaze to her own body. Having felt no pain, she could not imagine his reason for worry. Yet there, her wrist proved as flimsy as Nick's drooping ears, showcasing an imprint the shape of Analiese's hand, perhaps an inch deep. As if clay or dough, her body had responded to Analiese's touch, relinquishing any ownership to the space Analiese's hand requested.

"Heavens," she said. Her secret, revealed so soon. There for all to see, perhaps forever. Julia did not know how to undo a handprint. She had been concerned about so much more, and yet a single grasp was all it had taken.

"Don't worry, Jul'," Nick murmured.

"Don't worry," Julia repeated, still unable to look away from her arm.

"This is, well, embarrassing," Analiese said. "But I can fix this, promise."

"You claim to be better than all those doctors?" Julia scoffed, stepping back as she felt Analiese's warm breath encroaching her space.

"Oh, I can't fix me," Analiese amended. "Just you. And it took lots of practice."

"You have an ever unrecognizable appearance that could justify a name tag, but I've yet to see a problem of yours needing fixing."

"Just give me your hand." Analiese reached out and grabbed the wrist, gently massaging. Once again, like dough, Julia's skin moved to Analiese's coaxing, shifting form and slowly returning to what could be seen as normal.

"You have talent," Julia said.

"Talent? Try telling that to those I've marred for life. Took years to master fixing my sculptures."

"Talent?" Nick interjected, squirming to his feet without removing his hand from his nose and holding his other arm, twisted into a spiral, close to his chest. "Try tellin' that to the sculptures you break bones in without warning."

"Right." Analiese pointed his way. "It'll heal soon. Are the ears too heavy?"

"Oh, I'll manage."

Julia put her arm in front of her face, as smooth as it ever had been, only hints of scars encircling from her own abnormality—the imprint had been from Analiese's touch. Analiese had some abnormality, too, one that had evidenced on Julia. The circus group still had no way of knowing Julia's oddity. She was still safe.

"At least let me finish," Analiese said, still talking to Nick. "Your other arm isn't done."

Nick slowly took his hand from his nose, revealing a twisted spiral with finger indents much like his arm. Holding his unmarred arm toward Analiese, Nick cleared his throat and said, "Ready."

Analiese was slow this time, methodical, drawn-out as if a somber atmosphere had arisen from her accidental sculpting of Julia. The passionate, spunky, sadistic way she had forced her sculpting on Nick earlier was gone; yet Julia wondered if this was simply another side of Analiese showing off her art form to Julia. It was graphic, explicit, unfiltered by surprise, no chance of missing any detail as she watched the arm slowly sinking into itself, turning, turning too far. Then, the cracking—quick pops and lengthy crackles intermixing while Nick gritted his teeth to fight through the pain.

Should he grit his teeth? Can't they break? Not that his concern was necessarily on bones not breaking at that moment. In fact it seemed as if that may be the entire point.

Analiese scanned her work, but Nick averted his eyes. "Hmm, Nick? How's it look?"

"Oh, it feels like you're done."

"Seriously. A little more?"

Nick grimaced and glanced at his arm. "The wrist is crooked. I won't grasp rightly."

Analiese tugged, eliciting a snap, then cocked her head. Finally, she backed away. "Done."

"Yeah." Nick did not choose to peruse the completed product.

"So you just—" Julia scrambled for words to explain what had occurred, "—grasp and force the body to move in a way it cannot?" She once again found herself both intrigued and repulsed.

"My touch makes just about any material malleable. A curse and an art all at once."

"Curse," Nick muttered.

"Please, he enjoys it." Analiese beamed at Nick, and he returned it with something between a smirk and a grimace. Analiese looked upward, a bit somber, reflecting. "I appreciate the practice. It's not only forming something new, it's bringing the...object or human...back to what they were, mostly from memory. The ultimate art restoration project. Or an art forgery maybe, but without the original around for reference. And the symmetry combined with asymmetry makes it interesting. It's not... It's not always been easy. And some changes are more, well, permanent." She shook her head, smiled, and pointed at Julia's face. "I could never get a dimple like yours for instance, a secret that comes forth only when you smile. That's an exquisite masterpiece I have yet to achieve. It'd be lost forever, so keep your distance."

Julia didn't know how to respond to the...compliment?...threat? She wasn't sure. She'd smile out of decorum, except it felt a little showy now, so she pursed her lips instead.

"Anyway," sensing the tension, Analiese changed the topic, "it's time to get to Phoebe. She'll need me to chat her ear off—figuratively." Analiese quickly added the last word to reassure Julia, reaching out to pat her forearm, then changed her mind and instead dropped her hand to her side.

8

HERE IS THIS GALLOPING SNAIL off to?" I ask.

Fancy glowers, her chin outstretched to see over the steering wheel. "We need that Nick, and you lost him."

It suddenly all comes back to me what had transpired. That I'd been trapped in the brightest room ever, and then... I wasn't. It was a dark chasm, or I was a dark chasm, or... something that doesn't go into words or logic. And it seems like maybe Fancy knew and planned it. "Wait, so what was that back there with Nick? How did I—how did we...?"

"You had one job. ONE!" She lifts her index finger, but I'm pretty sure the middle one is in the running. "Just keep your paws on Nick when ya escape, but nooo."

"I didn't even know I was escaping, I don't even know what's happening!"

Fancy clenches the steering wheel, purses her lips, and mechanically turns her face to stare me down. "You," she whispers.

"Watch the road, Fancy," I say.

"Shut..."

"Fancy, I wanna live." I ponder pushing her face back toward the road, but she seems like the type to have a bite that comes with the bark. After all, Scrubs Two was downright terrified of her.

"Your..."

"Watch where we're driving. Wherever that may be," I add.

"Trap."

I sigh. We are getting nowhere with this line of conversation. Well technically we are going somewhere—leaving town even— she just isn't about to tell me where that somewhere is.

I clench my lips and make a hand gesture of throwing away the key. Fancy turns her eyes back to the road. Phew. Of course it's a straight shot and no one was coming, but the way she gambles with her life—and more importantly mine—it's as if she'd faced down the rider Death himself and defeated him. Or maybe she is Death herself. That'd be plausible.

Then, I see a barley field. A perfectly intact one. Perhaps comparable to the circus scenery once upon a time. "So where we going?"

She screeches to the side of the road. I've really done it now.

"Get out," she says.

We are in the middle of nowhere. If I were investigating a murder, this is where the body would be dumped: A vast field. Nothing to see for miles. And she wants to dump me here, probably alive, but still.

Fancy hops out of the car. Okay, so maybe she doesn't want me alive. Maybe she is going to dump my body here. If I go missing, no one will notice; to anyone I knew before, I'm already missing and nothing has been done about that. So if I'm murdered, no one would know to look for me. Right?

I briefly contemplate hopping in the driver's seat and running off, but that seems a little overkill. Sure, she's in the killing mood, an ever-present state-of-being for her I presume, but I still don't know if she is the killing type. And talk about embarrassing to drive off and later have to admit to her face that I had thought she would kill me. She'd get a kick out of that.

So against my better judgment, I risk my life to preserve my dignity, and hop out of the car. Still cautiously, just in case. I could outrun her, I figure, until my feet touch the ground. Then I remember.

"I need shoes, Fancy."

She wasn't listening, so I hobble up to her. "Dare I ask what we're doing in the middle of nowhere?"

Fancy surveys the field with her back to me, surely not the direction to face if on the verge of murder. She knows this place. Her gaze holds a mix of fondness and regret. It's what people must feel about home.

"It all happened here," she says.

"What?" I ask dumbly. In my defense, she didn't give me much to go on.

"Your search," she responds, more forthright than she's been yet. "Nicholas, Julia, the 'magical' circus if you must call it that... It begins and ends here."

A measly barley field. The circus had been here, though. The circus. Magical or not, that is something. And yet, this isn't where we'd been before. I am disoriented. No parking lot off a main road to the town, not like before. We are somewhere close, but different. I step forward and begin to walk further in, ignoring the squish of mud beneath my toes, too busy looking for signs of it—of the circus, of the people, of the magic, of anything.

Eventually, deep into the field, I see it. Across a small alley lined with trees, the raised slope, the packed in dirt, the beckoning wagons. Even a few peanut shells and apple cores I hadn't noticed previously.

We are approaching from some other side of the circus. Some part of the story that only insiders are a part of—no journalists, no audience—only the key players. Perhaps there is some truth to her tale. She knows something.

Fancy is right behind me. Oh yeah, I'm supposed to be cautious and worried she may kill me. Oops. A breeze plays through her wild hair, but all fierceness has left her eyes.

Something is gone, and I feel it. Or, I think I feel it. Maybe it's all this magic talk tricking me, but I feel an absence stronger than the feeling of the wind biting my face. It hurts.

Suddenly, tears splash the ground. I swipe my face. "Magic," I mutter. More a curse than any other word I'd say.

"You feel it, too," Fancy says.

But feel what? I don't know, and I'm not about to talk through it with this conniver, so I jog past her and back toward the car.

"Wait!" she calls.

But the tears are filling my eyes again. This cursed place has shaken something loose in me, and I can't wait. I have to run before it catches up to me.

Instead, I catch up to it first.

I trip in a divot on the way to the car. Or, something trips me. A body. Or should I say...a corpse.

Ten

NALIESE AND JULIA EXITED Phoebe's tent. Julia squinted and looked around, not due to the daylight though. Was she leaving Phoebe's tent already? She could have sworn the last thing she remembered was being in Nick's tent, maybe vaguely recalled leaving for Phoebe's tent. Julia glanced to the barley field. There, sneaking through the brush away from the circus, were two figures.

"Who would that be?" Julia pointed. Only after the question did Julia wonder if she had met them in Phoebe's tent and completely forgotten.

Analiese peered around Julia, catching a glimpse of the two men. "I don't know. Must be some patrons looking for free admission later. Keep an eye out once we open."

So Julia had not met the two in Phoebe's tent. *But I should know that*, she thought. *I should know who I have seen and who I have not.* And yet she didn't. She left Nick's tent, then all her memory held was darkness, as if a storm cloud had rolled in across the ground and blackened her sight.

As Analiese led Julia toward the big top, Julia watched the two men make their trail through the barley. The older had dark hair and an intimidating stature, the younger—barely more than a boy—had light brown wisps tugged by the breeze. With their backs turned, it could be hard to identify them later.

"I need to speak with Geppetto alone now." Analiese entered the big top and tugged the flap down without allowing Julia entrance, though Julia hardly noticed until she walked into the cloth, her gaze still on the barley where the figures could hardly be seen now. "If you don't mind," Analiese added from inside the tent.

"Sure," Julia said. She was actually relieved for the chance to be alone, and decided to follow the new path created through the field.

Once she ascertained that Analiese wouldn't return and others weren't watching, Julia climbed down the artificial ditch into the barley and wondered how many people this precarious ground had caught in its clutches. She watched the men ahead of her saunter through the barley, as if indifferent to her tailing them. As if she was not about to confront them about sneaking into the circus. As if they could not be fined or arrested for trespassing. (At least, she presumed there was some negative consequence of a sort.)

Julia stopped short. Was she going to confront them? *Genius, one naïve girl set on making demands of two men in an isolated field. More than likely capable of any number of atrocities on a defenseless lady.* She had to remember she could not play the sheltered rich girl anymore. She had to protect herself now.

Looking ahead, the men were nearing the edge of the field. Julia could still stand a chance of catching up if she hurried. Yet what would she say?

The older man turned as he exited the barley field. He looked Julia right in the eye and nodded. Julia squinted, shrugged her shoulders. She was having some sort of moment with this man. He was trying to tell her something, but what? He smiled and bobbed his head again. Julia started to jog through the trail, certain if she caught up to him he could explain his presence, the meaning of that look. But the malleable ground caused her to trip, momentarily catching hold of barley to steady the fall and keep her chin from smashing into the dirt, landing on her elbows instead.

Julia brushed the dirt from her arms and legs, carefully studying herself. No injuries, no abnormalities. Only the typical scarring that was as much a part of her as always. She was still safe. No one would find out yet.

Julia stood, brushing the wisps of hair from her face and straightening her dress as best she could. She looked through the field and felt blood rise to her cheeks as she thought of the two men seeing her clumsy footing. Yet all she saw was the field and a few outlying buildings on the way to the town. The men had left. She could try searching the town, or even explore the nearby buildings, but chances of finding them were slim now. Instead, Julia turned back and determined to keep her eye out for those men to return to the circus.

Eleven

EPPETTO HAD CHANGED from his drab brown suit into the circus attire, and was preparing to practice his presentation. Usually Analiese was here by now to help, but he assumed she was taking longer showing off to Julia. Which was expected, even encouraged; he needed Julia to be fascinated by the possibilities here.

When Geppetto heard shuffling feet outside the tent, he paused. They were headed his way. Sure enough, he would soon find out what Julia's initial thoughts were on the insider view of the circus. Even better when Analiese told Julia that she needed to speak alone with Geppetto—he could be quite honest with her about the whole thing.

"If you don't mind," Analiese said.

A muffled "sure" was heard from Julia, and Geppetto smiled.

"Geppetto, go ask Phoebe if I told her the routine for the night," Analiese demanded.

Geppetto patted his gold hat as if making certain it was still there. When its presence was sure, he did a half-spin to face Analiese. "Don't be silly. She doesn't know."

"Force her!"

"Why torment the girl for no reason?" Geppetto squinted. "And why don't you know, if you're the one who did or did not say it?"

Analiese grabbed the nearest equipment—juggling torches—and placed them by the ring haphazardly. "Because, I don't remember anything."

A crew member began to walk over to help with setup, but Analiese's glare gave her pause.

"Stop working. Sit down and explain." Geppetto began to squat down as an invitation, then stood straight again, realizing his suit could become too filthy right before the big show. Analiese was too focused on the juggling torches to notice, lining them up just so.

"I remember leaving Nick's tent and then there's only this dark, foggy memory, like nothing happened 'til I exited Phebe's tent. It doesn't make sense. I can't remember any of that time, just catching some guys trying to sneak in after."

"Okay," Geppetto said. "Hmm. Okay." He shrugged.

"Well?" Analiese finally stopped her work and marched up to Geppetto, awaiting a more satisfactory answer.

"Let me know if you see the men sneaking in." Geppetto waved his hand in dismissal.

"Well, yeah," Analiese said. "What about the memory?"

"Has it not occurred to you that we have a newcomer?"

"Julia. I led her around this morning."

"With a newcomer comes a new gift of a sort," Geppetto reasoned.

Analiese crossed her arms. "Wait. This is her problem?" Analiese glared at the tent entryway. "The freak didn't even explain it to me."

"She may not be aware it happened," Geppetto said.

"Yeah, yeah," Analiese said, storming out of the tent.

Geppetto wondered about this gift. How could blackened memories bring his circus success? Or perhaps this gift would be the demise of the circus. "Impossible!" Geppetto said aloud, hoping the word would make it so.

Geppetto looked at the juggling torches Analiese had abandoned. "Far from well done," he muttered, grabbing the bunch and waving one of the crew over to help, wondering if he'd have to practice his presentation alone today. He shook his head and laughed. Julia hadn't even joined the circus yet, and she was already turning it topsy-turvy.

9

Clue...6: A field on the edge of town, the setting of the mayhem. Clue 7 is worse: a dead body.

CAN'T STOP THE SCREAMS. The pounding in my ears is even stronger. A dead man. Not much older than I. Laying there. Still. Dead. I was right; this is the place you go to murder someone.

Fancy catches up to me, shakes me, jostles me until the screams die down.

"Pull yourself together and keep quiet," she says.

I scoot away from the body.

Fancy looks, studies it... him... I refuse to look any more and study Fancy instead. "Pinocchio," I think she says. But that makes no sense. "Goes to show the care that went into the investigation. They still haven't found the dead body right on scene."

I try to puzzle it together. She was saying someone died, presumably when the circus vanished, too. And here I was thinking I was merely looking into debunking some paranormal mystery. I'm in over my head.

"I knew him," she continues, with words that make marginally more sense. "I mean, sort of. I met him."

I swallow in hopes of my tongue regaining its mobility. "Who—no what—," I stumble, start again. "What happened?"

Fancy moves in, inches from his face. "Wrong place, wrong time." She lightly strokes the hair from his face. "Meddling, I suppose. Sound familiar?" She smirks my way, like it's some horrible joke.

That's what she brought me here for. To threaten me. To convince me to stay away, to not stick my nose where it doesn't belong, but mostly to insinuate that my corpse would end up like his, forgotten in a cursed field.

My stomach turns, from the body or the threat or the smell, I'm not sure. I puke, then wipe my face, hoping to gain some modicum of dignity back. I push myself to my feet, and see that Fancy is already on hers.

"So," I say. "Who are you protecting?"

"You," she says. "You're welcome." She walks back to the car, just leaving the guy there. If she were innocent, she should want to call the cops or something. If she were guilty, she should want to bury the evidence that's staring me in the face. But instead, she walks. No biggie.

I consider calling the cops. I really do; but I can't chance being interrogated by them, and I certainly don't want to become a suspect in this murder case. Fancy would throw the blame on me in a heartbeat.

I'm pretty sure I leave a piece of myself with the body. It hurts, the curse not wanting to give me up quite yet, but I plod along. I walk away. I follow her.

Fancy has me right where she wants me. Like always. I can't get ahead.

Two weary figures trudging their way to town, leaving behind the cursed magic that could no longer hold them. Something darn near poetic like that, I think. It had to be darn near poetic.

I am not convinced by this whole magic crap. I'm not.

But seeing a dead body messes with ya. The abandoned and "haunted" mansion suddenly feels quite homey. The dust and cobwebs starting to form are a nice touch for a halloween party. Then again, I'm not interested in guests. Or evidence of lives that are no more—even if it's spider lives.

So I take a cloth to the place. I guess I need to keep busy and get out of my head and into mundane tasks. I start in the grand entryway, work my way through the kitchen—which let's be real, should never have dust in it. I breeze past Fancy's door where she'd promptly locked herself when we'd arrived "home", and I begin up the staircase. Plenty of first-floor rooms I gloss over, just to work my way up the stairs, like I'm clearing a path. I know where I'm going, though I try not to think it.

Julia's room.

The doll is right where I left it, face-down on the bed, motionless. Too familiar. I toss the pillow over it, then worry that's a little too close to suffocation and replace it with a blanket. Better I guess.

I brush at the cobwebs but quickly come back to the desk, the note: She needs you.

I dig into the desk drawers, grab a stack of paper and a pen. And I begin drawing. A flowchart or mind map or whatever I guess. Clues.

They branch off in many directions: Nicholas, the mental ward, this mansion, the doll, the note, the cirque field, the body...and they all lead back to her. Fancy. Some whacked out journey she is leading me on, and to where? for why?

It all seems like good leads, but I can't make heads or tails of how to piece it together or what it leads to next. Probably proof that in my past life I was not in fact a detective of any sort and should never take up this career pursuit again. So instead I had let Fancy lead me around on my little leash like her little puppet, as she told me where to devote my attention. And none of it added up to an answer. None of it led anywhere except back to where I came from: Fancy.

I have two options at this point: Storm the gates and demand an answer, which in my defense I'd tried before. Fancy is pretty good with turning it all back on me, and then I get all flustered and end up at her beck and call all over again.

Soooo option 2. Sneak out and find some answers without her steering my path. That seems like more the Maxwell way. (P.S. Nope, let's never go by Maxwell.) Climb out a window. Or, simply walk out the front door. She stays holed up quite fine when I actually leave her be. Either a true mastermind manipulative trick to get me thinking it's my idea to involve her, or an actual indicator of her innocence, that hey I did in fact get myself into this mess while she was trying to mind her own business, I mean, I did kinda crash at her place uninvited. Couldn't possibly be the latter. Right?

I hurry down the stairs, snag the keys from the kitchen counter she'd plopped them on and the sneakers she'd dumped by the door that conveniently almost fit, then race out the door before she can notice I'm leaving—or maybe before I chicken out. It feels nice to have a sidekick, even an abrasive know-it-all one. It feels familiar.

I stop as soon as I'm outside. I am out, but... What now?

I have leads from Fancy: looking for Nicholas, notifying the police about that body, or exploring the field for more clues. I could of course browse the mansion more, except I'm avoiding Fancy.

Right, I'm avoiding Fancy. Going it alone. I can be a lone wolf, I tell myself. But it feels like I am missing my right arm; it isn't natural, all the silence. Companionship is my thing I guess, even if a little dysfunctional. I gulp. I have to do this alone for once, I have to learn to trust my own brain instead of leaning on someone else's.

What would I have originally done to investigate, if I hadn't been intercepted by all of Fancy's guidance? Where would my path have taken me without her misconstruing it?

The library. Newspaper clippings type stuff. That sounds like what a true detective would do. Funnn, perfect for a night on the town. Read all the dang articles for years into the past. Or at least, through the circus's rise and fall.

That day may come, but it is not today. Today, I want a little more excitement.

What else? Before Fancy, I led myself here, to the Trencher's haunted old mansion. I came up with that on my own. An achievement of my own. And it gave me an idea...

Me all on my own would look for a little guidance from someone involved that had nothing to do with Fancy. Before I came along, before Fancy came along, the circus turned things topsy-turvy for someone else. This story actually began before me and Fancy, in the same house I stood in front of, only with a different couple inhabiting and spatting and skeptical of the circus's magical pull.

It all began with...them. The Trenchers.

Twelve

JULIA DUCKED INTO PHOEBE'S TENT, hoping she could solve the mystery of the black memories. Phoebe was already in her dead-like state, head resting on the desk, eyes staring at the foam ball inches from her face. Surely the ball was supposed to resemble a crystal ball, probably in an ironic way since no one would expect her to actually see a future in the blobs of color on the cheap thing.

Still, Julia wondered exactly how Phoebe knew things about people—her name, Geppetto's upcoming invitation to the circus.

Of course all of that could have been staged, a not-so-clever trick to convince Julia of Phoebe's powers. Mind games seemed like an exaggeration when all that was needed was someone to tell Phoebe Julia's name and that Geppetto was interested in her joining. Still Julia presumed there may be more to the gift, considering the unblinking eyes in front of her, this puppet state they took on.

And the darkness. No memory of earlier events. The effect could be caused by some sort of drug, she supposed. The possibility of memory loss being a part of the circus gifts did not escape her notice either, but somehow it seemed too convenient, too exact. One memory gone forever, one entire scene in her life without even the foggiest recollection.

Why would the circus want her to forget everything that happened in Phoebe's tent? Was it Geppetto's doing? Analiese's?

Even Phoebe, kind though she may seem, had acted harshly last time Julia had entered the tent. Perhaps there was a big secret there, something she had uncovered.

Julia peered through a crack in the tent entrance. She could not see anyone nearby. Julia looked around the tent, but saw nothing suspicious. The desk with the ball, the chair Phoebe sat upon, the strings dangling, tied to Phoebe's wrists and ankles. Julia walked around to the other side of the desk. No papers or files, not even drawers to stash such items. She reached out slowly for the ball, touching it, feeling the grainy foam roll slightly away from her touch.

She looked down at Phoebe—still staring so persistently, still unmoving as the dead. Yet those eyes, watching the ball—did they see still? Julia clamped her hand on the ball more firmly, refusing to let it roll off. But it was only a ball, a chunk of foam from any old place, dabbed with paint. It couldn't be something worth the risk of being caught snooping. She slowly let go, carefully removing her hand to keep the ball from rolling again.

Firm steps approached the tent, and Julia jumped. As Analiese entered, Julia ducked down to feign studying Phoebe's breaths.

"What do you mean by this?" Analiese demanded.

"I want to understand the puppet show." Julia lifted her gaze to Analiese and crossed her arms.

"You mess with my mind without warning. I was at least apologetic when I sculpted you."

"I'm playing no game, I only—"

"You forget we all here have our own destructive force that can be used on ourselves or others. You'd be best to remember not to upset the acts. Next time my sculpting may not be so kind."

"I meant no harm, Analiese. I'll leave this tent." Julia edged around Analiese toward the exit, but Analiese quickly moved in front of the entrance.

"Remember, I don't have to return my sculptures to their previous appearance." Analiese backed of the tent and marched off. Julia felt her heart pounding and forced her breathing to slow down. Almost caught. There was certainly something the circus was hiding, and she had to figure out what that was. Until then, she should stay in the audience or in the background, never raising suspicion. Analiese was not one to deceive.

Julia exited the tent and wondered about lunch. She could wait; after all, not every person was accustomed to three meals a day. Yet still her stomach voiced its disapproval.

"Julia."

She started. She was not used to someone calling her name, certainly not an unfamiliar voice. Walking her way was a fidgety man, so nervous he couldn't even look her in the eye. Instead, he contented himself with studying the golden tent behind him, then the money collector at the entrance, next the puffy cloud to the side.

"Sylas," she acknowledged. The man she'd briefly met, mere minutes that were somehow long enough to convince her to leave behind the poking and prodding of the Trenchers and Doctor Wise. A man who claimed he was different, too, though not so outlandish as to care to take up with a circus, last she was aware. "Come to join?"

"Naww, I said I wasn't a circus performer. I meant it." His fingers gripped the edge of Phoebe's tent and rubbed the fabric between his fingers, studying the topmost point as if considering scaling the flimsy structure.

"Oh." Julia watched his gaze trail down to the dirt as he scraped his shoe in her direction. Glad for the firm boots she'd been wearing, Julia shifted from one foot to the other to avoid closer proximity to him. "What brings you here then?"

"Our discussion, of course. You up and disappear, miss appointments, your parents don't show their faces. And I think to myself..." Sylas sniffed and eyed the entrance again. "I thought 'where would Julia run off to if she's not with Dr. Wise?' Well we said it ourselves, there's only one place. And here you are."

"Right." Julia looked down at his feet again. His foot was tapping emphatically at the dirt. "Wait. You're stalking me?"

"Yeahh, no." Sylas said, finally looking Julia in the eye. "Silly, I've come to bring you home."

"Home? Why in the world would I go there?"

"I've been told the heart is there." Sylas shrugged.

Julia frowned. "Mr. and Mrs. Trencher don't exactly express affection."

"Oh I noticed. But let's be honest..." Sylas moved inches from Julia's face conspiratorially and whispered, making the situation more awkward by his inability to look her in the eye, and making them cheek to cheek instead as he stared off into the field. "Freaks don't want a circus anymore than they want a doctor's office."

Julia grabbed his shoulder and stepped away, holding firm to make sure he kept his distance. "What do we want?"

"You tell me."

Julia reached up and brushed her hair out of her face then rubbed her forehead. He was getting to her; the fidgets were contagious. "My parents," she tried the endearing term on for size. (It was a snug fit.) "They are looking for me?"

"Why would they confide such nonsense to me?" Sylas said. "I haven't seen them besides. They don't need the doctor now that you're traipsing about the world."

"The circus."

"Huh?"

"Not the world," Julia clarified. "The circus."

"Traipsing wherever you so choose to traipse. It' s not a doctor's office, and it's not home."

Julia paused for a moment, looking for an escape. "Not even home is home," she finally said.

"Then take me to see a show." Sylas walked in a slow, small circle, getting a good view of each of the small red and gold tents.

"What?" Julia huffed.

"One of the acts here. Any good?" Sylas asked.

Julia grabbed his sleeve in her clenched fist. "What about taking me home?"

"I thought you planned on staying here."

"I do, but you can't just change the topic." Sylas put his hand on her fist, gently pushing at a finger to release. She quickly pushed him away and stepped back, realizing her close proximity. "That's not how conversations work. You finish one before starting another."

"Well I thought that one was good and finished. Besides, since when did you become an expert conversationalist?"

Julia stuck her chin up and pursed her lips. "You're right, I didn't." She brushed past him and walked towards the center tent.

"So we seeing a show?" Sylas said, shuffling behind her. "Which one?"

"Actually I was proving my conversational ineptitude. I intended on leaving you without so much as a 'good day.'"

"What a stinger!" he replied.

Julia held the center tent opening up for Sylas to pass through and turned around, but he was walking away. She watched him duck into Phoebe's tent before entering the big top. She shrugged. "Good day."

Thirteen

HEN THE TIME CAME around for the individual acts to start, Julia headed straight toward Nick's tent. She couldn't help but remember his last show she'd seen, his eyes of terror and vulnerability. "Like I said, that sick a show," had been his words. With one last look at the barley fields, bent low now as if weary from their day of soaking in the sun, she ducked into his tent, as of yet the only spectator.

She realized she still did not know exactly what happened in the act, what sort of trickery or magic would resort a man to fear as a child does the closet monster or night mares. Yet she had to see again, whatever the cause may be, the state the "cost" of this circus Geppetto mentioned had brought to him. *Free, but rooted,* she hoped.

As she had seen prior, he lay prone with deathly appearance, only this time not disfigured by Analiese. Lanterns surrounded the perimeter, flickering out then on to reveal him in a seated position, before the flash happened again and left him lying deathly still once more.

Julia did not leave the vicinity of the tent opening, remembering the total darkness that had enveloped for such a slow passage of minutes. Sure enough, after waiting a length of time the lanterns all were doused again. Julia waited, listening closely. Outside, an object slapped along in the breeze. Other spectators murmured in some nearby show, and shoes rustled against the ground. Some insect droned in and out of earshot. With all the noise outside the tent, Julia could not hear any rustling, feel any presence, within the tent.

She reached her hand behind her to grasp the tent fabric. To allow only a trickle of light through, she carefully nudged the cloth a hint to the side as she scanned the tent. She started when she felt more than saw Nick standing in the light right next to her arm. She stepped back, allowing him space as she held the tent opening to assess him. His eyes were wide. She could nearly hear his heart pounding as his breath came rapidly, jaw set tight as if an attempt to hide the gasps.

"Close the tent," Nick said.

"Are you frightened?" she asked.

Nick looked away, into the darkness still covering most of the tent. "Let go of the tent," he reiterated.

Julia grabbed his arm and turned him to face her again. His eyes made a brief twinkle of recognition before returning a hard stare. "Geppetto'll—"

"What's terrifying you?"

"It doesn't matter." Nick grabbed her arm that held the tent open and released her grip. The room darkened for the slightest moment before she reached back and allowed light in again. Nick stepped closer to her, yet again mere inches from her face. This time she wasn't sure if she felt his chest pounding or her own; it was as if they were in sync from the close proximity. He stepped back, ducking his head in brief embarrassment.

"You win," he said. "But if another person comes, I gotta act."

"You're terrified," Julia said.

"That's life."

"It shouldn't be."

Nick shuddered. "It is. Some children are scared of the dark. They don't know that darkness itself feels fear, too." He clenched his jaw. "You scared o' shivering?"

Julia gripped her arm across her stomach. "It shouldn't be."

Nick looked beyond Julia out of the tent, and his face froze. Julia turned at the sound of footsteps.

"You're cheating." Analiese stepped into the tent with a smirk. "Save the flirting for later and get on with the show."

Nick looked between the two of them and rested his hand on Julia's shoulder. "Don't make me go." The words came out somewhere between a command and a plea, as if an attempt at assuredness.

Analiese tsked. "You know the rules." She grabbed the tent opening, waving her other hand as a threat to Julia. Julia let go, then Analiese stepped in and released her hold on the tent opening. As the darkness closed in, Nick shoved Julia away.

"You b-" Nick yelled, but was cut off as the darkness took over.

Julia's arm twisted with the force before she landed on top of it, hitting the ground with an "oomph."

"Surprise." Analiese said. "Someone could walk in at any moment, actually wanting a show." Analiese opened the tent, Nick standing in front of her with clenched fists. "Hope you understand." Analiese patted his cheek, softly enough not to cause any sculpting, before walking out and letting the tent return to darkness.

Julia scrambled to her feet and stumbled to the exit, looking in and seeing Nick a couple yards away. "It shouldn't be," she repeated. He didn't acknowledge her at all, instead staring wide-eyed out the tent opening in a way that made Julia wonder if he was looking at something that was no longer there—something he had seen moments before in the dark of the tent, that gripped him more fiercely than this dusky reality could.

Fourteen

ULIA HAD NOT SEEN Sylas since their earlier run-in, but she wondered if he had been as intrigued by the dead-like puppets as she had been.

Perhaps he sat with Phoebe, as companionably as Julia had with Nick. Perhaps he sat with her even now, gazing into the ridiculous ball, eyes wide like a goof as she told him what a fraud he was. Or perhaps he called *her* out for being a fraud, catching with his ever-moving eye some proof of the hoax.

Whatever the case, Julia once again entered Phoebe's tent, but this time it wasn't to search. The acts had awoken and Julia was hoping Phoebe would more readily reveal in this performance whatever premonition she had, perhaps even reveal whether she knew Julia's abnormality. With a glance she knew that Sylas had left and briefly wondered if he had moved on to another tent or left the circus altogether.

Phoebe gazed at her curiously. "You are an oddity, Julia."

"Try harder." Julia put her hands on the desk and looked down at the blue foam. "You could have known that from earlier."

"Geppetto will invite you to join our circus. Why is that?" Phoebe scooted her chair back and crossed her arms, causing the strings to cross and trail along her face.

"You tell me."

"You think you're a tough one?" Phoebe said, the X of the

strings' shadow bouncing around her nose. "I don't need to impress you. I offer what I offer. You don't like what you're getting, move along. I already know you'll be back."

"Will I?"

"Yes, you accept." Phoebe raised her eyebrows and inhaled sharply. "Y-you accept Geppetto's invitation," she stuttered.

"Of course you say that." Julia looked back at the foam ball again for a moment before turning to leave.

"You should know something before dismissing all that I said." Phoebe stood, scraping her chair further along the floor in the process. Julia tilted her head back towards Phoebe and noticed the shadowy X was gone. "I only see one moment of a person's life in my head."

"And you see me accepting?"

"And it's no small moment." Phoebe pursed her lips. "I wonder, what life-changing decisions have you made already?"

Julia considered her choice to leave home quite a sufficient twist to her life trajectory.

"Now," Phoebe continued, "imagine a decision even bigger than that, one of utmost importance."

"The biggest decision of my life. To what end?" Julia questioned.

"I don't read your soul, I merely see an important scene and relay the message. See it as you will." Phoebe sat back in her chair and leaned back until it sat on two legs.

Julia walked back to the desk and scooped up the foam ball, holding it away when Phoebe swiped at it, nearly tumbling forward as her chair righted itself.

"Look into this sham of a ball," Julia instructed. "Imagine for a moment it showed you what you needed to see. For now we'll go with your best guess."

Phoebe's nose flared. "One thing's for sure, I would've seen you stealing my ball away to use against me now. You do realize I can make another one for pennies."

"Humor me. Two paths diverge before me. I head back to the Trenchers, or I stay here. What vision might you see?"

"Perhaps this becomes the home you always dreamed of," Phoebe surmised. "Isn't that what we're all here searching for?" Julia sat the ball back on the desk, and Phoebe grabbed hold of it. "Who knows, maybe you'll make this circus a big deal, like none of us could. Geppetto's not got this whole showmanship thing down yet. Or..." Phoebe shrugged and looked up at the tent strings. "...Or I suppose the strings could be your worst nightmare, you despise your puppet life, and make enemies of us all. I'm not gonna make this all roses." Phoebe moved her gaze back to Julia. "Doesn't matter, though. I already know it's your decision, so best make the most of it and choose the first 'home you always dreamed of' scenario, no?"

"Yes," Julia replied. "I mean, we shall see."

"Oh we shall. No worries. I'm eventually proven right."

10

KAY. SO I *DO* go to the library, but only long enough to find the Trenchers' new residence. The whole "abandoned" thing is mere folklore; they actually still own the house and also purchased another nearby. They aren't hiding or anything. The sale is listed right in the paper as going to "The Trencher estate."

The idea of the circus causing them to vanish from a "haunted" mansion is all hype, and I'm satisfied to see that superstitious element crumble. It's the start of a domino effect of superstitions collapsing, I reassure myself.

And so, I am off to some new bougie mansion of theirs, I guess because their abandoned place wasn't bougie enough.

Fancy's car I borrowed putters into their driveway, which stretches far enough that I'm pretty sure they could use it as a runway for their private jet in the meantime. Pristine. That's what I'd call the place. A manicured lawn and well-maintained foliage. Not a weed to be seen, not a branch out of place. The yard is watched over by a statue at the center. A marble girl. I could imagine her beckoning each flower to bloom just so. With a glance of her eyes, weeds would wither to nothing and with a flick of her dainty wrist, leaves would rise from the ground back to the tree they'd leapt from.

Still, even amidst her immaculate domain, the statue doesn't gaze at the foliage; she gazes longingly out at the world from whence I came. One foot forward, ready to explore the world beyond her own yard. The grass is always greener or something like that. Enchanting.

I continue eyeing the statue as I hop from the car and amble towards the door. I suppose that's why I don't see the man in my path.

"We're not interested," he says. I start, step on his shoe and trip, all in one fell swoop. Way to get off on the wrong foot.

"I-I... Sorry," I say. "I'm not selling." Sheepish grin.

He isn't buying it. "You should turn the car around and get out of here before it takes its last breath in my drive."

"No, you see, I'm here to, well..." I brush off my shirt, as if that would take out the wrinkles, transform it into a bespoke suit, or make me feel at all to belong in this neighborhood.

"Nice statue," I comment. "Very, uhh... ornate..."

Mr. Trencher frowns.

"I'm here about your daughter," I finally say. His eyes widen, but his scowl deepens. "Julia," I say. "And what happened to her..."

Mr. Trencher grabs my shoulder and glances back at the house. I assume he's about to throw me curbside. Instead...

"Keep your voice down," he says under his breath. "I won't have that talk, and on my very own doorstep no less."

He cautiously looks around, taking in our surroundings, then whisks me off to the side, ducks behind a bush, and huddles against the stone walls of the...home?...can I call this gargantuan grim building a home? The better for prying eyes to not see when he decides to strangle me as a sacrifice to the magical garden guardian.

"You... you have a message?" Mr. Trencher whispers, peering from behind the bush.

I'm not about to join him all the way in there—I want to live!—but I squeeze between shrubs a bit, slightly acquiescing in hopes of gaining his trust. I keep a watchful eye on the street, my last hope.

"There's been some confusion, sir," I say as loudly as I can muster without sounding conspicuous. I straighten my posture, as if that will project my voice. "I know nothing. I only—"

"Hush!" Mr. Trencher insists, waving his hands frantically. Not a hint of decorum. "Keep it down. You'll be heard."

Exactly, I think. The ideal scenario when hiding in the bushes with an eccentric stranger. Reluctantly, I inch a little closer. "I said I know nothing. I'm here to find out what you know." Mr. Trencher frowns. "About Julia," I clarify. He frowns deeper.

"You're no use to me if you have nothing to offer," Mr. Trencher says. "Get your junk car out of my drive before it stalls out."

I can't lose him. He seems at least somewhat invested in the concept of talking to me. He is voluntarily ruining his suit in the landscaping.

"I'm trying to find out what happened," I say. "For all of us. For Julia, too."

"You want a story?" His face darkens, and his eccentricity turns from quirky to unsettling in a heartbeat. "They *all* want a story, every high-strung reporter out there has already bombarded this sanctuary and left to tell the fairy tale. You're late to the party, so you best get!"

The last sentence ends with a loud ring. He isn't concerned about the neighbors hearing now. He doesn't want to strangle me. He just wants me gone.

I try one last tactic. "I came all this way," I edge toward the window to peer in. "Maybe Mrs. Trencher would—"

"Get down!" Mr. Trencher leaps on my back and tackles me.

I yelp. He quickly crawls off of me as I struggle. He has smudges of dirt on his face, and his hair stands on end. His suit will never be considered fine dinner attire—or any attire really—again. "What is wrong with you?" I yell.

"Sshhh," he says. "She'll hear you."

Then it hits me. He isn't trying to hide me from prying eyes outdoors. He's trying to hide me from prying eyes indoors. Mrs. Trencher?

I hop to my feet, hands out as my act of surrender, however temporary that may be. "All right, I get it. I'm gone," I say. I jot back to the junk car and drive away. But only so far. Only to find a parking lot to stash the car, head back to the park across the way, and sit by a tree to keep watch.

I feel a little bit like a stalker or a thug. But I remind myself that detectives, reporters, and private eyes are all about watching a private place while staying in what's technically a public space. So I think I'm okay.

I sit against that tree 'til my bum is sore, then I stand and pace 'til my legs complain. So I sit again, but not as long because my bum still hasn't forgiven me from the last time.

I don't know how long I am there, with nothing happening to show it. But I'm a patient man. I mean, I don't remember ever being patient, but apparently I can be, because I stay.

Wait. Maybe I'm a *stubborn* man. That seems more accurate to the (albeit limited) memories I have. Stubborn. I should add that to my list of character qualities.

Eventually my stubbornness pays off. Mr. Trencher leaves the vicinity. It has to happen at some point, and I'm glad in this case it happens the same day and not after I'd camped out for a week and got all stinky and starving.

I approach the house again, nodding in solidarity at the goddess of the garden, hoping she will bestow her blessing on this endeavor. A sense of foreboding fills the place, probably because I am sneaking around where I don't belong. It doesn't stop me.

I tap on the door. No response. I tap again, a little louder, but I can't bring myself to knock at a decibel that anyone could hear unless they were directly on the other side listening. It goes as no surprise that nobody hears, nobody answers.

I turn the knob, but it's locked. Of course. Nobody would leave a place this classy open to the masses. I frown and step back.

I turn around to the statue. Her back to me, heading away from the place I'm trying to enter. Foreboding. "It's not safe," she whispers. Or perhaps more logically, it's the wind and my paranoia playing tricks on me.

She doesn't look back. That's not what turned her to stone. She looks forward. Leaving the place is what's a curse, not staying, I tell myself.

I pound on the door finally, then move into the brush to peer into the window. Last time I was in this precise location, Mr. Trencher had tackled me. But now, I get to look. It's a nice place—no, nice doesn't cut it—it's a lavish place. Refined and untouched. No one lives here, they inhabit here. It's what the old Trencher place felt like, before the dust settled and spiders moved in to decorate, before Fancy and I moved in and decorated our respective rooms with life and clutter.

Behind me I hear a click and a small swish—the door. "Hello?" a mousy voice asks.

"Mrs. Trencher!" I belt out before remembering that I'm

hiding out in her bushes. She doesn't seem to notice, though. I clamber through the landscaping and up the steps as if that's completely normal.

"Such a pleasure to make your acquaintance," I continue. I grab her hand in an overzealous handshake, eager to act the part of fitting in around these parts. Hint: I don't. Her lips tilt upward stiffly, either from an uptight personality or from the operation she'd had on the right side of her face at some point to hide some wrinkle or blemish or something *undesirable*. Or, okay, I suppose the stiff response could be because a stranger climbed out of her bushes. That could do it, too.

"Won't you come in...?" a little rusty on proper decorum for this situation I presume. She gestures down the hall, and I duck through the door as she says, "I'm afraid you just missed him, but do sit. I'll bring you a cup of tea."

She whisks past me and leaves me alone in the entryway, as pristine from the inside as from the window. More glamorous though; everything has an extra shimmer to it.

I tiptoe through the hall to a parlour on the left. Bookshelves line the walls, though they don't quite look right. Bookshelves are meant to have dust collecting in long-forgotten corners while the most treasured section has a certain gleam to it. Here, though there are hundreds of books that couldn't have possibly been read recently, not a speck of dust is in sight. The place is for show as much as for use, if not more so.

Plump chairs invite me further. I am eager to finally have a moment of rest that isn't on the ground. I slump into the firm cushion. I could get used to this. I should be investigating, but I reason that I could use a moment to collect my thoughts, to strategize my next steps.

And then I'm out...

...

...

...

"You!" the voice booms, and I jerk awake. "Scallywag, this isn't some sleazy motel."

I'm sure I am gonna get thrown out in no time. "So sorry, Mrs. Trencher," I mumble as I rub my eyes to wakefulness.

"You can't barge in here and drool all over my furniture. Drink this tea to wake you before Mr. Trencher returns." I wipe my mouth—she's right about the drooling—and accept the cup she has extended.

"Thank you." I sip the tea, grateful for the warm comfort. She helps herself to another inviting seat, though she brushes it with her fingers first as if it is coated in crumbs. It isn't, of course; it looks like it's straight from some rich folk catalog.

"Cream and sugar," she gestures toward an end table where sure enough, there are all the tea things. Never been one for additives to my tea, though. At least, I don't feel like I've been one to add things to tea. So I gulp the tea down readily enough without it.

"Tell me," she says. "What business have you with my husband?"

I quickly move the cup to my mouth, to give more time to come up with a response. A moment later, I say, "To be frank, I'm here to see you."

Mrs. Trencher stands and begins to leave the room, not even glancing my direction. "If you're a journalist, my husband insists you leave at once. If you're a doctor, however, I'm the one to insist you leave."

"Wait." I sit my cup down, sloshing a bit on the end table in my haste. "I'm neither, Mrs. Trencher. I'm a friend."

She pauses, but doesn't turn back. "A friend," she scoffs. "Come to chat a spell, have a laugh at my expense, tell Mr. Trencher I'm off my rocker and should be committed immediately. Yes, what a friendly thing to do.

"Tell me... I invite you in, prepare you tea. I do all that a dutiful hostess should, and have been quite reasonable, I should say." She wags her finger, though otherwise still frozen. "While you... you scrounge around my bushes in all manner of filth, doze and drool all over the furniture like an untrained house pet. Yet you have the audacity to say I'm the uncivil one because I can't bear to think about what... how she..."

Finally, Mrs. Trencher turns to face my way. "I'd like my tea cup back now."

I lightly set my cup on the end table and lift my hands in surrender. "I believe you." I say it in a hushed tone, maintaining eye contact, scrambling to remember what body language conveys non-threatening vibes. My selection is probably a horrifying mashup that instead screams untrustworthy, hiding something. Of course it would be; my body is even hiding something from itself, so why wouldn't it be hiding from everyone else as well.

"If you truly mean me no harm—" Mrs. Trencher sniffles, like I've created some stench in the house. "If you truly are a friend as you claim, you will leave this house at once and take no mad fairytales with you. No rumors of the crazed lady cooped up in quiet luxury, no fanciful stories of ghosts and hauntings. Choose wisely."

I nod, stand slowly, and tread toward the entryway. It's the "choose wisely" that catches me. There is a hint of an answer here, but I would never get it if she didn't feel safe. I'm playing the long game, so I agree to leave. Her wary glance follows, and I avert my eyes as I pass her. She follows me to the door.

I wish I were taking something more concrete with me. More than ravings of lunacy and hauntings, but it's a start. As I step onto the porch, I see her. The garden statue. The uncanny resemblance to the woman I've just had tea with. The immovable stature. And though the fervent gaze and pursed lips are turned away from me, it too is a reflection, I remember.

"Julia!" I exclaim. "It's her."

"Julia?" Mrs. Trencher pushes past me out the door, looking every which way. "Julia..."

I rest my hand on her arm and she startles. "I meant the stone, Mrs. Trencher. Your garden statue."

The light leaves her eyes and her brows furrow in resignation. "Oh..."

She sighs. "That—That isn't Julia. If you knew Julia, you'd know it's nothing like her." She gazes at the girl who's turned her back on this life then froze. Then she spits out: "It's an imposter," and turns back inside, calmly shutting the door as if this has been some normal chitchat with a friend.

Right. That's what I'm wanting to be. A friend. I can leave now and prove my trustworthiness for a time, then return to gain some actual clarity.

For now, I have to leave and wonder: the statue bears such a resemblance, how could it not be Julia? What am I missing?

11

USED TO WRITE CLUES here, goshdarnit.

What is this mess of a story anyhow? I feel like there are a thousand "clues" or questions every which way, but none that point in the direction of an answer. What do I write? What is worth documenting and what is mere fluff? I can't decipher. I'm traipsing haphazardly from one place to the next, not because anything led me there, but because of some speck of hope that something substantial will present itself. The asylum, the circus grounds, the Trenchers' old place and their new one...they all are filled with answers, but the walls can't talk and the people won't, at least not about anything of use.

Is this what actual detective work is like? No wonder there isn't a substantial investigation into this, because I'm so over it already. If I wasn't personally invested, I sure would not be professionally invested in this case. I'd simply move on with my life. But I can't move on, because my life is tied up somewhere here, if I can just find out how.

I drive home and expect Fancy to be all up in my case, if not about investigating without her then at least about stealing her junky car. Instead, I find a sleek replacement in the driveway. Either Fancy got a new and nice car (unlikely, "nice" isn't her style) or...someone is here.

I debate whether I should enter or run. But do I have anything to run from? I don't think so. Then again, I don't know.

120

I choose to risk it. When I enter, I hear a polite giggle from the living area we never touch. A forced one, not actually lighthearted, but still... This is not the haunted mansion or the Fancy I expect.

She must hear the door because she bustles around the corner. "Max! You're missing everything. Get in here and meet RaeChae."

RaeChae. I know that name from somewhere. But where? I walk in and immediately recognize the elegant beauty from one of the circus posters. Ah, right. RaeChae, short for RaeChaeline. Research is good for something.

She is as radiant and poised as I imagine she's always been. Like a peacock or some bird that towers taller than its height and doesn't deign to associate with lesser beings. Though the furniture is inviting, she hasn't made herself at home. She stands, uptight as ever, abrasive and jumpy, eyeing Fancy's movements as if she has a gun; Fancy looks as harmless as ever—all talk and nothing to show for it.

RaeChaeline smiles at me as a courtesy, but her eyes are piercing, like a hawk.

"Nice to meet—" I start to say, but she interrupts.

"I'll keep this brief," she says. "I caught wind that you invaded...Fancy, is it?..."

Fancy shrugs. "His pick."

"...Fancy's space in some delusion of 'investigating' a circus that closed up shop, same as many businesses in this economy close."

"RaeCh..." Fancy begins.

"Don't you 'RaeCh' me, 'Fancy,'" she warns. "You've no right to 'RaeCh' me."

Fancy frowns.

They have history. Not friendly history, though.

"You two know each other?" I ask 'RaeCh'.

"Let me finish," RaeChaeline says. "You're welcome to write about the economic travesties all you want, researching any other business that's closed. You can traipse the world digging into the collapse of circuses near and far. You can even make Fancy's life a living hell here for all I care."

Definitely not friends.

RaeChaeline continues. "But sniff around this circus, drudging up old wounds, concocting preposterous notions... You will regret it."

I decide to shake things up a bit. "You're a little behind the times. Fancy's already threatened me. She showed me the dead body."

RaeChaeline's face drains of color. She turns to look at Fancy. "Dead body? Fancy? How...?"

Fancy shrugs again. She is trying to look nonchalant, but I see the look. She's trying to tell RaeChaeline...something, I don't know what...with her eyes. "...that's right. I took him to the field by the circus grounds. He would have gone there anyway, so best to get past that now."

"Oh. Oh!" RaeChaeline says. "The circus... Right. There's a...?" RaeChaeline is wracking her brain for something. It's like she knows what they're talking about, but is still trying to put some piece together.

But then she recovers and turns back to me as if she hadn't lost a beat. "Sounds like you've been threatened, but not properly. Cops haven't found that body, but when they do, they're gonna need someone to pin it on. I'd hate for it to lead them back here to you two..."

RaeChaeline shakes her head and walks out, leaving our lives as fast as she arrived, like the whirlwind of a hummingbird sighting.

Clue 8: RaeChaeline is hiding something. Fancy is hiding something too, but what's new there?

12

ARK. MENACING CLOUDS ARE MOVING in as RaeChaeline storms out, and for a moment I wonder if this is some of the rumored circus magic, if RaeChaeline has sent a storm as a grand finale to her threats. "Impossible," I mutter. Then: "So, Fancy..."

Fancy is already meandering out of the room. I'm about to lose her. "Uh-uh. I am not getting into this."

I zip around her to the doorway to block it before I remember it's the size of an elephant. Darn extravagant mansion life.

I stand firmly in the center anyhow and rush the words out before she can walk away. "What does she know, how does she know it, how does she know *you*, and what's with the dead body secret message between you two thing?"

Fancy glares me down, then scoots around me and leaves.

"I'm not giving this up, Fancy," I yell.

She returns, pen and paper in hand. "I'm gonna skip over those questions and make you do the work, Mr. Investigative Genius. At the very least, it'll get you out of my hair for a bit. I've got my own life, remember." She hands me the piece of paper, an address scrawled on it.

"What's this?" I ask.

"More questions," she tsks. "Who knows. Maybe you'll get lucky and find answers, too." She emphasizes the unlikelihood with an artificial smile. I try to remember if it's the first time I've seen a smile on her face. Then I wrack my brain to try to remember the last time I saw a genuine smile, on Fancy or anyone really. I can't remember.

With that grim realization, I leave to check out the address. "I'm taking the car," I say.

She laughs. "And I'll get groceries, hon." Quite the couple we make.

DRIVE OUTSIDE OF TOWN, behind and past the circus lot. Past the field, past the circus wagons that stand like sculptures of remembrance. They look menacing amidst the storm, the garish scenes painted on the facade flashing with each crackle of light. For a moment I can believe they're haunted, too.

The address leads to another high-end community, a suburb of vast lots where the car doesn't fit in. And I figure I stand a better chance going incognito. I park blocks away, closer to town, where the junk car would—if not fit in—at least not stand out. I hope this plan is worth getting caught in the storm, which has escalated to a torrential downpour complete with loud booms and cracks. I approach the address nonchalantly, as if I'm not drenched head to toe and worried about being struck by lightning from a mystical, intimidating acrobat. I creep up the drive, though with the cloud cover of gloom I figure no one will be watching for visitors. It's a nice enough area that there could be security cameras everywhere; I don't see any, so I remain hopeful.

Oh yay, another mansion with a haunted appearance. At least this one looks well maintained—like the new Trencher home, not the old one. This one is lived in. It has turrets, almost like a more modernized castle. It towers over me as I approach, when I still have a ways up the walk.

And, wait: another medical facility. I come to a halt in front of it, not sure if I am frozen in fear or simply pondering. Let's say it's pondering. 'Cause the other medical facility wasn't traumatizing at all.

Actually, come to think of it, the events from the other one feel like one big delusional dream. Foggy and unreal and larger than life. It did happen, right? And dang it, I should have been watching the TV for something about dangerous fugitives escaping the asylum or whatever. Are we wanted? Is there a manhunt I should be worried about?

Anyhow, back to now: this new place isn't like anything you'd think would exist. What well-off physician would want his workplace built right next to his palatial residence? But here it is. A gargantuan home and a small pristine workplace separated only by an immaculate lawn.

The sign reads "Physician Laboratory", quite vague like people don't visit it on the regular—which makes sense for it being at his home. At the same time, there's a sign, so someone must need to see it, need to drop by on occasion for lab work or lab results or something. His work must be specialized or niche, or I suppose maybe he's just rich enough to do bare minimum generalized work with mediocre branding.

I duck behind the sign to be less conspicuous. I could go in maybe. It's not a mental institution so I needn't worry about getting locked up. Right?

I figure I could pretend I am a—patient? Colleague? No, not colleague. Med student?—I probably couldn't even effectively pretend that. I'll have to go with patient. If they say patients don't come here, I could say I must have been given faulty info. Or something. I'm definitely winging it, and we know how that's gone before.

I take a deep breath and approach the door. My palms are

sweaty as I move to push it open—wait, it's stuck. No, not stuck. Locked.

"The doctor is out" I whisper. "Come back during office hours." Another locked door, another dead end mocking me.

I peer through the glass but can't make out defined details. Maybe a small office area—desk, chair, lamps, the usual. I still don't know what I'm looking for, why Fancy sent me here, but I won't find out if I give up now.

I creep around the building, looking into windows. Most of the time my view is blocked by closed blinds. Doctor-patient confidentiality, of course. It would be just my luck if one of the windows was ajar, but if you've been following along, luck isn't really my thing. I did find a "staff only" door hidden amongst the landscaping, a more flimsy outdated thing that seems untouched for centuries or millennia or maybe just years.

Here's the thing: It doesn't seal against the storm. It's creaking back and forth with the wind, just a smidge, like a flimsy lock holds it in place. Otherwise the entire thing would collapse, or so it seems. Which gives me an idea. It seems quite reasonable that the storm is going to take this door out at some point. And maybe, I mean, I could help the storm out a bit.

Am I a criminal? I don't think so, but the idea of vandalism— oh yeah, and breaking and entering, maybe theft depending on what I find—those ideas slip into my mind too simply, too desperately, and I wonder. Yes, I am more likely to have been a criminal before than an investigator.

I give an exaggerated kick to the door and it cracks, but doesn't give. It feels good, though. It feels freeing, like I am finding myself. Maybe, I can't remember.

Anyhow, the second try is more successful, the door banging

open with an accompanying whine of weariness. Thankfully, the sound of the storm masks the noise. Miracles in disguise are the best kind.

A concrete slab of a hallway is before me, with flickering fluorescent lights. A spider scurries off in complaint at my intrusion. With the stormy backdrop, it's the perfect haunted setting.

I creep up the hallway, listening for a hint of humanity here. Though the place appears empty, I couldn't be sure. Plus, I should also probably be listening for ghosts and werewolves and such, with the horror movie vibes and all.

The hall turns and I enter the entry room, an office space as I'd surmised. Clutters of paper and file folders are scattered about. Coffee stains: typical. Reading glasses. Nothing to see here unless I want to read all the documents—which, maybe, but let me check out the rest of the place for something more exciting first, mmk? Besides, who knows how much time I have before I'm discovered or arrested for trespassing. I should see as much of the place as possible before I lose my chance.

A bookshelf lines the wall, leading up to the doorway into the rest of the building. Books are strewn about in piles, defeating the entire purpose of the bookshelf, and most of them dog-eared with sticky notes and copy paper jutting out. There are books on the brain. Books on human behavior and psychology, but mostly books on the brain. If I find a shelf full of brains in jars, then I am for sure in a horror film and probably not one with a happy ending. Also, crap, this isn't a mental institution, but it's the next worst thing. Yep, I am in the middle of a horror film.

A rumble comes from outside as I approach the doorway. "Drumroll, please," I mutter as I creep around the corner. The hallway before me has a few doors, the first opening to a bathroom, the second to a closet. Nothing to see there. But peeking into the next one is more intriguing. A typical lab with white lab coats, microscopes, sinks, and tools I couldn't begin to identify. No brain jars in sight, but perhaps those are in the locked cabinets or mini fridge. Heebie-jeebies. I figure I'll come back to this one after peeking through the last door. (I am predictably wrong.)

If I thought the last room was eerie, the next is downright macabre. Even before opening the door I have prickles, because a rack at the end of the hall holds scrubs, a box of latex gloves and face masks, plus hand sanitizer as a backup to the gloves, I suppose.

The large metal door is sealed tight. I am pretty sure the place is quarantine. Am I about to contract some plague that will eat me from the inside out?

I put on gloves and a face mask, hoping it's unnecessary and I'm scaring myself silly for no reason. I grab the door handle tentatively, pull on it tentatively. The door gives with a hiss, and cool air hits my face. And then, I see what's inside.

It's a freezer, but suddenly I feel very hot, and I run back to the bathroom before I crap my pants or puke my guts. Turns out the face mask only gets in the way. When I have collected myself and replaced the mask and gloves, I return to the freezer.

I don't plan on touching the body, but in the chance it's some airborne thing, ya know. I open the door, again, and look—again.

A corpse lays on a metal table. I don't want to see any further, but then again, I have to know. Ya know?

I step cautiously into the freezer. The door whirs shut, resigning itself to the fact I'm not heeding its warning. The burly man is wrapped in an extravagant costume of shimmering red and gold, and it's then that I know, or at least have a hunch.

His presence is larger than life, at least back when he was alive,

I imagine. I can hear his booming voice radiating through my bones, but maybe that's just tricks of the thunder outside. As I get close enough to see his face, I recognize him, I'm certain. Icier in death than in the photos, but there is no denying the face of the man of such renown, to my own life at least.

The door hisses, and I bolt, before I realize there is nowhere to go. I duck behind the table, but with a clang in my haste. She probably has seen me anyhow, but if not, she sure hears me.

"Would you believe he was colder in life?" she says. As if she's heard my thoughts prior. "And yet... You probably wouldn't believe that this is the best thing that ever happened to him."

I stand straight to look her in the eyes. She stands on the other side of the table, looking affectionately at the corpse as if it were her prized possession. I realize she has no mask, no gloves, so I remove mine in hopes I'd escape easier without the additional layers.

"Why should I?" I ask.

RaeChaeline turns her gaze toward me, her stare sending icy daggers. "Because I cared for him, and I killed him."

I gulp, but try to hide it. I have found a psychopath's lair. Correction: Fancy has led me to a psychopath's lair. Probably called RaeChaeline to warn her, or maybe they planned it all from the beginning, the sneaky lot.

I begin to walk around the table, edging toward the door without looking at it, hoping she won't notice. Oh yeah, I'm supposed to distract her with some sort of question, get her on a villainous monologue.

"Why?" I say. "Why would you kill someone you care about?" I have made it around the table. The door is less than ten steps away, though RaeChaeline is now only three steps away. We are face to face as she replies.

"Destiny." Typical villainous answer. Not the typical length, though. She is still staring me down. The good news: She isn't stalling, that's what villainous monologues are for, right? Still, I as the unlikely hero need one.

"Care to elaborate on destiny?" I ask.

"Your pet project Julia gave destiny a push." She looks down at the lifeless Geppetto with something almost resembling affection. "That's all that matters."

This is my moment. I bolt clumsily toward the door, just in reach. But pushing the heavy door gives her all the time she needs. She doesn't even have to chase, only walk nonchalantly, I imagine. I don't see though; I am too busy putting my effort into leaving. One good quality I suppose, I don't look back at the villain when I'm running away—isn't that always a character's downfall in the horror movies? So if I were in a horror film, I should get away. But I'm not, so I don't. As the door gives a large enough opening for me to jet through, I feel the needle prick.

I step outside the freezer, but that's all I can do. "Not again," I mumble. I've escaped just in time to collapse.

"Julia stuck her nose where she didn't belong. Sound familiar?" RaeChaeline stands over me, looking down at her prey. That's when I realize. A vulture. That's what she resembles.

Clue 9: Hey, I think I know what RaeChaeline is hiding. Another dead body. At some medical office by a creepy castle-y mansion. Beware.

14

WAKE. I'M NOT DEAD. Or if I am, there's a groggy afterlife. I feel the pain rising up in me, the killer headache and the nausea, and I stifle a reaction. Not until I gauge my surroundings. I can't draw attention to myself.

I am laying on a cold slick surface—hard, not a bed. My wrists and ankles have a weight on them, some sort of restraint more than likely. I hear a clack clack clack close by. In the distance, the roar of the rain. No voices, no other movement. That is all I can decipher without my eyesight.

So, I peep my eyes open. Bad idea.

She's right there. Psychopathic RaeCh, and in a lab coat now, which somehow makes it worse. She is staring me down, as if she's been watching me the entire time I was out.

"Good, you're awake," she says. I wish I were dead.

I let out the groan I've been holding in. It takes all my energy to look around, to take in my surroundings. I am in the lab, not the freezer. I suppose I should see the bright side of that. RaeChae hovers over me. And the clack clacking is a warning. It isn't her nails or a pen or something innocuous like that. It's a knife—one of those small surgical knives that could probably slit right through your bones to your soul. I am dead after all. This is hell.

"Here is how this will work: I ask, you answer and remain intact for the full conversation." She raises the knife to the light

133

and grins at it. "Or, if you prefer: I ask, you don't answer, I slice and dice 'til you are a broken little man who will divulge anything."

I pull at the restraints, but they remain firm. RaeChae notices and laughs. "Also," she waves the knife around like it isn't an instrument of mass destruction, "believe it or not, I'm no doctor. Not my fault he's away. I mean, you did come outside office hours. And maybe, just maybe, I'll get lucky and cut something I shouldn't, watch you bleed out or lose a limb or something more... permanent."

"Okay," I resign myself. Really, I've been resigned; she didn't have to say a single threatening word. "I'll tell you anything. I'm not hiding anything. In fact, Fancy knows all I do, so really, this was an unnecessary waste of time." I force a laugh, but it comes out as a whimper. Oops.

"Oh, Fancy knows much more than you do." RaeChaeline touches the knife to my wrist, then slides it up my arm. I freeze. She moves gently so it presumably won't cut me, but I wouldn't trust that to be the case.

"First question: What did Fancy tell you?"

I blubber it out real quick. "I don't remember. Hardly a thing. She took me to Nicholas Cirque, and to the dead body in the field, but she is pretty tight-lipped."

"What did Nick tell you?" She trails the knife down my chest now. I never felt so thankful for a shirt in my life.

"Gibberish. Something about light and a contract, but I couldn't make heads or tails of it."

RaeChaeline moves the knife to my other arm, and in the brief space between I take a deep breath, realizing I've been holding it.

RaeChae purses her lips. "Either your investigative skills stink or you're not telling me something."

"I definitely stink," I laugh. Yay, I'm going mad with fear. "No skills to speak of. Haven't found a darn answer anywhere. All of you are tight-lipped actually—you, Fancy, even the Trenchers. Threatening, too. So many threats." I hate to admit it, but at about this point I begin to break down and a tear rolls down my face. It's a good thing I don't have classified intel.

The knife freezes. She is either about to slice or about to give up. And I don't know which, which somehow amplifies the terror. If I only knew I could maybe deal. Okay, probably not. But maybe.

Then, I have what seems like a wild-eyed epiphany, though hindsight says I'm actually in panic mode. "But not Nicholas," I say. "He's not tight-lipped, just...broken... Did you torture him too, is that what causes it?"

Nicholas, the one person who has nothing to hide and is conveniently locked up—I mean, until we broke him out or whatever happened.

But RaeChaeline has come across her own epiphany, a better one. "The Trenchers," she says. "You've seen the Trenchers. What do they know?"

I shake my head. "They're in denial. Blocking it out. They won't talk about it, lash out if ya try. Whatever they know, it's way deep back in there, ya know?"

She removes the knife from my skin, holds it to her side. Satisfied. It's only then I realize there's snot running down my face; real dignified like, I know. I'm glad I used the restroom immediately prior to my capture, otherwise there would be a proper stink in here.

"So, you're running helter skelter, and still all you know is there's a bunch of people who won't talk and two dead bodies?"

Technically, I now know that she murdered the Gep guy since she told me, but I'm not gonna remind her of that now. I nod furtively.

"Pathetic," she says.

"Right?!" I say a little too emphatically. I blame the adrenaline of the moment.

She looks to the side, deep in thought. I pull at the restraints again, but of course I don't stand a chance. "Okay," she says. "One last question."

"Anything," I say. I shouldn't have said.

"Why do you care? Who are you really?"

It's two questions, technically, but now isn't the time to correct her. Except, those are the exact questions I can't answer so I need to deflect. So... "Technically that's two questions."

Her eyes light up and she puts the knife to my cheek. "I'm sorry, what was that?"

I was ashamed of the tear before, but now it's joined by dozens streaming down my face. "I'm sorry," I whisper.

"Why," she growled. "Do. You. Care."

"I—I can't," I say more to myself than to her. My will is betraying my body, throwing it to the wolves.

I feel the prick, really much lighter on the pain scale than I'd imagined, but then again, we are just beginning. She has all... well, all my life, however long that is, I guess. I'm not sure if it is blood or tears dripping into my ears, but considering the timing, high likelihood it's the latter. That understandably concerns me.

"That was easy," RaeChae says. She leans in close to my face, admiring her handiwork. "So easy. And it could get a lot worse."

I nod. "I know."

The knife slides down to my neck, thankfully bypasses that, and goes straight to my chest. "Hmm, I wonder what's in here. Anything vital?" She beams at me like we are having a lovely chitchat about the latest romcom.

"We'll come back to matters of the heart," she continues. "Vanity clearly isn't your thing. You weren't too worried about your face. So the question is, what are you worried about? What piece of you is more important than any other?"

It's a valid question. In fact, she makes me wonder about the answer. Do I care if she sliced somewhere specific? Isn't it all slicing I'd equally want to avoid?

She rests the knife on my pants. Yeah, there, that part. You catch my drift. I don't flinch. "Interesting," she says. "Huh."

She is as shocked as I am that I'm not too invested in saving that piece over another. As she slides the knife up my stomach and under my shirt, I realize she is gonna keep trying until she finds it. The piece I supposedly care most about. Is there any way to get her to stop on a piece I could sacrifice to avoid her performing open heart surgery? Only if I give her the answers she wants, probably.

The knife pricks the skin on my stomach.

I whimper a bit. Probably a few vital somethings in there. But she isn't going deep, not yet. Does that mean I'm okay? I could only hope. I have to feign indifference or she'll probe until something breaks—either my silence or a vital organ.

"You gonna talk?" she asks. I shake my head.

"Hmm," RaeChaeline says. "You know, if you're not interested in vanity or lust or greed... We're down to only a couple more places before I have to try something with more long-term effects."

She moves the knife to my hair. I thought we've already handled the vanity thing, but apparently I am about to get a haircut. Then I realize... nope, it isn't for a haircut. There's something most people value underneath the hair.

"There's all sorts of things you could lose in here, depending on what I hit," RaeChae said. "How do you like keeping your IQ, personality, memories, identity...?" I roll my eyes. I didn't feel the piercing this time. I feel my hair dampen. Then I feel the pain. But I have only the same amount of fear as before.

"Surprisingly calm even still," RaeChae says. "I'm not an experienced torturer, but assuming you're not an experienced torturee, I'd say most people would have broken by this moment."

"My mind has already betrayed me," I respond. "I no longer trust it."

"If this has anything to do with why you care about the circus, please elaborate. Otherwise, I don't care about your sob story, so let's continue with the torture, k?"

I sigh.

"Elaborating?" RaeChae asks.

I shake my head. A tinge of pain shoots through my neck. Probably not a good sign.

"Didn't think so." She grabs my wrist where I am strapped in tight. The naive part of me hopes she is about to let me loose. Admit her defeat, that I'm too tough to break.

But of course that isn't the case. Instead, she opens my fist, lays my hand flat against the table, palm up. Then my naive self leaves, and the potentially-useful-to-this-situation cynical guy returns. I realize what is about to happen and squirm.

"I'd hate to hit a nerve and render your hand completely useless," RaeChae says. She looks me in the eyes.

Don't look afraid, I think. Seem nonchalant. But I can't think how to look that way. My eyes are surely saucers, and I can't shrink them. My body is tense and I can't relax.

All I can do is try to put my hand in a fist again. But given the situation, she holds fast, smiles, triumphant. "Found it."

As the knife approaches my palm, I almost give everything away. But miracle of miracles, my mind decides to throw me a bone and provide one little crucial detail—it's my right hand. And I am left-handed.

This is my moment. I could make her think I cared, I mean, because I already did. And she would slice up something relatively unimportant instead of what is apparently the most valued part of me.

The knife pierces my palm, preparing me for some ritual sacrifice from one of those ridiculous movies I must have watched. I flinch.

"Please," I whimper. This time I am okay with sounding pathetic. It is part of the act. I think.

She digs the knife deeper, then drags it across the width of my hand. "Never would have taken you for a physical labor guy, unable to part with your hands of all things."

"You and me both," I say through gritted teeth.

"Talk," she says. "And it's all over. You can leave with a chance that your hand is still intact instead of shredded."

I sigh, try to look exasperated, like I am about to give in and fighting it. That isn't too far off, because really I am mentally preparing myself for the anger I am about to incite, the pain my hand will go through. I still am about to be tortured even if I don't care particularly about this hand.

"I—I can't," I say.

"You can," she says. "You can save yourself, your livelihood."

I laugh. My livelihood. Then I realize the laugh could blow my cover, and I start sobbing. A pretty convincing portrayal of hysterics considering I'm not too far from it anyway.

"I won't," I whimper. Then louder: "I won't."

She roars and slams the knife into my palm. I cry out. My heart pounds. It knows, I am losing blood, and that is still pretty dang vital.

RaeChaeline breathes heavy, but otherwise has calmed herself a tad, I suppose. "Let's make the hand useless then," she says. She draws ribbons through my palm with her knife, ribbons of my blood that I feel pooling.

I relax. The worst is over: my body has grown accustomed to this level of pain, and now I only have to wait it out. Wait for her to realize the hand is useless, the torture is useless, and to—well, hopefully let me go, but I guess murder is an option, too.

Or, maybe, just maybe, escape. I may be delusional from the loss of blood, but it seems feasible. You see, my wrist is getting damp, so damp with all that blood. But first, she has to give up on the slicing. So I calm myself as best I can. My heart still pounds, I am still covered in tears and snot and blood of course, but I don't flinch, don't whimper, don't let her cuts get to me.

And, she notices. She pauses, takes a sigh. "You really don't care anymore, do you?" she says. "Hmm," she wipes the hair out of her face, smearing blood across her cheek and into her hair.

"But you care about your hands, which could only mean one thing."

I purse my lips, willing her not to say it.

"You've resigned yourself to losing this hand as long as you can keep the other," she says matter-of-factly.

She said it. She turns her attention to my other hand, my left hand, the hand that did matter very much, and I freak. I squirm and buck and pull at the restraints.

My one relief is I feel my right hand slide a bit, not enough to escape, but enough to bring a sliver of hope.

RaeChaeline laughs. She plays the villain well. She walks to the other side of the table, the better to slice me with, my dear.

I clench my fists, but quickly go lightheaded as blood comes pouring out the right one. I unclench my right hand and recover.

I figure she'll grab my left one and try to pry it open. But she doesn't. She takes the knife and shoves it in the crack between my thumb and my fist. She doesn't care if it jabs through the skin, but I do.

I quickly unclench my left one, but she has already pierced deep, the knife stuck through into the center of my hand. Probably more detrimental than what she'd done to my other hand. Dang it. She lets go of the knife and gazes at it proudly, her workmanship.

Now is my moment. I clench my right fist for another gush of blood, and I go woozy. I unclench and twist my hand back and forth, trying to spread the blood as best as possible.

"You care more about this one," she says thoughtfully. She looks me in the eyes now. I have to keep her distracted. "It's not manual labor. It's something else. Sports or arts or something. Isn't it?"

"It's my memory," I relinquish. I begin to pull my wrist through the restraint. It wouldn't go very far, but I continue to work at it, letting the blood loosen things up. "I don't care about my mind because it betrayed me. The words I put to paper are more reliable than my thoughts."

RaeChae raises an eyebrow. "And you're left-handed. Huh. Wonder if you'll be able to write after this.

"I wonder," I say.

"So, short term memory loss or what?" she pries.

My hand slides out up to my thumb. So close, yet too far. I have to keep her preoccupied longer. I have to give it away if I am going to stand a chance at escape.

"Long term?? Maybe?"

"Maybe..." she smiles. "Don't remember?"

Here it is. I pull at my hand again, but it isn't coming. I have to say it. "I don't remember my life prior to the day the circus disappeared. That's my only clue to who I am."

RaeChae laughs. "That's what this is about? An identity crisis?"

I clench my fist for but a moment and use my fingers to rub the blood against the restraint. I feel myself weakening from the blood loss, eyes getting heavy, brain getting fuzzy.

RaeChae looks off at the doorway, likely pondering the information I've divulged, since no one is coming through the door. "If that's all this is about, I got news for you."

I pull against the restraint and finally, it gives. My hand slides through, and I reach across my body and pull the knife from the other hand.

"The dead guy in the field is your clue, not the circus," she says.

But self preservation has overcome my curiosity, and I push myself up and thrust the knife at her chest. She looks down just in time to see the blade, to yelp, but not to deflect. I grow nauseous from the loss of blood and upright posture, and right as the blade hits her skin, I collapse and go unconscious.

Fifteen

ULIA WOULD HAVE HEADED for the big top. She would have. That's where the dozens of other spectators were heading, at the beck of Geppetto's booming voice promising enchantment, so why shouldn't she follow the piper as well? But she was intercepted.

RaeChaeline meandered outside, head high, perusing the fields as if assessing the land she owned and finding it wanting.

"Come." RaeChae barely gave Julia a glance as she brushed past, but the demand was undeniable.

"I know you don't want me here," Julia said.

"Hmm," RaeChae replied. "It's like someone threw some magic potion of optimism in the air, and everyone's caught it. You're just a girl. An important girl, sure, but when did everyone forget reality?" RaeChaeline paused. "And yet, Phoebe says you will join."

"I'm not supposed to make my decision yet."

"Geppetto is flying sky high with your arrival. Nick is, of course, quite taken with you, and Phoebe and Analiese, well they're no help now. I thought it time you hear it straight."

"What do you mean?" Julia turned to look RaeChae head-on, but RaeChae turned away and started walking toward the circus entrance.

"I mean that Geppetto is holding his cards close."

Julia did not follow her, forcing RaeChae to turn back around in order to be heard. "I mean," RaeChae jabbed her finger at the big top, "what if your big decision is to free us from this hellhole? Not placate us in it, make it a little more cush for us."

"Hellhole?"

"This isn't your prissy, sheltered lifestyle." RaeChae finally made full eye contact with Julia. "There's a whole slew of futures you're messing with here. Phoebe's, Nick's, mine." The last word came out with a hint of a growl. "There's a whole ordinary world out there waiting to be lived in, a nice dull lifestyle. I for one want to die in it. And so did they!"

"So leave," Julia said.

"We're trapped. The whole lot of us, but see if you care to do anything but ensnare yourself as well. Your decision could be to end the whole ordeal, not implant yourself in it."

Julia looked back out at the barley field, waving so gaily at the world, at all who would look.

"What, you think the biggest decision of your life is in hopes of millions of gawking stares, pestering tabloids, and a whole new scientific branch of research? What a waste of a life."

RaeChaeline stiffly began moving backwards toward the big top. Her feet ground into the dirt, like she wanted to stay to chew Julia out a bit more, yet something in her was hopelessly aware that the show must go on.

RaeChae cleared her throat. "Something to think about." And with that, she turned and stomped into the big top.

15

S O. MY ESCAPE DIDN'T GO QUITE AS PLANNED. I wake, still on the table, but this time no restraints. She's bandaged me up. My head pounds, my heart is running 300 miles a minute; yes, I'm using mixed metaphors because hey, I was quite recently tortured and my brain is scrambled. My cheek is sore from the slicing, but my hands are completely useless. They scream like they'd been amputated. Or like I wish they'd been amputated. I don't know. Pain. Lots of pain.

I don't want to move. That's the point. I know I should probably be hightailing it out of here, but I'd rather sleep in the dragon's lair for the next century or so if ya don't mind.

But RaeChaeline won't have it. She is waiting, of course. We look at each other. She raises her eyebrow and purses her lips. I frown, grimace when that pulls at the wound on my face, then close my eyes.

"Come on," she says. "You're alive, your wounds are treated... for trespassing and B&E, I'd say I'm being pretty darn hospitable."

"Let me sleep," I mumble, trying not to move my mouth.

"You've already slept. Hours, days, years...way too long."

It's my turn to raise my eyebrows. I instantly regret the movement. That one hurts my head wound.

"I have a proposition," she says. "I think you'll like it."

"I won't marry you," I say.

She sighs. She is not amused. "A proposition, not a proposal. Just..." She grabs my shoulder and I wince. "Get up."

I pry my eyes open. She begins pulling at me, trying to get this dead weight into a sitting position, and I figure it would probably be less painful if I help her out. I scoot up, avoiding the use of my hands. I wish there was a wall to lean against, but the table I'm sitting on is in the middle of the room. I settle for slouching, legs dangling off the edge of it.

RaeChaeline offers a glass she's pulled from somewhere I don't have the presence of mind to notice. "Water," she says. "No poison or sedative was involved in the making of this drink."

I glare at her, and instead of taking the glass with the bandaged hands, I lean forward until she takes the hint. She rolls her eyes and puts the glass to my lips. I take a sip.

The water soothes my throat, momentarily, so I squeak out, "I'd thank you, but all things considered..."

"Yeah, yeah," she says. "So the proposition. You leave us alone. By us I mean me, this property, Nick, ...Fancy, and circus folk in general. And the Trenchers."

"That sounds like the 'what's in it for you' part."

"The part you care about is I let you go, no more threats—"

I squint. "No more carrying out of the threats?"

She crosses her arms, indignant, and huffs. "Or carrying out. But I was getting to the good part."

"Here I thought avoiding torture was the good part," I choke out. I motion at the glass again. None too enthused, she offers another drink.

"The good part is I give you a clue to your past. The big clue."

"You mean the dead guy," I say. "Not the one next door, the one you left rotting in a field. Big help."

"He was left rotting in a field because he has nothing to do with us. We aren't about to go near him and incriminate ourselves."

I cock my head, and regret it again. "If that's so, how come you know he's my clue?"

She clears her throat and gestures at my head. "Because of your... malady..."

"I think 'memory' is the word you're looking for."

"The lack of it. That guy, he..." She pauses, purses her lips. "You almost got me. No more talking until you agree. Leave us alone and I tell you everything I know."

I don't have much choice, really. "Sure, I'll leave you alone if this lead you give me doesn't end up pointing right back to you."

"It might sound like it does, but it doesn't," she says. "Agree in full or you get nothing but dead."

I try to come up with some way this could lead to my advantage. "How 'bout two dead guys for the price of one? You tell me both stories, let me live."

"Bargaining right now, ambitious of you..." She squints, weighing her options.

"I'll leave you be even if it points your direction," I add in.

"And all other circus folk?"

I'm not sure if I'm an honest fellow, but I can figure out that part of my identity later. For now, I have to agree if I want to get the information and get out.

"Yes."

I grab the glass of water as a show of confidence I shouldn't pretend to have, and lift it to take a drink. Half of it spills down my bandaged hands and shirt. I would have played it off with maybe just a cough and a wince, but she pulls the cup from my hands before I have a chance and frowns.

"I don't have to elaborate, I only give you the facts," she qualifies.

"Would you get it over with so I can take a painkiller and zonk out?"

"Very well." She sits the cup on the table next to me and proceeds to tell me the supposed facts: "The dead guy in the field. Has some sort of magic about him. Up and died in front of us all, but none of us remember. Never seen him before, then saw him dead in front of us and didn't remember what happened leading up to that moment. Memories just gone."

"First off, none of that is real," I say. "You gotta come up with a better lie than that."

"You don't have to believe it. I'm just saying. Clearly he has some magic of taking away memories, like all the other circus magic except not part of the circus. And you're missing memories, so I'd suggest you figure out who he is and where he came from if you want to find who you are."

She's right; I don't believe it. But it's worth knowing what sorta lie she's concocting anyway, a magical one based off the concept of the magical circus. She either figures I believe the whole magic circus thing or at least she wants me to believe that *she* believes in the magic circus to perpetuate that mythology.

"And the dead guy next door?"

"I told you I care for him. It's true, more than anyone else. We've been through..." She gestures at the room like that means something. "...all this together. Killing him was the only way to break a curse." She pauses. "But it wasn't murder; at least, it won't have been murder."

"Won't have been?" I say. "What's next, you gonna tell me there's time travel?"

"Time travel?" she says. "Don't be silly. No, but... We agreed that I don't have to elaborate. All that matters is that you know it won't have been murder."

My mind is reeling with questions. Mostly along the lines of *What's the real story, because you're totally making all of this up*, but my brain is too rattled to ask. Come to think of it, this is all likely a hallucination. So instead I say, "I'm gonna go back to sleep now."

"Wait," she says. "I gave you the intel, now you have to leave us alone; go on your quest for that dead guy to find your identity or whatever."

But instead, I lay back down on the table. She grabs the glass before I knock it off. "After I sleep," I say.

"Max, come on," she shakes my shoulders and I wince, but mostly, I go to sleep. "You gotta leave, before it's too late," is the last thing I hear before it's too late.

Clue 10: Supposedly the dead guy in the barley field causes lost memories. According to RaeChaeline, so take that with a grain of salt or 20.

16

 HE WORLD IS A SCRATCHY PLACE. Or the afterlife is. That's what goes through my mind as I come to. This time, it isn't a table in a lab that I feel, no clack-clack of a surgical knife. The surroundings are much more itchy than that. And wet.

I am laying in a puddle of brambles; that's what I tell myself, anyhow. Brambles are scratching my face and arms and side, too, though it's much preferable to a knife, I have to admit. And every so often, cold droplets plop onto my face, and a cool breeze brushes over me.

Am I in hell? No, it's more subtle than that...

I am outside.

I open my eyes to investigate further. Apparently I was dumped in the bushes on the side of the building. Mulch and shrub branches are my bed and blankets.

I prop myself up and scoot to the corner of the building, peer around. There is the door I'd broken into. RaeChaeline is showing some guy the door. Not like walking him out, I mean literally showing him the damage I'd done to the door.

How long have I been outside the lab? Which one dumped me here? And why?

I'm not sure if the guy is trying to save me from further torture by hiding me from RaeChae, or if RaeChae is trying to hide me

150

from him so he can't stop her from torturing me. But I'm not going to stick around to find out.

I push myself to my feet, but immediately feel dizzy and lightheaded. I go to my knees instead. How far is my car? A few blocks? A few miles? I can't remember.

I crawl out of the brush before noticing that the drive has no cover. Without the dark of the storm, anyone could see me leaving.

I listen for their chatter. It's gone. They could be right around the corner on the verge of discovering me, or they could be inside dissecting a dead guy. Who knows. I crawl to the side of the road, then push myself up to a crouch, moving a little faster.

But not fast enough.

"Intruder!" the man calls out.

It takes all my effort not to look back to see if he is barreling down on me. I told myself he was far, far away—likely not true— and that if I kept going, I'd be fine—also probably not true.

I hear a car engine. Nope, I won't be fine. I pick up the pace, in vain, I know. I can't help but look back at the car. The man is driving right for me, an enraged gleam in his eye.

I turn back toward the road. It's too far away, but I keep moving, refusing to look back again at the car bringing my doom. What am I in for? More torture? A prison cell? A harsh talking-to?

The car approaches, but I keep moving as it crawls along beside me, taunting me. I hear a whir of the window rolling down, then:

"Would you stop your tunnel vision and get in?" A high pitched voice.

It's RaeChaeline. Not the man. He's not even in the car. I look behind us to see him jogging, almost caught up.

I turn back to RaeChaeline, not sure who to trust. But for now, she is at least pretending to be an ally, and he is fuming. I fumble with the back car door and pile in. I take a deep breath as RaeChaeline jets off, reaching the street in no time.

"What's going on? Who is he? Where are we going?" I look out the back, but see no one chasing. I sit back in the seat.

RaeChaeline scowls at me through the rearview mirror. "I'm taking you to that dead guy you care about."

I am not about to go traipsing around a crime scene with her. "Nonsense, my car is over—"

"Your car was towed—and by 'your car', I mean Fancy's."

I'm trying to piece together what's happening in a fairly confusing situation with memory loss and torture on top of it. I'm failing. "Her car was...? How would...?"

RaeChaeline smiles at me through the mirror. It's not a kind smile. "She called me wondering what was up when you didn't return."

"So she didn't know about the whole torture thing?" I say. Then: "Wait a sec. You skipped my question. Who was that guy? Why are we running from him?"

"Let's call him Dr. Evil."

I wave my bandaged hands at her. "Sounds more like a name for you."

She sighs. "I'm Assistant Evil. You don't want to meet Dr. Evil."

I realize I'm still clenching the door. Ready to jump out if I picked wrong I guess. "Dare I ask why?"

The car falls silent. I'm not clear if or why she's helping, no matter what her Evil honorific is. Then she ends the conversation with, "You're welcome."

When Fancy had brought me here, she'd suddenly veered off the road and parked in the middle of seemingly nowhere, like an unexpected pitstop to relieve herself.

This is different. RaeChaeline parks as if this is her destination and she is staying here awhile.

At the corner of the field closest to town, a small patch of trees separates the field from a dirt path. RaeChaeline turns onto the dirt path, or I should say mud path with the recent storm, then pulls between a couple of trees as if they were delineating parking spaces.

We exit the car in silence. Though the body is mid-field—I remember that much—RaeChaeline begins walking down the muddy pathway. It then occurs to me—she could leave, right now. She was only dropping me off. But she isn't walking toward the dead body, and she isn't driving back to her evil lair.

"Where are you going?" Figure it doesn't hurt to ask.

RaeChaeline yells back to me. "You too! Don't you want to know where the dead body came from?"

When my options are tromping through a field in the heat of the day towards a decomposing body or trotting down a quaint path alongside my torturer—it's a tough call. I wish I had a weapon of some kind, that I'd snuck something from the surgical torture chamber. I follow her cautiously, a good deal behind, preparing to defend myself but not really sure I know how.

We progress a good ways, and the whole time I'm huffing and puffing from the mud gluing my shoes to the ground. Meanwhile, RaeChaeline carries on in peace, as if she floats above a romantic meadow, the complete picture of dignity and grace.

"Why didn't we drive further? Why the long walk?" I ask.

"I care more about the state of my car than the state of your outfit," she says. Then she smiles ruefully. "Besides, it's better watching you suffer."

Easy for her to joke about torturing me. When ya know, she actually tortured me.

I clomp along in silence until we reach the edge of the ashes. The dirt path was the border, the grayed out sign that told the fire "no trespassing" and it actually obeyed. On the one side, a normal field, save for a dead body, hidden within. On the other, an ashen wasteland. A scene of destruction and mystery, with faces on circus wagons looking on. It smells musty from the recent rain, the burnt smell wafting through, not yet carried off by wind and time.

We veer into that foreboding field, and eventually she approaches a spot that meant something, I guess. No idea how she recognizes it as different from the rest, but she comes to a stop.

"It happened here," she says.

"The dead guy?"

She nods solemnly.

"But he has no burn marks." She doesn't respond, so I continue. "I'm no coroner—at least not to my recollection—but I can pretty much guarantee an autopsy won't say the cause of death was 'burnt to a crisp.'"

RaeChaeline stands there, remembering whatever atrocities had happened that day. The crowds, many of them kids, running for their lives, escaping. No casualties, a miracle if ever there was one. No found casualties I should say, and that's the mystery of it. No bodies, only a number of vanishing persons. Not missing persons. Vanishing persons. There is so mystical of an air around the whole event that even the public statement says "vanishing" as if it were of their own accord to disappear. And who knows, maybe it was. No one knows, or the ones who do won't talk, like for instance...

RaeChaeline had been there. What had she seen?

She points her foot at an ashen spot on the ground with bits of charred wood. "This was a fire pit," she says. "We were standing around it. He was dead...somehow. Just showed up, at the edge of our collective memory. We began to move the body away, avoid suspicion. Truthfully, we don't know what happened, whodunit. Pure luck he was carried across the road, where the fire didn't spread, and then... then that night began. Who would have thought the dead guy would be the lucky one, the one only just out of harm's way."

She shakes her head, throwing the memories aside. "But that's not got anything to do with you. That's all I know about the guy. A blank spot in my memory, then him, dead, and chaos next."

There is this feeling, fuzzy, at the tip of where I don't remember. A suggestion in my gut that maybe I should remember a fire right before my actual memories begin.

The problem with lost memory is ya don't know if these inklings are legit or merely wishful hopes. I wish I could solve what happened when my mind went dark. A fire could cause that trauma, right? A sensible reason for brain loss is more preferable to this magical dead-guy memory-stealer hypothesis. And seeing something horrific no one should have seen.

Maybe my mind is doing me a favor, then. Perhaps after all this work, I would finally achieve my goal, bring back my memories, only to realize I don't want them. That my body was right all along. That could happen.

And yet, if you can't trust your memory, what can you trust?

There is one thing I decided I could trust, only one. My handwriting. My written memory. I could jot everything down and lose it all again, but if I have those papers and could see my writing, that is enough. I'd have a written memory. So here I am, writing all this down like some drama queen diary. Half investigation, half desperation.

But wait... Out of my musings, back to the memories I'm supposed to be jotting down before I forget again.

RaeChaeline shows me where he died, then leads me back across the dirt path, showing me how he was taken.

We walk a ways to the corpse. Bugs are making their home here, settling in. It is no easier seeing him a second time. My gut churns, remembering its past encounter.

"What now?" I say. My investigative skills are superb. Lead me right to the clue and I'll stand there dumbfounded, figuring nothing out. No wonder everyone sees through my lies.

Clue whatever the number is: I'm not an actor. No skills in that arena.

RaeChaeline approaches the body. There is a hint of uncertainty as she creeps up. But I can't be sure. It is still much quicker than I'd approach if I ever had to. At any rate, she stoops down and brushes bugs and dirt and who knows what else to the side. She digs into the guy's pockets. Of course. What any detective would do. A torturer I suppose would have the stomach for it.

RaeChaeline doesn't worry about fingerprints—like no detective or successful criminal would do.

Nothing in the front pockets. She pushes the corpse over—

eww!—and reaches in the back pockets. A wallet. She pockets the wad of cash inside without a second thought, then tosses me the wallet. It's damp and smelly, and I pray the dampness is from the rainstorm and not the body's internal goo. I wonder for a moment if I am the praying sort. I fumble with the wallet through my bandages and manage to get it open. One identification card. That's all the guy carried—a wallet with a wad of cash and an ID.

"Ferguson E. Tibble," I say.

"That's the most fake name I've ever heard," she responds.

I shrug. She's right. "Maybe I can look up the Tibbles, see if they are magicians or sorcerers or memory thieves."

"You loon." RaeChaeline rips the card from my hand and reads it. "Go check out the address—apartment 103. Don't say I never did nothing for you."

Of course. The address. "Oh, I could never say that," I whip back. "You helped me escape the torture chamber you put me in."

RaeChaeline points her finger at me. "Exactly."

Sixteen

J ULIA SAT BEHIND PHOEBE'S TENT in the dirt and barley, pondering Phoebe's claims and RaeChaeline's warnings. The grainy texture and musty scent of the soil was surprisingly relaxing. She nearly believed that she could stay there forever as her eyes fluttered shut and open, only kept from sleep because of the thoughts cluttering her mind.

She accepts Geppetto's invitation. And that is the most important decision she ever makes. The claim seemed overstated; could it really be true? And was this future set in stone, with no choice of changing? After all, the entire point was that it was her decision.

"Julia."

Julia startled and peered out of the barley. "Sylas," she mumbled. "Stop doing that."

"Doing what?"

"Saying my name."

"What else would I say?" he asked.

"Just about anything else."

Sylas shrugged. Julia crawled out of the field and stood, brushing herself clean as best she could with her hands. She then brushed her hands together, but the soil clung to her skin. "Okay, take me home," she said.

"Why?"

"That's what you came to do. Be productive."

"You didn't want to before," he said.

"I'm fighting my supposed destiny. Humor me."

Sylas sauntered off in the direction of the town, and Julia assumed she was meant to follow. They walked for a time in silence, but Julia stopped him to duck into a small building tucked within an alleyway.

"Wait. I should freshen up here. I look positively disheveled."

Sylas shrugged as they walked through the door. "Positively nomadic."

Dinah's Fine Dining the sign read, though the words were faded and the building peeling in such a way as to contradict the name. Upon entering, rickety tables and chairs, waning lightbulbs, and a grumpy waitress confirmed the outward appearance.

Julia paused at the bulletin board by the door, full of notices for missing children, dogs, even a cat. Why was her picture not there? Shouldn't they be looking for her?

Julia felt Sylas's breath on her, and she turned to see his face. He was scanning the pictures in quick succession, memorizing every face and name, she imagined.

"A washroom?" Julia whispered to the lady, eyeing the few customers downing coffee, studying the newspaper or watching the miniature television mounted in one corner. A newswoman seemed to be detailing a marathon of some sort. Julia wondered if her face ever made the local news with a flashing red sign that read "Missing."

"Thataways," the waitress jerked her head to the other side of the building.

Julia entered the stall while Sylas continued studying the bulletin. She laid out the used dress from her bag, then pulled off the dress she was wearing and laid it beside. Both looked worn, wrinkled from the bundle, with faded colors from a layer of dirt. Neither were presentable by Mr. and Mrs. Trencher's standards, not even for working the garden.

She sat down on the dress she had been wearing and picked at the hem of the other. Destiny. Destined to join a circus. Destined to not return home in a filthy outfit. Wasn't that a positive turn of events? Certainly better than Mr. Trencher's pursed lips and Mrs. Trencher's sniffle at the sight of such attire. Yet didn't she have a choice in the matter? Did she have no say all because a self-proclaimed non-psychic said she saw a vision of Julia joining?

Julia put on the dress she had just taken off. Perhaps this would be more aired out than the dress that had been laying filthy in her pack. She spent a time detangling and braiding her hair, applying soap liberally to the most visible and mud-covered areas, and perfuming herself from head to toe. When she finally exited the restroom, Sylas was sitting in the hall, fingers tapping each small floor tile in quick succession.

"Let's go." He leaped to his feet and rushed to the door.

Dinah was not so eager to watch them leave though. "Just you wait here, missy. Paying customers only."

Julia opened her pack and pulled out her coins. "How much for a treat to eat on my way home?"

"Cookies are $1.29 each."

Julia counted out the coins while Sylas gripped the door handle in a firm fist, switching his weight from one foot to the other. Dinah set a cookie on the counter and extended her hand impatiently, beckoning the money. Julia placed her hand above Dinah's and released the coins. Her hand, however, joined the coins, detached at the wrist and plopped into Dinah's open palm.

At first, Julia did not notice what had happened. Why was her hand resting on Dinah's? Why was there blood on the countertop? Why was Dinah screaming curses and flinging her hand, along with the coins, across the room?

Julia shuddered, her abnormality finally there for all to see. She clutched her arm to her chest and gripped it in the one hand she still had left. Her eyes began to water as she slumped to the floor, muttering under her breath. Sylas was by her side, holding a hand that wasn't his, a hand that should be hers. He reached towards her other hand, but she edged away. "Don't," she whispered. Then louder, "Don't don't don't."

"Let's go home," he said. "Come on."

Dinah was still screaming over him. "What have you done? You demon child! What have you done?"

Julia hung her head down, wishing her hair was loose to cover her face from the stares of the few customers present.

"Dr. Wise..." he said.

"Soulless scum! You have no right to be here!" Dinah was scrubbing her hands in the sink as if evil itself had sunk through her pores and into her veins.

Julia mumbled through the sobs, not sure even she could identify what she was saying, but knowing she must say something.

"Let's go home," Sylas whispered in her ear, scooping her into his arms and standing with a small grunt.

"How...?" Dinah had stopped in her tracks and stared absentmindedly at the cookie. "How did this...? How...?"

"No, no, no no no no." Julia pushed at his face with her intact hand until she began to fall out of his arms.

"Okay. Okay." Sylas consoled. "What then?"

Julia screamed, "The circus. I have to go. To the circus. Take me back, just take me back."

Sylas grabbed her pack. He pushed the door open, but Julia didn't follow. Her feet were frozen. Not some abnormality frozen, simply frozen at the realization of her predicament. That she did not, could not, return to the Trenchers where she must always be fixed. That she would rather risk a circus that many warned her away from, where she may never be fixed again.

"Do you want to stay here?" Sylas asked.

Julia shook her head.

"Do you want me to carry you?"

Julia didn't know what to do, so she nodded. Sylas placed her pack in her lap and once again lifted her into his arms, clutching her detached hand between his hand and her leg. With a sigh, he pushed the door open again and began his walk toward the barley fields.

Seventeen

THE PERFORMANCE HAD STARTED, so Sylas and Julia walked toward the big top. He had stopped carrying her awhile back. "Put me down," she said not long after the incident, having calmed herself down enough to realize she was unacceptably close to him. From there she walked in silence alongside him, holding her empty arm to her chest to cover the absence. Sylas carried her pack and held her detached hand carefully. She wondered if she should demand rights to her hand back, yet did not want to expose her incomplete limb.

Sylas held the tent open for Julia as she creeped in. The show had already started, Geppetto front and center with his flashy suit. RaeChae stood to his left, with Nick to his right sporting the stretched-out ears, twisted nose and arms again.

"-sight may deceive," Geppetto was bellowing. "Behold, the wonder!"

Looking around, Julia saw Phoebe and Analiese in the crowd. Analiese seemed to be a spectator, though an unusual one with her face redesigned outlandishly again. Phoebe was walking down the aisles slowly, scanning each face as if reading some invisible ink across their faces.

"There," Julia whispered.

Sylas followed Julia's gaze to Phoebe. "She's awake now."

"She could help. She—she has visions. She might already know."

Julia walked over to the aisle Phoebe was walking down and stood in her path, Sylas behind her. The crowd applauded some great feat in the front.

Phoebe saw Julia and Sylas ahead, took a deep breath, and approached.

"Help me," Julia whispered.

"There's plenty of seats near the end." Phoebe pointed toward the edge of the half-circle of benches.

"No. With my..." Julia realized her voice had risen and people were staring. The audience may see a greater oddity than the show, and their sight would not be deceived. She hunched over slightly to make certain her arm was completely out of view. "With my problem," she whispered.

Sylas raised her hand up with no subtlety, a triumphant grip.

Phoebe looked from the clasped hands to Julia's arm and back again. "Oh," she said. "Oh." She grabbed Julia's intact arm and tugged her towards the exit. Julia gripped her arms to her chest tightly but followed.

Phoebe did not release her insistent pull until they had entered her small tent. "What do I do?"

"I don't know," Julia said. Sylas sat the hand and bundle on Phoebe's desk next to the foam ball.

"Don't know? It's your problem. What fixed it before?"

"Dr. Wise."

Phoebe raised her eyebrows and sat down in her chair, kicking her feet up on the corner of the desk. "Dr. Wise? Seriously?"

"She's serious," Sylas interjected. He circled the desk, hands in pockets then out again, folding them across his chest, then moving them to his back pockets.

"He'd put me back together," Julia explained.

Phoebe raised her head and pinched her nose, staring at the puppet strings. "You haven't joined yet, have you?"

"The circus?" Sylas said. "Nah, she's heading home after this is fixed." He glanced at the lonesome hand on the desk, then trailed away to the foam ball, suddenly entranced.

"I'm still weighing options," Julia corrected. "How is this related to my hand?"

"You have no idea," Phoebe said. Then to Sylas, "Dude, you're spacing." He gave no indication of hearing, so Phoebe returned her attention to Julia's predicament, tentatively picking up the dislocated hand and studying the wrist. She could see the inner workings, like a medical diagram, yet it lived on and remained intact with itself while detached from the body it belonged to. Somehow, be it magic or a curse. "Did it fall off like this?"

"Something like that," Julia said. "As if it's not meant to be attached."

"And Dr. Wise-guy attaches it again? Like with a bunch of stitches or something?"

"Or something."

"Well, I know how to sew. We can give it a shot."

"Are you medically trained?" Julia asked.

Phoebe laughed. "No, I sew. Want me to try or go back to Wise?"

Julia slowly released her arm from her firm grasp and rested it on the table. Phoebe furrowed her nose. "I gotta be honest, I'm totally disgusted. Let's get this over with before I lose my cool."

Phoebe pulled a small container out of the desk, opened a pouch and pulled out a needle, some black thread, and scissors. "Always prepared," she whispered.

Phoebe rested the hand in front of Julia's arm. Julia winced as

Phoebe punctured the skin and began her knot. Julia bit her lip, then considered that wasn't the best option and tightly pursed them instead.

"What's so interesting there?" Phoebe said to Sylas, still in his own world, staring at the ball. "It's just foam."

Sylas didn't respond.

Phoebe tried again. "I mean, you haven't stopped fidgeting once since I saw you, and now I can't get you to distract my mind. Hint hint."

Julia reached out and tapped his arm. Without removing his gaze, Sylas said, "It's not just foam. You have no idea how foreign this is to me." He finally looked up at Phoebe, who was intent on her work, shoving the needle one way then another. "It works more wonderful than anything I've ever seen."

"Works?" Phoebe laughed. "Doesn't do enough for me as of late." She raised Julia's arm and hand, careful to grasp them together, and flipped them to face up as she began the underneath.

"Careful with the vein." Julia looked away for the first time, unable to watch as Phoebe pricked through the fragile skin.

"It's funny," Phoebe said. "I never had to deal with specks of blood popping up while sewing before. I mean, on purpose. Sometimes I'd accidentally nick myself."

"It's funny?" Julia said.

"No, not funny at all." Phoebe shook her head and turned to Sylas. "You want a turn?"

"Nope. I've no experience, medical or artistic." Sylas looked back down at the foam ball.

"You're a quality gazer, though."

When Phoebe finished stitching, she tied a knot. "Can you move your hand now?"

Julia lifted her arm slowly, but the hand slumped, useless as a lump of clay.

Phoebe returned to her pack for a first-aid kit. "I know we're all freaks here, but 'til you have an act, I'd rather you not scare away the clientele." She pulled out a bandage and dressing. "This'll take care of the little blood, and maybe after a few days you'll be able to move it. Unless you want to see, ya know, an actual doctor."

Julia smiled halfheartedly. Perhaps her secret could last a little longer, if the sewing worked, that is. "No, I would much rather be one-handed. I think."

"Ideally, that's not necessary." Phoebe tied up the bandage. "There, now it just looks like you had an injured wrist."

"She did," Sylas said.

"An ordinarily injured wrist," Phoebe clarified.

Julia lifted the fragile arm and rested it against her stomach again, clasping at the wrist with her other hand. "I would appreciate it if this incident did not leave this room."

Sylas laughed. "Keep trying."

"Don't you worry," Phoebe said. "It's as if it never happened."

Eighteen

YLAS FOLLOWED JULIA out of Phoebe's tent. "Ya know, I'm not gonna carry your pack around for you everywhere."

"Toss it here," Julia nodded at the ground behind Phoebe's tent. "This is my space for now."

Sylas dropped it and sat on the ground, running his hands through his hair then tapping his knees like a drum. "Your space could be a bed with a roof over it."

"Your fidgets are back," Julia observed.

"We all have our battles."

"I'm not going home. My back will get used to the ground." Julia sat down as if to prove it.

"Eventually. Doesn't have to, though."

"There are as many secrets at the Trenchers as here."

Sylas stood up.

"Where you going?"

"Home. As should you." He walked toward the front of Phoebe's tent. "No one trusts anyone here. You know this is just another cage, another way of not fitting in. It's all stares, only a question of if it's for laughs or for pity."

"I'm joining the circus tomorrow," Julia called out.

Sylas turned and studied her face. The tight eyebrows, the pursed lips, the jutted chin—she was serious.

"What's this I hear?" Nick came jogging around the corner, flashlight bobbing in his hand. His grin stretched as far as a grin could stretch without Analiese's coaxing. "Join us? Naww."

Sylas studied Nick—the loping gait, the crooked grin. "I hope it's all you want," he said, then turned and continued his walk home, beginning the drumbeat on his legs again.

Nick glanced back at Sylas, then plopped down beside Julia.

"Is the show over?" Julia asked.

"Yep, it was a'ight. Should've seen it." Nick laid back on the grass, lifting his hands behind his head. "Speaking of, where ya been? Didn't catch ya at the big top."

"Around."

Nick looked down at her injured arm, then his eyes met hers. As if in a moment of clarity, he reached his hand out and grabbed the bandage slowly. "What happened? Is your arm still hurtin' from Analiese?" Nick nodded at the arm clutched to her stomach. Was it the same arm Analiese had twisted earlier?

"No." Julia moved her hand to show him the bandage. "I injured my wrist. Phoebe bandaged it."

"What'd ya do?"

"Oh, it's stupid." Julia shrugged, but Nick waited for her to continue. "I, uh, was buying food and my hand...hit the tabletop too hard...?" Her voice lifted into a question, like she didn't quite believe her own lie.

Nick frowned. "Seriously? A tabletop?"

"Something like that." Julia rubbed her eyebrow. "It all happened so fast."

"That food better've been top-notch." He laughed.

Julia shrugged again. "Anyhow, I should be told the exact terms of this circus so I can join."

Nick sniffed and sat back up. "Isn't a big deal. Basically givin' Geppetto full authority over whatever oddity you've got."

"As in Analiese can only do her sculpting if he lets her?"

Nick shook his head. "She isn't an act. She's got whole different terms."

"Terms of a contract?"

This time Nick nodded. "Exactly. But if she were an act, she'd be a puppet during exhibit hours, then only sculptin' during show time. Rest of the time she's practically normal."

Julia put her hand to her forehead and squinted in thought. "So hypothetically, if my abnormality was, say, shivering—"

"It's not, is it?"

"Hypothetically," she re-emphasized.

"That'd be so boring." Nick shuddered as if the thought was contagious.

"But I would hypothetically sign some contract with Geppetto that makes me enter some almost-dead state, then—hypothetically—shiver for the show, then be completely normal during all other times...?"

"More 'r less."

"Where's the part I don't like?" Julia asked.

Nick blinked and smiled forcefully. He counted off on his fingers. "Uhh, first the 'til-death-you-part contract, which so you're awares, doesn't necessarily include wedded bliss. You gotta find that one in a different contract and still have it workin' the bounds of your contract to Geppetto. Second, the puppet times. Next, the—hypothetical?—shivers. And the normal on his terms." Nick wiggled the four fingers in front of her face. "Some would find a problem here."

"Not as bad as the ever-imminent hypothetical shivers."

"Why ya think we've signed?" Nick grinned and spread his arms wide.

"All right. What is this puppet dead state like?" Julia's stomach growled.

Nick glanced down for a moment before correcting his line of sight. "Thought ya got food for the injury?"

Julia wiped her bandage. "Yeah, the food wasn't at the forefront of anyone's mind after the incident."

Nick jumped up. "Get up. We'll find a spot for you to crash in Phebe's wagon, and you can feast on some leftover crap. But it's only 'cause you let me know after all the places'll be closed. Your fault, put it on record."

Julia stood and grabbed her pack.

"And you can quit draggin' that stuff 'round. Leave it in Phebe's wagon 'til we get you your own. All the start of a new circus life, right?" Julia nodded, eyes wide equally with hope and fear.

17

Clue 12: Ferguson E. Tibble is the dead guy in the field. Has an address on his (probably fake) ID and everything.

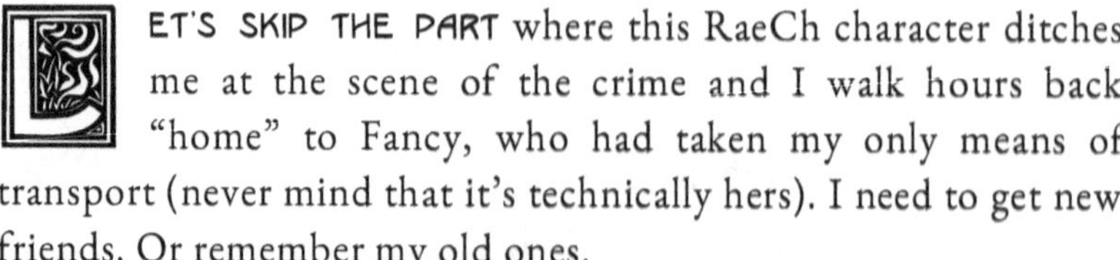ET'S SKIP THE PART where this RaeCh character ditches me at the scene of the crime and I walk hours back "home" to Fancy, who had taken my only means of transport (never mind that it's technically hers). I need to get new friends. Or remember my old ones.

I return bedraggled, covered in sweat, and—on top of that—probably stinking of corpse, so my priority should be a shower and a nap. But with my past just out of reach, my priorities aren't exactly in order.

Fancy is waiting in the entryway, beaming.

"Oh, the cleverness of you," I mumble.

"Oh, the cleverness of me," she returns. "Seems I had time to file a police report for a stolen vehicle, locate the car and leave an anonymous tip, have it towed, pick it up, and return home all before you completed your excursion. Which by the way you owe me money for. Goes to show you to 'I'm taking the car!' as if you own it."

I cross my arms and feel the need to harrumph like a cartoonish grump, and I wonder at what point it's read as a devilish smolder versus a childish pout.

"And yes, I went to all the trouble just to see this look of indignation on your face," she continues. "But tell me: How was your field trip?"

I lift my bandaged fists in the air to show her the result. "Did you know you were sending me off to be literally tortured, or was that a happy coincidence?"

"You'll never know."

I roll my eyes.

"Are you taking the car keys again?" She dangles the keys in my face. "They're all yours."

I'm not about to risk being arrested for some falsified police report, but I need to get to this address, and alone. Desperate times and measures, I have to choose one or the other, and I wonder if there's a chance I may be a more dangerous driver than Fancy with my injuries.

I sigh. "You drive."

Fancy prances out to the car, victorious. I'm not convinced she hasn't won this round, not to mention every other round of our sparring. "I don't have any money to help with the tow bill, you know," I say in hopes of getting a little bit of an edge on her.

"Oh, I know," she responds. "We'll sell a chandelier or vase or something." She says "vase" like "vawz" to emphasize the high-class living we're imposing upon ourselves.

She steers us straight to the apartment before I realize I hadn't provided the address. "RaeChaeline gave me a little tip over the phone. Be grateful I waited for you."

"More like keeping an eye on me."

"Hmm," she says. "That's possible, too."

We approach the door, and I realize...I'm not sure what to do now. We're here, but clearly dead guy is not. I did what anyone would subconsciously do when approaching a door; I knock. Fancy rolls her eyes. "He's dead, genius. You expect his ghost to answer?"

"Shh. If he has anyone here, they're looking for him, and we don't want to become the lead suspects by saying he's..." I slash a finger across my throat. "...err-err...right on their doorstep, genius."

She huffs, crosses her arms, and looks at the door. I turn to look at the door, too. But nothing.

I should be thinking of some story for the landlord, a plausible one that won't lead straight to me when the cops inevitably find that dead guy. I rest my head on the doorframe as I think.

Fancy stoops and lifts the welcome mat. No key.

I could tell the landlord that investigator angle, though that hasn't worked too well in the past.

Fancy stands on her tiptoes and rubs her fingers across the top of the doorframe. Still no key.

Maybe Fancy could pretend to be the investigator; she can be convincing. Although, trusting her in the past hasn't worked too well.

Fancy peers behind us at the shrubbery. "Looking for a fake turtle or rock or something?" I say.

"I was thinking a real rock," she says.

"Huh?"

"For the window."

"Fancy, stop, this is a bad idea." I'm not the squeakiest of clean guys in terms of criminal past, at least not now thanks to the creepy torture chamber place, but B&E with a rock is a little above my bravery level. Stupidity level? No, definitely bravery level; Fancy is much more clever than me, so if she is throwing rocks when I won't, it's not about stupidity.

While I am thinking through all that, Fancy has, of course, ignored me and picked up a nice fist-sized rock and marched right back toward the window.

Then it hit me. Not the rock, she's got better aim than that. The realization. That I am her scapegoat. That's why she'd throw a rock when she isn't an idiot, because she has *this* idiot by her side ready to take the fall for it.

"I'm leaving, Fancy. I'm not getting caught in this." And I begin to walk away, hoping that I catch her in her own game and foil her plan. Not that I have a backup plan, but a broken window would certainly get the cops investigating and finding a dead body with fingerprints and vomit and all sorts of evidence around it.

I hear a thud. The rock dropping, not a clash of a window crumbling to bits. "Come on," Fancy says, jogging up behind me.

"Not gonna hear it," I say. "Any other plan."

A couple of people are walking straight for us, would have arrived in time to see the window and catch us climbing through probably. I feel a blush of pride as I realize I'd made the right call.

"Well, there's the option of picking the lock-" Fancy begins. I whirl around and cover her mouth.

"Shh."

She raises her hands like I have her at gunpoint, although I'm pretty sure somehow she's the one about to set off the gun. She lightly touches my wrist between two of her fingers and lifts it from her mouth, then whispers, "but I'm not quite trained in that, and I doubt you are either, so you're gonna have to find a new way to contribute to this relationship and have your own backup plan."

The couple walks past, though at this point I realize it's likely a prospective tenant and some staff member. He is telling her all about the security lights to keep scoundrels at bay. Ironic given we are in broad daylight scoundreling around here.

I smile at Fancy, trying to look normal, like we belong here. With my slew of bandages I probably look maximum scoundrel-y. "I'll get back to you on that, but we better jet before we're late for the meeting." I throw in the fake line and hope she catches my drift.

Fancy smirks. "The meeting."

The staff member turns and gives me a quizzical look. Darn torture making me conspicuous.

I smile at him. "Act normal," I think, then promptly wonder what is normal, and how should I know when I have no memories earlier than a couple weeks ago.

"Jasper?" he asks.

My eyes must leap wide like craters, and my jaw must drop into the core of the earth. My heart is pounding, and my hands are sweating. I know that much. Once I take a breath, I reassess my face, and my smile is still intact so maybe I pulled it off.

"It's been awhile," he says, oblivious to the earth shattering event that has just transpired. "Are you all right? How you liking the place?"

I clear my throat. "Just grand," I squeak out, still clueless as to what he means.

Fancy sidles up to my side and places her arm around my waist. "He was about to show me around," she says with an exaggerated pout, "but just realized he left the keys back at my place so we're off to fetch them."

"Really," he says. "Didn't seem to be the type."

"Oh, he's been very forgetful lately. Must have been someone he just met." She giggles. First time I heard her giggle, and it still is way too false to be her actual giggle. But this guy is buying it, and I'm not even sure why we need him to buy it.

"Well, we better, uhh, go, uhh, honey," I stammer. "Get that key or whatever."

The staff member waves his hand. "Don't worry about it. I'll let ya in quick."

"Perfect." Fancy is practically purring as she glides behind him and leads me along. I don't understand what is happening, even as he walks straight to the Ferguson guy's door and unlocks it for us. I don't understand even as the staff member moves along with the prospective resident to show her some unoccupied residence. It only hits me when Fancy grabs the mail in the doorway and hands it to me.

It's addressed to "Jasper Tibble".

Jasper. The guy who works here called me Jasper, and the guy who live(s)(d) here was Jasper. I either am a coincidental clone or... I just found who I was. Am?

18

Clue 13: I'm Jasper Tibble. Or at least, some landlord thinks I am.

ASPER FEELS LIKE PAST TENSE to me, a separate entity, and I'm not sure how to merge Max and Jasper into one whole human that I refer to in first person. But exploring Jasper's apartment could maybe be a start.

Fancy has already moved to the dining table and begun rifling through the mail for more clues there. I'm still in the doorway, taking in the new information and the unfamiliar space. There should be a semblance of a life, a memory, a home here to me, right? I see a worn couch that I must have sat on; I walk over and touch the scratchy surface and smell the space for familiarity. But I got nothing.

There are no knick knacks or mementos or hints of a life lived. I'm not sure if that's an ominous sign, or just a typical bachelor pad.

Which reminds me: I share the fake-last-name of Ferg. Who is he to me? Brother? Partner? Prison mate? What sort of person am I, and do I care about the man who is rotting in a field? And if I do, if there's some connection, do I really want it all to come flooding back to me by treading any further?

Trauma. That's what can take away memories like they were never there. It's a protective mechanism; the body knows what it needs and holds itself together in interesting ways. And what I'm pursuing is sabotaging that protective layer. Maybe I should be thankful for the wall in my memory, that clear line that no one can pass. And this apartment, it could be the tightrope I could lose my balance on, and fall down, down, down into a darkness worse than I have now.

Fancy is finished looking through the mail, and she glances into the kitchen area that isn't in my line of sight. Must be nothing interesting there, because she begins to walk down the hall. And that's when my gut knows what I'm gonna do regardless of all this shock and processing. I rush to her and grab her shoulder. She freezes.

"Let go," she says.

"I go first."

"This some sort of patriarchal 'protect the girl' nonsense?"

I know it's not that, but I don't know if explaining will convince her to let me lead.

"Because I can handle myself better than you any day," she adds. "Maybe you should stay back."

"It's my place," I spit out. "I mean, maybe. I don't know, but I should get to see whatever is here first."

"Ahh, you're all caught up now." She laughs and moves to the side. "Fair."

No photos on the wall, no decor at all. I wonder if I will find two bedrooms or one. I wonder again who this Jasper was, who I was. And I begin opening doors: a bathroom. A closet with a couple shoes and coats, still no memories or hobbies or life. What were we hiding, Ferg and me?

The next door is a bedroom, and that's where there's finally an atmosphere of home—not my home, but someone's. Most prominent are the golden yellow and deep red curtains over the window, the first sign of color in the place. Nothing else on the walls, and sparse furniture—a rundown bed and desk and wooden chair. But there's clothes hanging over the chair, and the desk has paper and pen at the ready. Signs of living.

I venture toward the desk to search it. One piece of paper has a crudely drawn diagram, a blueprint or map maybe, with shapes and X's and squiggles. And when I open the drawer, I find... a flyer for the circus. An old one, years old. A bright, sheer scarf is folded neatly underneath.

I look under the bed and let Fancy have at all that stuff. There's an empty suitcase, ready to pack and leave, I suppose. In the closet there's clothes, but nothing more of note.

I head to the other room, hoping I could look without Fancy for a time. As I near the door, I hear her call "Max, err, Jasper...whoever!" I hurry into the room as I hear her footsteps coming my way. I slam the door shut, and am relieved to find a lock to latch. Fancy groans. "Really Max? I found something."

"It can wait," I say through the door. She sighs and walks off. Is that a moment of understanding or empathy or something? Whatever it is, I'm grateful for it.

I turn around and breathe in this room. Any sign of home here? Once again, not mine at least. Which makes me wonder which room was mine. Should the scarf have held a memory for me? Or will this room hold my memories instead?

This room is equally sparse. No cool curtains, so I secretly hope the other room is mine, or Jasper's should I say. This one has a smaller bed, with the blankets tossed about. A dresser instead of a closet. A lamp. A chair—although this one is at least a chair you can sink into instead of rigid wood, so maybe I'd prefer this one.

I feel like I am shopping, like I could pick which life I want to sink into based off what the rooms says about the person. And who knows, maybe I can. Maybe I could be whoever I want if I stop trying to remember. But I am compelled. I check under the bed—nothing.

That leaves the dresser. It mainly holds clothes, as you'd suspect, but in the middle drawer underneath the clothes... I can't choose who I am, which room is mine, anymore. There is pen and stacks of paper, but not blank sheets. Almost all of them are filled with scribbles, notes, a life. And the handwriting matches my own.

These clues I've been parsing together, here, in this notebook. That isn't some new thing to document as a pretend detective. Who I am has been seeping out in inconspicuous places all this time. And I suddenly have dozens of pages of reading material to learn exactly who this Jasper was, who I was, and maybe find other innate pieces of me that haven't changed or new things I've never tried. Maybe I'll learn that I speak Finnish or juggle or have a third cousin who's been searching for me high and low.

I stuff the pages under my shirt and hope it doesn't bulk me up to where Fancy would notice. I search the rest of the drawers; only more clothes, and it occurs to me that these pages were hidden. The pieces of each person were behind bedroom doors, not in the shared area. This Fergie guy I lived with—there wasn't trust there. Sooo brother probably, I think.

I open the door, and Fancy isn't pouncing at me. I walk down the hall and find her at the dining table. I quickly scan the kitchen, still no signs of a home, open the fridge for at least a hint of their food palate—or my food palate—but it must be bland bachelor palate. Just bread and a few condiments.

"Nothing in the other room," I say, hoping my voice doesn't betray me. "It's like the people who lived here have no personalities, except that curtain. What personality do you suppose that is?"

"Either room seem like yours?" she says. "Are you the curtain personality?"

"Who knows." I realize I have a chance to say something honest and make the most of it. "Still no memories jogged. Nothing seems familiar." I tap my hands on the countertop, the counter I'm supposed to recognize.

"Doesn't help jog memories when you have no personality to drudge it up," she teases. "But I found a clue in the other room."

"The circus flyer? They must have seen the circus back in the day or something."

"Not that," she says. She holds up the paper with the squiggles and X's. "This."

"Care to enlighten me?"

"It's the map of our circus here, recent, not the old layout."

"Wait, back up," I interrupt.

"I'm not backing up, this is good intel."

"But where do you get this intel? How do you know the layout?"

"Connections, obviously, not like I haven't been there or don't know the people or anything. Now let me finish."

I consider pushing the issue, but have witnessed how fruitless that is in the past. So, I drop it and get to the intel, to the part she is already disclosing, the path she's already leading me on. "Fine. Let's go, take a look at what's mapped out."

She smiles, triumphant yet again. "Actually, I was thinking... This is your place. A personality-less one, but your place nonetheless. You should stay here for the night while I go live it up at the mansion, and we reconvene in the morning to find out if you acquired anything during the night. Like say bedbugs, or a personality."

I'm not sure about this. I'm not ready to live in this place, haunted with memories I can't see. But I also need time away to read all the pages of my life I'm missing. I am frozen, pondering, and Fancy makes the most of the opportunity to walk backwards toward the door. "I'll pick ya up in the morn' and bring a breakfast bagel or something."

And like that, she is gone. I am still here; back to the life I have been looking for all this time, and I'm not sure I like it.

Clue 14: Journal writings by Jasper—pre-memory me—at the Tibble apartment.

19

 PULL THE PAGES OUT OF MY SHIRT and jump in at the beginning. The first thing I notice is that either Jasper's time or patience wasn't what mine is. I use the paper and ink to encapsulate everything, to meander through my life and ponder and make meaning from it. He approached the paper with caution, like what it said could and would be held against him. He would jot with precision after much pondering away from the page, brief snippets of a life, the most meaningful peek behind the curtain into his head.

He doesn't like to admit the curse he's put on me, the spotlight I'm under. He only peers at it from his peripheral vision, won't even glance at it for a moment. He's in denial, bound to break if pressed. And so, we pretend this is what we always wanted. That we're unlikely kin that wouldn't want to live without each other, never mind that we couldn't.

But here, this, these words here... This is my ultimate rebellion. This is my insurance policy.

If the darkness comes for me, or if I choose the darkness one day, these words will be my memories. These words mean I can go on living, without him, even. And if he ever found out, well, that wouldn't be looking at what he's done in the periphery—that'd be looking with full blinders into the blazing sun.

I quickly learn that the beginning of the pages aren't the beginning of the story. Jasper doesn't tell me where I was born, who my parents were, all about grade school and lost tooths and skinned knees over climbing trees. More similar to me, he hadn't always been writing and he wasn't working on a biography. He wasn't destined to be a writer from birth. Something sparked it, some outside force or event compelled him to write.

And for both of us, the motivation was so that we would have our memories, so we wouldn't forget. He foresaw the darkness and fought against it in this small way. And that, of all the abject pieces of my life I've encountered so far, that may have been the first part of my identity I feel a small kinship to, a small pride in knowing "Hey, that's me; I did that." A pride in the actions of this Jasper fellow, yes, but more and better than that, it was also the first bridge, the first characteristic where I see myself and think maybe we're not so different after all.

I still feel like I am intruding in a stranger's house, like any moment a Jasper with my face will barge in the door and demand to know why I'm rifling through his things. Fancy would probably love to see me arrested; maybe that's her end game. So, I don't take the couch or Jasper's chair; I halfway sit at the dining table, sideways on the edge of the seat, ready to jump and throw my hands in the air and say "It's all a huge mistake!"

And I read on.

He, Jasper... me... I... write about this codependent obsessive relationship. This Ferg guy saved Jasper at some point, in some way, and it doomed them to a dreadful life together. Jasper isn't great with specifics, he's more into the poetic, fluffy-feels description. And I think, maybe, if this Jasper guy saw this person on the verge of death, a person he was bound to in an unhealthy but compulsive way, that could be enough to cause a psychological break where memories disappear. And I worry that maybe I don't want to learn more about this Jasper who is probably me.

A small apartment, essentially the exact right size. The right size to be inseparable as he intended.

Ferg has one aim, and sometimes I'm a pawn in that, but there's also out of necessity a link, a connection, a bond. We both know we shouldn't care for each other, that's too much of a risk, too much trust required that isn't there. And yet, our connection, this codependency we've become intertwined in, it's messing with our heads. We're bonded for life now.

And I wonder if he could go back, would he make the same choice? Would he choose me all over again?

~ ~ ~

He saved me. That's what I remind myself on the worst days. Two roommates that can't separate because he just had to save me.

~ ~ ~

I want to write real direct, talk straight, here's everything "you" need to know when the darkness comes. But there's a more imminent threat than the darkness, and that's the light. We got a good thing going. This paper is too discoverable, yet no one else can find this information. So, I'm easing into it. Speaking in code. And the center of the circus is the key to the end.

I gotta give it to Jasper, his use of metaphor is impeccable, and I'm a bit jealous. I tell myself it's because he had the metaphors stewing in the back of his mind all day, to make myself feel better; that I could write with that precision if I only had more time. But I also am betting he had less time than I do, that he just made the most of it, whereas time is more abstract to me and I take it as it comes. The memories are what give time meaning, what make the abstract tangible.

And here is where he admits it, so close to the beginning. The circus is at the center of everything that happened.

Back it up. I go by Jasper. You can use that name too, or pick a new one, whatever ya fancy. If you're wondering about a career or even a job, a family or even a life, there's not much I have to offer. You can go make your own better than I could now. Meanwhile, I'll try to fill in the blanks. It all started with sjqfbf. At least to my understanding. And I'm worried it'll all end then and there, too. There's no happily ever after for me, but there could be for you maybe one day if you leave this behind.

I stop here, at the jumbled letters. It's too consonant-heavy to be a mistake. It's a code. Jasper too nervous to spit it out, came up with a code to say what he wasn't yet ready to say. And writing it in code wasn't necessarily going to solve everything; it's more a mental patch than a legitimate fix, but at least he wrote something.

And the good news is, I'm Jasper. He's me. I don't think he's some super-guru when it comes to riddles and logic games, but whatever skill level he has in that, I have that same skill level, too. So I try to think through what code he would use.

He's needing something quick to translate into code with his short writing spurts, and something simple enough for me to later decipher. I would guess he's less concerned about making it so complex someone else can't decipher it—this isn't some government intelligence thing, I don't think—only a mental framework to feel comfortable divulging others' secrets right under the nose of some complicated roommate situation. All of that adds up to an easy code that I should decipher in two minutes.

sjqfbf

Shifting a letter ahead makes it *tkugcg*, and shifting a letter behind makes it *ripeae*. Both still a mishmash of random letters that mean nothing. Unscrambling any of those combinations don't seem to bring me to a word, unless *Pierae* or something like that is a neighboring town. I'll have to check with Fancy later on all the local knowledge I'm missing.

I think back to earlier. About the circus being the key, and I wonder if that is the key to unscrambling this. I re-read the sentence: *The center of the circus is the key to the end.* Of course it's a riddle. It sounds exactly like what some vague wizard would say right before keeling over and leaving the unsung hero to solve it over the course of a bloody battle to save the world. Or in this case, for the wizard to say right before keeling over and forgetting who he is, and having to remember from this one vague sentence to save...well, his memories I guess, or his future, or...I don't know yet what I'm trying to save, because I don't know enough to know.

The center of the circus. I grab the map thing that Fancy had, and look at the X's. Neither are near the center. Of course there's a large circle in the center of the map, which I assume would be the big top. I could possibly go check the area later, but let's be real. Jasper wrote this before the large fire took everything. Whatever Jasper was pointing to is probably long gone.

The last clue to the center would be the word itself. The center of the word "circus". The space between "r" and "c" which is technically hardly a space. Or, it says the center of "the circus". And the center of those letters is "I", so I am the key? If that's not some adventure tale savior story trope, I don't know what is. I'm not ready to be the key to it all, and maybe I'll have to come to terms with that eventually, but I move on to finding any other interpretation and hope something else is the key.

I go back to the word I've been looking for: *sjqfbf*. 6 letters. What else has 6 letters? Julia doesn't. Ferg doesn't unless I make it like Fergie, but Jasper has never referred to him by any cutesie name like that, at least not yet in this writing.

But circus, that's six letters. And the two c's repeat, like the two f's. So, in theory, it could be the word "circus" in code and then scrambled up. Although I have no idea how the circus would be the key to scrambling up the word circus and how that would all somehow make Jasper okay saying "circus" *in* code by using "circus" *as* the code. That feels like a stretch, and the code would seem too complex for Jasper to use quickly.

I dump the code for now, hoping against hope that I'll find out it's some town name that the circus camped in or something once Fancy returns to shed some light on the local intel I'm missing. And I keep reading, hoping something here will bring it all together in the end. If Jasper was counting on me figuring out this code, he may have put this all together in vain. But maybe he'll loosen up down the road and I'll put some pieces together.

If you're diving into your past, you'll approach it with a healthy dose of skepticism. Of course you would. It's not like we had much trust to begin with, let alone when you don't know if each individual you bump into is a friend or foe or stranger. But you're also going to need to approach this with a healthy dose of faith. You're going to have to be open-minded because it's a magical world you've left. A lot of your history is based on prophecy. And if we make it through this, then all of the prophecy is behind us and the rest of your life is wide open for the taking without some magical hand guiding it. But for now, we are what the prophets foretold.

We are a curse and a deliverer, a sacrifice and a new start. We've come to shake things up and flip the tables, break chains and bring life and...well, death, too.

And now you think I've lost my mind, and I probably have. But these are the memories you're looking for.

Prophecy isn't all there is. You already know about the darkness. You have the darkness now. But there's other curses too. There's a twisted sort of alchemy or sorcery. And this all may sound too fairytale to you, and it's too fairytale for me, too. This is the real world we're in, this world where things are just...ordinary... and magic can be found within children's books and nothing more. But that magic is seeping out of somewhere into this concrete logical realm, and logic isn't enough any longer.

~ ~ ~

Everything has brought us to this point, the greatest

moment. It's finally here, and I don't know if we're ready for it—or at least, if I'm ready for it. Everything would change, the duo becomes a trio, and suddenly I'm a third wheel. And that makes life more volatile, the darkness more imminent, awaiting around every corner.

He's smitten, Ferg is. We're going to take her away from her life, and she won't know. She won't know what she's missing. But it's what she wants. She just doesn't know it. She can't know it, she can't remember. But Ferg remembers. So we need to convince her. And that moment has come, the second prophecy becoming tangible.

Great, so now we're being obsessive. He's convinced we'll free someone—Julia, I suppose, and that she'll like it. Totally not creepy at all, Ferg. I feel like Jasper me probably said the same thing at some point to his roommate, and he's sorta swept along in this for vague reasons he still hasn't quite clarified. Whether or not Ferg is well-intentioned is still to be determined, but Jasper and me at least are on the same page on this—Ferg needs to tone it back and play it cool.

I remember the note in Julia's room with the flyer: "She needs you." And I wonder if that was all a ploy of some sort to lure Julia out under the guise of helping...someone. To then whisk her away with these Tibble folks to the circus. There are still holes in the story, though, and I can't be certain.

He and I saw her today. Lynka. The prophecy is being fulfilled. Ferg has laid out the plan, and the chess pieces are in place. A fire, pieces of paper; that's all it takes. So simple, yet so dangerous. Because the puppet master controls all of the chess pieces. I know, I'm mixing metaphors. Keep up. Remember the magic? Now imagine the wizard whose incantations control every move of each person, all with the jot of a pen, a simple signature that gives him full control. And the only way to free them is to burn those pages under his nose. Ferg has done it before, Ferg freed himself. And now it's time to free everyone.

~ ~ ~

Ferg is getting more, ehh, sappy? Obsessive, with a hint of sappy. He was obsessive before, of course; going to right wrongs of the past and free his one true love to live happily ever after... but now it's all coming together, and he's grasping tightly at that. He won't sleep, he'll be up pacing all hours of the night. He's muttering and scheming on paper the same thing over and over, plans we've already hashed out, brainstorming all the possible obstacles and ending with the same conclusion. It might be sweet if the girl remembered he existed, if he wasn't so irritable to the one person glued to his side 24/7, if his foggy sleepless brain wouldn't be the death of us.

Finally we get to a part that feels just a stretch out of reach rather than the deep chasm the rest requires me to leap into. Something that ties into the story I'm living in, like it was one step prior instead of ten.

It sounds like Jasper is claiming these people were trapped by some sort of representational magic—the contracts Nick mentioned!—

and Ferg and Jasper were freeing them by burning the source. Which may be what led to the great fire? Like, maybe they couldn't find the representational magic and instead lit up the whole place to hope to catch it?

And then it must have worked. The crew had disbanded. Only, supposedly Ferg died unrelated to the fire, which would mean... Did I finish his work? No, I wouldn't have burned a site with a crowd of people there at risk. I'm not that type of guy. At least, I hope Jasper isn't. I hope I'm not a monster.

I'm at the last pages. I have all the clues I'm going to get from here. I should get some sleep and revisit things in the morning with fresh eyes. But even with the late hour, I can't. My mind is running a million miles a minute with the possibilities of who I could be, of what could have happened, or what I hope wouldn't have happened.

Jasper was supposed to have all of the answers laid out for me, but he brought more questions instead. I pace the floor. I revisit the riddle, the key. I stare at the curtains from Ferg's doorway and think of the circus. I collapse into the dining chair and stare at the circus map again. Finally, without realizing it, my head hits the table into a fitful snooze.

Trust your eyes. Trust your ears. If you stick around for this instead of running, then don't brush off what you've seen and heard as an illusion or a scare tactic. Be afraid. Change your mind, and build your life elsewhere, far, far, away. You've been given this second chance, so take these words and run. You don't need to see it for yourself. I've seen and heard it for you, and that's the only difference between you and me, that divide that created a before and an after, the split in our identity, where we went from first person to second person. So don't bridge that gap. It's fruitless and could get you killed.

Run.

Nineteen

JULIA HADN'T YET PERUSED the circus wagons, an equally fantastical part of the circus world, yet one hidden from the public view. They were lined up parallel to each other behind the big top, boasting circus history for very few to see. Julia pursed her lips to keep from gaping at the workmanship.

The towering murals on either side gave an overbearing presence as you approach, a larger than life glimpse into a fairy tale world that delighted children and terrified adults. They were works of art in their own right, yet hidden away, simply used for the functional day-to-day of the performers.

"How did you come by these?" Julia asked.

"Let's just say a generous but overbearing sponsor, "Nick said. "Nothing more than the practical joke of the well-off, but these are... breathtaking."

First they passed a tableau of a princess dancing with a monster, a woman and her beloved beast. The streaks of red in the background brought a sense of frenzy and despair to the piece. One wrong step and the monster would prove to lack a princely decorum.

The next wagon bore a tableau of a woman with a shoe. "RaeChae's" he said. Julia peered around the other side as they walked past to get a second glimpse. She bumped into Nick, who had stopped.

"Sorry," Julia whispered.

He cleared his throat. "This is mine." Julia looked ahead at the towering wagon, a picture of a man with candles. "Jack be nimble."

"Nick be nimble," Julia replied.

"Yes. I'd much prefer jumping over the light like Jack." Then, he led her to the next wagon, Phoebe's. It displayed a lady in a pumpkin patch. The rustic orange and melancholy green of a perhaps dull life, with a cozy hope of the cottage in the distance. Waylaid on the path to her happily ever after. The prince peered over the wall, ready to find her, to save her. Presuming she needed and wanted saving of course.

"The pumpkin eater," Nick said.

"Huh?"

"Kept his wife in the pumpkin patch. A nursery rhyme."

"Oh." Julia reconsidered the fairy tale she was pondering. The man wasn't there to save her; he was there to…keep her. Perhaps tending the garden was her escape from the trappings of a cooped-up home. Perhaps the pumpkin patch was preferable.

Nick had approached the door and was explaining to Phoebe that Julia would be staying. Phoebe seemed confused but welcoming. The interior of the wagon was simple: Phoebe's bed, a sofa that Julia would now sleep on, a closet for clothes and other meager supplies. Phoebe welcomed her in, but did not acknowledge the bandaged hand—like she had agreed, it was as if it never happened, and Julia was relieved.

Julia's makeshift bed was more comfortable—and let's be honest, more bed-like—than the night prior. It was still more inviting than the elegance of the Trencher house. *Just right*, she thought. *Or, closer at least.*

Still, her sleep was fitful. When she awoke early in the morning,

Phoebe was already awake, sitting up at her bed, frowning and pinching her nose.

"Is everything all right?" Julia asked, sitting up on the couch and leaning forward.

"No," Phoebe said. "I don't know."

"I'll be out of your hair soon," Julia said. "Or at least, I think I will. Once I accept the contract and join, Nick says I'll have my own wagon."

"Hmm," Phoebe said. Then she gathered herself. "Oh wait, no, it's not that. You're welcome here, any time."

"Nick said RaeChae requires her space, and Analiese might kill me if I intrude on hers, so you were the safe bet," Julia laughed uncomfortably.

"I'm happy to help." Phoebe sat up and joined Julia on the couch. "I uhh, am having trouble with my memory this morning."

"Oh," Julia said. "Do we need to take you to the doctor?"

"No, no. Not..." Phoebe grimaced, struggling to decide how much to divulge. "Do you know me?"

"We've met a bit. You mean your visions?"

Phoebe snapped her fingers and nodded. "That."

"Well yeah, you saw that I join the circus," Julia said. "I know that."

Phoebe scrunched her brows and shook her head. "No, that's not what... At least... I don't think..." She paused. "Yes, maybe I mean. It's uhh... dark now. I can't see it now."

Julia patted her knee carefully. "Has that happened before? Maybe when it's about to come true?"

"No, that's not how it works."

"Hmm," Julia said. "That does sound worrying. I'm sorry."

Phoebe shook her head quickly, to clear her mind. "Never mind that. Let's get ready for the day. Safe to say these clothes are mine?" Phoebe pointed to the open closet that displayed patchwork skirts and bohemian style flare, directly contrasting Julia's more classic outfit.

Julia nodded. "Can I ask you a question first? About your memory?"

"Sure," Phoebe said. "Can't guarantee I'll remember the answer, but give it a shot."

"Nick said Geppetto's contract means the oddities are only during showtime. The rest of the time you all are back to ordinary. Since you signed the contract…shouldn't your memory…" She trailed off.

Phoebe shook her head and pulled a few hangers out of the closet. "Nick sounds wonderfully optimistic. You give Geppetto too much credit. He has some semblance of control, but he's not omnipotent." Phoebe whirled around with a couple outfits in hand. "Do you have a change of clothes? You can borrow mine if you don't mind the style."

Julia looked at the patchwork skirt, the billowing sleeves, and smiled. A change of appearance could be precisely what she needed to change her identity. She wasn't ready to chop her hair off or anything, but lightening up her wardrobe could convince her she had done away with the past life she was running from.

Twenty

ULIA STORMED OVER to the last wagon—Geppetto's—armed with her new identity, thanks to Phoebe's gracious assistance. Julia hardly took notice of the tableau of a grotesque frog wearing a flashy crown alongside a frowning princess.

Julia had considered Phoebe's warning, that Geppetto's power had its limits, whatever those may be. And sure, she didn't like to hear that news, but it only spurred her forward instead of back. If everyone here was stuck in this place under false pretenses, there had to be a way to freedom that they could find together.

She pounded on the door, and it took but moments for Geppetto to open. It's not like it was a big wagon.

A probable-Analiese stood next to Geppetto, frowning at Julia for the intrusion. She now had a prominent, pointed nose and towered at a height a touch higher than the entryway, a touch higher than most she would encounter. *The better to look down on you, my dear,* Julia considered.

Then, Julia reminded herself of the reason she'd come: *This is the moment Phoebe sees. Or saw, at least.* "Give me the contract."

"Take some more time to consider it," Geppetto crooned. "The consequences and all."

"The consequences are precisely what I'm considering." Julia's gaze darted to Analiese.

Geppetto moved back into the wagon, and Julia entered. While his wagon was as small as Phoebe's, it was packed with decor. A red and yellow curtain framed a window in the back to let in natural light. A small ornate wooden table set. A lush sofa with pillows, tapestry on the floor, a massive wardrobe. It was clear Geppetto either had come from money, had money stashed away, or this wagon sponsor had afforded Geppetto some extra luxuries.

Geppetto set a piece of paper on the tabletop and motioned to Julia. "Well if there's nothing more to it, I suppose it's good I had Analiese write up the contract for you." He held another sheet in his hand that she hadn't noticed earlier. "Read it well before you sign, will you?"

Analiese lifted a pen in invitation with a tentative smile. Julia snatched the pen. She didn't read the contract. Instead, she scribbled her name so fast she wasn't sure the scribbles could be considered a signature. "Should I sign better?"

"Any penmanship will do." Geppetto shrugged and handed the signed contract to Analiese.

"Congratulations," Analiese said. "You're now 'free.'" She opened a drawer in the wardrobe and set the paper inside, then nodded and ducked out of the wagon.

"Care to say what this is about?" Geppetto asked.

"I'm done considering," Julia responded curtly.

"Here," Geppetto patted the paper he held before handing it to her, "is a copy of what you signed in such haste. So you know what you agreed to and all." Geppetto gestured out the door, and Julia took a few steps backward before turning and exiting.

She jolted to a stop as she exited, the wagon before her showing a side she hadn't yet seen. Phoebe's wagon didn't have the pumpkin patch tableau on both sides. Instead, there was a girl in a red cloak, hand outstretched, offering flowers in an act of kindness. *You're treading on dangerous ground, Hood*, Julia thought. *Run.*

But this was the moment that would change everything. Her most important decision, they said. And how could she fight that? She'd tried before and failed. So, instead, she was choosing to use the greatest moment, make it count for something.

Julia lifted the paper and glanced at the words, not yet actually reading. She had signed her life away perhaps, hadn't even batted an eyelash about the notion. Would such certainty turn to regret once she saw what she'd agreed to? Julia sniffed and rubbed her forehead. No use worrying about it now. She had made the most important decision of her life and had no intention of that choice being a waste.

I, ___*Julia Trencher*___ *(herein referred to as the Signee), do give all rights to my actions, occurrences, and abnormalities of any type to Geppetto (herein referred to as the Contractor), of The Great Geppetto's Circus of Strange Marvels (herein referred to as the Benefactor.) When the Contractor gives instructions, commands, or requests of any type in the direct or indirect interest of the Benefactor—whether in fact or intent—the Signee must and will follow through with no regards to the Signee's own thoughts, desires, well-being, or lack thereof. It is with complete understanding and in clearness of mind that the Signee agrees to this strict, lifelong obligation. The Signee recognizes that upon the Contractor's retrieval of this signed form, there will be no expiration date, no amendment clauses, and no superior claims on the Signee's actions, occurrences, and abnormalities. Though this contract is in no way legally binding, once signed it remains both binding and irrevocable.*

___*Julia Trencher*___
Signee

___*Geppetto*___
Contractor

20

ANCY ARRIVES RIGHT ON SCHEDULE, and by that I mean, of course she catches me unawares, barging in as I drool all over the map. It was at that moment I realize I hadn't locked the door. She scowls at the wet page and sets a bagel next to it, true to her word.

I rub my eyes, and when I open them again I realize the error of my ways. Okay, yeah, there already was an error of my ways with the drooling and the unlocked door, but I mean a bigger one. I've left Jasper's writing strewn across the table. I imagine myself turning and looking into a mirror, arms crossed, and my face staring back at me shaking his head in disapproval.

Instead, Fancy's arms are crossed. "What's all this? His desk have more clues in that pile of papers?"

I think about lying, agreeing. She'd think the curtain bedroom is mine, then. But something tells me the story wouldn't quite add up, that the map is more of a Ferg thing, that I'd be the obsessed one instead of Ferg if I claim that bedroom. So I go with the truth. Sort of.

"Other room, buried under clothes. Guess my eyes aren't what they used to be."

"Good thing you checked it twice, then."

"Right." I bite into the bagel, thankful for something a bit more fresh and flavorful this morning. "There's this interesting code I thought you might be able to figure out. Is 'Pierae' or some scrambled version of that a nearby town by chance?"

Fancy squints her eyes at me and purses her lips. "Really?"

I shuffle through the pages and find what I'm looking for. "See here. The circus is the key, and all I can come up with is something like 'Pierae', unless there's something physically in the center of the circus field we should be searching for."

Fancy pulls up a seat, reads the sentence, then laughs.

"What is it?"

"Phoebe." She says it with such a certainty as if she's reading the word off the page instead of gibberish.

I grab the page from her. "Where'd you get Phoebe? What's the code?"

"I don't know," she says. "But it's six letters with the 4th and 6th being the same, I'm telling you it's Phoebe."

"But maybe it's 'circus' scrambled then," I say. "Two c's."

She laughs. "Circus can't be the key to the circus or you would have said circus the first time. Obviously. You think your past self is more clever than your present self. Don't think too hard; your past self didn't. Six letters, tangentially related to all this circus stuff—it's Phoebe."

She points at the other page, the crudely drawn circus layout. "This map here, you know what X marks the spot of?"

I wait, and she waits too, smiling, taking a deep breath for dramatic effect.

"Drumroll please..."

I don't oblige. Remember, I apparently have no personality, not even a curtain one.

"X marks the spot of...Phoebe's tent."

"What about the other X?" I ask. Oh yeah, did I mention there are exactly two X's on the supposed map?

"We're not talking about the other X, we're talking about this X," Fancy says.

I don't back down. "I'm asking about the other X."

"And I'm not talking about it." We stare each other down. I know there's no use pushing.

"Can't you be grateful for this information at least?" she asks. "It's exciting, isn't it?"

I squint. "So, it sounds like I was part of the circus then, at some point."

Fancy jumps out of her seat. "No, where did that come from?"

"The flyer, the map, the curtains…"

"What do the curtains have to do with it?"

I lean back in my seat. "They're the color scheme of the circus, obviously." If she can be so certain about that gibberish being code for Phoebe, then I can draw conclusions from patterns, too.

"No they're… Anyone could have red and yellow curtains. But no, you're not part of the circus, you're just…"

I gesture my hands at the papers, but more widely at the space in general. "…Then what are all of these signs pointing to if not that I was part of the circus?"

"You're stalking the circus, obviously."

Now it's my turn to stand. "What?!"

Fancy nods affirmatively, satisfied with her assessment and oblivious to her indictment of my past self. "Probably for Phoebe, she could be quite vulnerable and valuable in the right or wrong hands."

"And am I the right or wrong hands?"

"Both. If you're kidnapping Phoebe, you're both."

I put my hands to my head. "I'm not kidnapping Phoebe."

"Of course you aren't, I'd never let you. Besides, you're not that clever." She smiles.

I scowl and begin to gather the notes, ready to storm out and solve this on my own. "I'm clever enough."

She shakes her head and reaches toward the papers in my hands, but I step back and continue picking up the other pages.

She doesn't try to stop me this time, at least not with her hands. Instead she says, "You're trying to convince me you're clever enough to successfully kidnap someone? Is that really an argument you want to win?"

I pause with my hand halfway to the bagel, the last item on the table to confiscate. Sigh. "...No."

I wasn't about to tell her that her hypothesis was making a lot of sense. Jasper did say Ferg was gonna take some girl from the circus; he made it sound like a partial kidnapping, partial eventual voluntary roommate... Okay, thinking of Jasper's less than willing roommate situation and looking at this one...yeah. Pretty sure I was involved in a kidnapping. But I want to live in denial a bit longer, and I certainly don't want Fancy to catch on. I skim the pages with the new horrifying framework she's proposed.

"What did the rest of it say?" she asks.

"Not much. Something about magic and prophecy being real, and about burning paper to set everyone free."

"That lines up with the fire."

"How come you haven't been such a snoop and pest since yesterday?" I ask.

She steps back like I just delivered a blow. "What's that supposed to mean?"

"Letting me go down the hall first, not entering the second bedroom, not ripping these pages from my hands to devour them yourself...and generally actually letting me in the loop on my life here instead of sabotaging me at every turn."

Fancy shrugs. "This is your space, whether it feels like home to you or not. I guess I can relate to wanting my own claim on a space I don't belong to but should, my own time to process and explore and allow my body to remember who I am deep down."

"The circus, you mean?"

And there I see it—her eyes harden, her jaw tighten. Fancy closes back up again, the vulnerable moment past. "Of course not. Can't I be nice without you interrogating me for it anyhow?"

I pause, consider pushing, but pretty quickly admit how futile that conversation would be. "All right, let's get out of here. We've got places to be."

"Hold on, let me check the closets for any tied up circus folk first."

I side eye her, and she laughs. She grabs the bagel and passes it to me as we walk toward the door. "Anything come of that fire, did it say?"

"I don't know what happened, that's where it ends." I shut the door, intentionally careful not to lock it this time since I'm still not sure where the keys are.

I once again consider how the fire must mean I went through with it, and maybe with the attempted kidnapping? Without Ferg, once Ferg was dead. I hope I don't have Phoebe locked up in some basement I forgot about. And I wonder whatever happened with this paper-freedom-burning thing. I'm not even sure if it was a success, if this is how we intended things to end, or if there was a snag somewhere.

Twenty-One

JULIA SPENT THE MORNING in Phoebe's wagon, pondering, thinking... she'd say "planning" but there wasn't much to come of it. She perused the document. Nothing too shocking—quite extreme, but all to be expected from what the others had alluded to.

Of course Julia felt trepidation about what was to come. Her stomach had been clenched up all morning, and she couldn't eat. And deep under that feeling, there was a worse feeling. Not a sense of fear or excitement. A sense of despair.

If her most important moment had passed, what did the rest of her life hold? The most dramatic scenes were behind her, then. And what hope was there of anything of significance now, knowing that? She couldn't imagine how difficult of a gift (curse?) it was for Phoebe to manage, entrusted with such personal moments. Even just knowing this one moment, her moment, Julia felt her mind fighting this curse of knowledge that had been bestowed on her.

The individual shows must go on, but not quite yet Julia's. Geppetto wanted to introduce her tonight in the big show before opening a new tent act. So, after the shows had started, Julia left the wagon and took the contract copy to the tent show she hadn't yet viewed—RaeChaeline's.

RaeChae was in front of a meager crowd, balancing the tightrope and performing flips in the small space. Her graceful movements defied logic, so unaware of the meager string that held her above the ground.

There was a tap on Julia's shoulder, and she turned to see RaeChae grinning at her. Julia looked back up at the tightrope—the tightrope that had held RaeChae seconds before. The string was empty now, pulled taut and waiting for an acrobat.

"Shouldn't you—?" Julia pointed at the stage.

"Naw, the audience is still getting their show," RaeChae said. "A little more redundant of one, but I'm still doing my act."

Julia looked at the group of spectators, and sure enough they still watched the tightrope as if an acrobat were present, pulling off magnificent, or at least acceptable, stunts to hold their attention.

RaeChae grabbed Julia's arm and tugged her out of the tent, noting the paper on the way and grabbing it from her hand.

"He asked," RaeChae sputtered. "So soon, that overeager zealot."

"I signed," Julia said.

"No." RaeChae's eyes got wide. "No, you didn't. You can't do this to us."

"I did this to help. My decision will not be wasted."

"That's not the way. Your *decision* was your most important mistake." RaeChae fumed. An eye twitched, and her cheeks turned red.

"I can help now," Julia said eagerly.

"You can rot with the rest of us now. You think you helped, but you just made the biggest mistake of your life and ruined it for all of us—all of us, not just you."

"No, I'm going to get us all out of this," Julia said.

"You're stuck in this as much as we are now." RaeChae shook her head. Dropping the paper on the ground, she went back inside her tent to finish the show.

~~ ⛺ ~~

When the individual acts were over and the small crowd was moving to the big top for the show, RaeChae trotted ahead of the crowd. Geppetto stood to the side, all grins and bobbing his head at the approaching spectators. RaeChae wondered if this was the same welcome he gave for each show or if his anticipation had escalated to this overeager spectacle due to Julia's signed contract.

"Geppetto, I need to speak with you now."

"Oh. Oh!" Geppetto jumped, but recovered quickly. "Dear, I hadn't noticed you there. Here, to the side." He motioned around the tent; they edged back, yet stayed in sight of the spectators, receiving a few curious stares but no more.

"What is it?" Geppetto attempted to give RaeChae his full attention, but it was obvious he was distracted by the public. His eyes roamed from meeting her gaze to the final few stragglers, offering them a wide smile.

"She signed."

The topic choice caught Geppetto's attention. "Oh, yes she did. RaeChaeline, it's finally happening." He patted her back conspiratorially. "We have her now."

RaeChae stepped back. "You think this is the best way?"

"Well of course it's the way, what are you talking about?"

"I'm talking about our—" RaeChae gripped his arm and leaned in to whisper, "your—problem."

Geppetto leaned in close to RaeChae's face. "I know. She's our solution."

"You think she'll fix this by signing?"

"Well, how else would she?"

"She's as trapped as we are now. But her big decision could be to set us free."

Geppetto harrumphed. "Thank you for being thoughtful enough to say 'could.'"

"You know you want out—we all do."

"Nooo," Geppetto said. "We don't want to lose what we've gained."

"This is no life!" RaeChae lifted her fist. "She could be the end of it all, and you're only concerned about an audience for our personal freak show."

"RaeCh, I understand your concern. You and I started this all, and we will bring it to an end. 'Will,' not 'could.' You must trust me. I'm not concerned about this now. We're winning."

RaeCh shook her head.

Geppetto placed his hand on her arm. "You'll always have my heart, you know."

She frowned. "And you mine. Doesn't mean I don't think you're making a mistake."

Geppetto laughed and walked away into the big top. RaeChae wiped her eyes and followed him, defeated.

Twenty-Two

THE BIG TOP HAD THE USUAL meager number of spectators. A ladder was perched to a great height with a thread of a string across the tent top for RaeChae's performance. Julia stood with Nick and Geppetto in the center.

Geppetto whispered to Julia, "All right now, before we begin, I need to know that we're not about to all lose our memory of the show."

"What do you mean?"

"Your gift. You make people forget, yes?"

Julia gripped her bandaged arm. "No."

"Oh?" Geppetto's brow furrowed. "Well then, there must be some other explanation for this memory loss."

"Memory loss? You've lost memories as well?"

"Never mind that," Geppetto brushed away her comment. "All's good if you won't make the audience lose their memory. For tonight's show, when I motion to you, activate your ability."

"I can't activate," Julia responded. "I can't control it."

"You're right," Geppetto nodded. "But I just did. Don't worry about it."

Geppetto turned towards the small audience and beamed. "Distinguished guests, young and old..."

Julia looked around and saw Nick and RaeChae up front beside her, while Analiese and Phoebe were amongst the audience.

"Have we a show for you tonight! Prepare yourselves for the splendor, the awe, the spectacular."

Geppetto moved to the side of the stage, and RaeChae stepped forward. RaeChae's performance involved intricate contortions, acrobatics, and aerial stunts. She began twisting her body in ways it should not twist, even with great flexibility—her legs over her shoulders, then crossed in her lap, with hands resting lightly to keep them down. She then moved to a ladder and flipped up, first gripping with hands while her feet flung a few rungs up, then her feet gripped while her hands moved up to grip the next spot, all happening in mere seconds. Nick stood alongside, stoic, as RaeChae had her moment in the spotlight, prancing across the thread and back, as if there was no danger.

Moments later, she walked to the center of the rope, leaned over the edge, and spread her arms wide as if to fly. She dangled one foot then the other over the ledge and began a count as she leaned back and forth precariously. "One...two..." On "Three" she yelled and slipped over.

For a second, she was floating above the string she'd walked, arms flapping to hold her in the air. The crack on the ground drew everyone's attention long enough to see RaeChae was in fact not flying above the tightrope, but dying on the ground. She had been high above the ground moments ago, but now the dirt was collecting her life force. Nick gripped Julia's arm so she wouldn't race to her side, broken and purple, eyes staring wide—only Julia doubted this time she would awake from this puppet state.

Geppetto smiled. Had he expected this? Planned it? Perhaps RaeChae had exposed her plan to be set free and upset him. He did seem quite manipulative, his smile never going deeper than his lips, his words dripping with guarantees of all he wasn't saying.

A brave spectator was heading for the exit to call for help. Analiese was already at his side. "Wait..." She pointed up to the perch at the top of the ladder. RaeChae posed with a smirk, bracing against a barely visible rope, and sneered at Geppetto. No one lay dying on the ground anymore. It was some illusion, some grand grotesque illusion.

"But...she was dead," Julia whispered.

Nick released his grip. "You'll find that's not as uncommon as you think."

The audience slowly began clapping, not too enthusiastically, furrowed brows showing confusion amidst glances between proud RaeChae atop the platform and the empty space beneath. Julia approached the spot RaeChae had been dying—dead—scooped and touched the dirt. Dry.

"There's no blood." Julia raised her eyes to RaeChae, smiling her reassurance down on her.

"Now," Geppetto boomed once again from the center of the tent. "If I can remind everyone that no electronics are permitted during the performance. For this next portion of our show it is very important no electronics are used while we control the lighting."

Nick stepped up to begin his act.

RaeChaeline came up behind Julia. "Ready for your turn?"

Julia shook her head. Then changed her mind, and nodded. She had to be ready. She signed up for this willingly.

RaeChaeline patted her shoulder. "Remember, your art is not your act; it's your persona. You're not creating a show, you're creating a character you're portraying. It's not really you. It's just a show."

And with that she walked off to join in Nick's show. He was

moving great lengths in an instant of darkness. It was a similar act as in his tent, only with more space, greater distances, and the other performers involved. Lanterns would turn off and on, and Nick would appear in different places around the tent. Phoebe and Analiese stood on opposite sides of the audience, alternating who had a lantern lit up, and Nick jumped back and forth within seconds. The back and forth ended with RaeChae lighting a lantern up in her perch, and Nick standing next to her, grinning and bowing with great pride. Then all the lanterns were lit again, and Nick climbed down the ladder for another bow.

"And finally," Geppetto moved back to the center of the tent for the climactic announcement.

Julia inhaled slowly and blew the air out her mouth. Her turn was up. Could she do it? "It's only a character," RaeChae had said. "It's not you." But Julia wasn't convinced.

"We have a special treat for you today. May I introduce to you our newest act."

Nick nodded a reassuring smile her way. Her eyes began to water and her body trembled as Geppetto motioned her direction. In an instant, Julia crumpled in on herself, every piece of her body detaching and piling on the dirt in a big heap. She heard screaming. Someone cursed. Not again.

Twenty-Three

ANALIESE JOGGED TO THE PILE OF BODY PARTS in the middle of the tent. Nick was kneeling next to it, hand covering his mouth. "Nick," she said. "Keep the spectators back. I got this."

"Huh?" his eyes glazed over as he glanced her direction.

"Get the audience out of the tent."

Nick looked behind her. Some of the people were still in their seats, stuck in shock. But others were past the shock and moving in for a closer view.

Geppetto was trying to calm their worries, as if the whole thing was planned, gesturing them toward the exit. "That's a wrap. Thank you for joining us! Come back tomorrow night for more wonders."

Nick stumbled to his feet. "All right, move along, people, move along. Show's over," he mumbled as he nudged their shoulders one by one in the direction of the exit.

Slowly, the audience moved out. Nick returned to Analiese's side, Phoebe and Geppetto right behind him. RaeChae was already crouched next to Analiese.

"Well." Geppetto paused. "You have your work cut out for you, Analiese."

"How are you at puzzles?" RaeChae asked.

Nick's nostrils flared. "You can't possibly mean that. She's in pieces. You can't –"

"What do you suggest, Nick?" Analiese said tersely.

Nick didn't answer. He shuffled his feet and ruffled his hair. "Just fix it," he finally mumbled.

Analiese began sorting pieces—a third of a finger here, an ear there. Phoebe collected the strands of hair and began forming them into a loose disheveled braid.

"There's bandages," Analiese commented as she pulled the bloody dressing and sat it to the side.

"Phoebe did it," Nick said. "When Julia hurt herself."

"I did?" Phoebe asked.

Nick nodded.

Once the finger pieces were sorted to hand, RaeChae took each piece and compared them to determine its location, one fingernail to a knuckle to yet another knuckle and finally to the intersection of the palm. When Analiese came to the pile covered by Julia's dress, she had the men leave the room. Eventually, she had all of the pieces sorted into a semblance of a shape of a body.

"Hmmm..." Analiese picked up a piece of a finger and the palm, studying the point of intersection. She positioned the two pieces and molded the skin to adjoin. Stretching some skin out, pinching some skin together, mashing other skin out of the way. She did the same with every piece of Julia's body, slowly making a semblance of a person. As she neared the halfway point, Analiese wiped her face, smearing a streak of blood. But she couldn't worry about the spectacle right now, not with Julia laying in pieces. Hours later, Analiese and Julia rested side-by-side, both covered in blood, but intact.

"I vote for washday to be today," RaeChae said as she exited the tent.

Twenty-Four

JULIA GRIMACED AND PRESSED her hand to her forehead. "What happened?" she forced from her burning throat.

"If I were to take a gander, somethin' like shivering—a lot."

"Ha. Ha." Julia sat up. She was in the big top, and it must be late at night, because the only way she could see Nick sitting next to her was the dimmed lantern between them. "Did I scare everyone?"

"I was worried you'd not wake up. I mean, Geppetto said you had to wake, seein' as Phebe's vision of you hadn't happened yet. But you were so—so dead, more than a puppet. I couldn't be sure."

"I-I'm fine, I think," Julia looked at her hand, attached as well as ever before. "Did you take me to Dr. Wise?" She lifted her other hand and saw it intact as well, though her wrist was swollen and red.

"No doctor. Analiese fixed ya."

Julia looked up at his face, ascertaining his honesty, though she couldn't imagine why he'd lie. "She can do that?"

Nick shrugged. "Looks like."

"What about all the people who saw?"

Nick shrugged again. He couldn't care less about anyone else at the moment. "The audience got an extra odd show, and the crew wrapped up same as any other night. They have their own

Geppetto contract, keeps them from worrying or talking about the things they see here."

Julia touched her head again and leaned back.

"Lie down," Nick said. "I brought water, tryin' to get ya rested." He handed her a cup, and she slowly sipped.

"I don't feel all right." She lay back down and closed her eyes, hearing his "Rest up, Jul'" before she drifted.

Twenty-Five

 HAT'RE WE GONNA DO?"

"She's the most important decision—"

"No, not that!"

"Yeah, most important 'cause she dies, causes an investigation and ruins it for us all."

"It's impossible, no doctor could understand."

"Focus, what about the Wise Guy? She told Phebes 'n I..."

"No, there's no Doctor Wise listed in the phonebook."

"Geppetto, what about—"

"Absolutely not."

"But we need—"

"I said no."

"He's the only chance."

"Who?"

"We gotta do it. It's the only way."

Twenty-Six

ULIA FELT THE COOL STIFFNESS underneath her—not a dirt floor or a field of barley, not even Phoebe's sofa. This was an actual bed, but a rigid impersonal one. She rubbed her eyes until they could open.

"Well, well." Her thoughts were interrupted by a spry sort of fellow that put her in mind of Ichabod Crane. "The catalyst awakes. They claim you're the cirque's salvation." He bumbled a laugh. "Let him try."

Julia sat up. "What happened, where am I?"

"A nasty infection, some crazed idea to mold your body like clay gone awry. I was the last reso-"

"You are the *last* of last resorts." Geppetto waltzed in with a trail of his circus folk behind. "Think of him as Dr. Evil, that's all you need know."

"Dr. Evil, really?" The doctor bounced back and forth on his feet. "Bitterness does not become you, Gep, old pal."

Geppetto glowered. "After all we've been through..."

"Exactly, after all we've been through, I should think a proper gentleman's introduction would be requisite, not to mention courteous."

"He's the scumbag who offered a medicinal remedy, that's all."

"Medicinal remedy or medicinal malady? You won't tell them the whole story?" Dr. Evil tsked. "For shame...."

"Come on, Julia," RaeChae beckoned. "The deal was only until your fever broke and you woke up. Let's go."

Julia, still groggy from the medicine, stumbled to her feet until Phoebe grabbed her and held her up.

"She should stay longer." Phoebe put her hand to Julia's head.

"She's fine." RaeChae grabbed Julia's arm and pulled her towards the door. Julia's head was swimming, but she kept walking.

"Dr. Evil," she whispered. "Ichabod."

"Never you mind that," RaeChae said. "Better we're out of here."

"Let the game continue," the doctor yelled after them. "Eh, Gep?"

Julia knew they were exiting a grand property, even more grand than Mr. and Mrs. Trencher's land. She knew they had piled into an empty bus, though wasn't certain who had paid or how it was empty for them. She even knew she had sat in a seat next to Phoebe, but she couldn't ascertain more than those meager details when all she wanted to do was prop her head on the window.

"'Right, RaeChae, Geppetto, someone talk. Jul' nearly died—"

"Shut up," Analiese interjected.

"—and she deserves t'know what ya done."

Julia forced her eyes open, saw Nick hovering over Geppetto and RaeChae, with Analiese on a bench watching.

"Done?" Geppetto said. "We haven't done anything but use a mortal enemy to save her sorry excuse for a life."

"Calm down, j-just everybody calm down." Analiese pulled a paper sack out of her duffle bag and retched.

"Dr.—" RaeChae cleared her throat. "Dr. Evil betrayed us, that's all you need to know. He should be avoided at all costs, excepting, of course, the cost of Geppetto's greatest moment."

"How did he betray you?" Julia said.

"He stole everything—left me with nothing but you fine folk." Geppetto smiled in an attempt to ease the blow of his contempt. "There are always detours, but determination cannot be stopped. You fine folk are what will set this whole story aright. With Julia's help, of course."

RaeChae stood and squeezed past Geppetto and Nick, moving to the back of the vehicle.

The occasional bumps had grown from cracks and potholes to gravel and grass, and soon enough they had arrived back at the circus.

Julia rubbed her eyebrow, felt the roughness of its shape—she really was becoming less a Trencher and more a circus-side-show every day. She was losing control in even as little a thing as the shape of her brows.

"Next time," Julia said, as she climbed down the stairs of the bus, "Let me give you Dr. Wise's number and we'll avoid Ichabod Arch-Nemesis."

"Julia, wait," Analiese caught her arm. "Is that what...? Every time?"

Julia nodded. "My body parts detach. Or act in an...illogical fashion. I suppose."

It was Analiese's turn to shudder. "You should know, these past few days, the circus..."

"It's got swarms, news and audience and people, asking about you," Geppetto chimed in, beaming.

"You're a hit," RaeChae added glumly.

"If you near-die over and over again," Analiese spat.

"We'll work it out," Geppetto dismissed, "just takes more practice, hmm Analiese?"

"I won't be charged with manslaughter, either by cops or my own conscience. Keep yourself together." Analiese stormed off to her wagon.

Twenty-Seven

 ULIA FELT WEAK, but need not worry for anything with Phoebe and Nick hovering. She slept most the day on Phoebe's couch, with the two of them refusing to let her leave.

"Rest up, Jul'," was uttered more than she'd like to hear in her lifetime. "Gotta get your strength back for tonight."

Julia's heart pounded, finally understanding the repercussions of her contract. Geppetto insisted on another performance that night. She wouldn't have to create an individual act yet, but he guaranteed their profits would increase enough to purchase a small tent for her soon.

Still, Analiese refused to patch her up again. Julia was shocked to discover that Analiese did not have a contract, and was not bound by what the others were bound to. She could refuse Geppetto's commands, at least to the extent that Julia's life was now at risk if Analiese didn't put her together.

"At least let me go to Analiese, convince her to try to put me together if—when—I go to pieces."

"She won't," Nick said. "Positive she'll kill ya if she tries again. Geppetto won't let us take you to Dr. Evil again, and An'liese is scared of infection."

"Okay then, we need to find Dr. Wise. He helps with these abnormalities."

"You think we got money for a legitimate doctor?" Phoebe said. "Catalyst or no, we can't afford someone else."

"Was Dr. Evil illegitimate?" Julia asked.

"No," Nick corrected. "He helped from the rocky knowin' of Geppetto. No charge, just gloatin'."

"I'll die!" Julia yelped, half-jokingly. Phoebe patted Julia's arm.

Nick shook his head. "Nahh, we'll figure something." Brushing hair out of his face, he squinted in thought. "Phebes, Analiese can mold anything she touches. How could we convince her to mold Jul'?"

"Seriously?" Phoebe said. "Ask Geppetto. He's the tricky one. Convinces anyone to do what they never planned on."

Nick beamed. "Phebes is right. No need to worry. With his catalyst dyin', Geppetto will have a plan. Won't give that up."

"You trust him too much." Julia laid back down, pushing Phoebe's arm away. "I already got the circus its audience. That's all."

"No," Phoebe said. "You're most important moment isn't here yet. But Geppetto isn't worried about losing you when you still have life ahead. He's got no plan, only knows you'll live 'cause you still have events that haven't transpired."

Julia resignedly shook her head. "My most important moment was telling Geppetto I would join, you saw. Saving the circus." She gave a wry laugh. "Can't save it if my big decision is signing up. I'm done."

"You aren't!" Phoebe grabbed her hand. "Your decision is with me, not Geppetto. Talking in my tent and then..."

Julia clenched Phoebe's hand, more subconsciously than out of malice. Phoebe *didn't* see a vision of her joining. It wasn't her most important moment. It wasn't even a moment that had to happen if Julia had wanted to choose a different path. Which means, she had a different vision of a different moment in Julia's life. One still approaching. "...Then what?"

"I don't know."

"But you said....I decided the circus. I chose this, you said." Julia clenched her skirt to stop the shaking. "I couldn't decide. Because it was already for sure. Destiny."

Nick placed his hand over Julia's. "You're not the only one who does whatsoever Geppetto says. His word's decision enough."

"I'm sorry," Phoebe said. "I can't remember. But I'm sorry."

Julia leapt up and brushed past her two caregivers. "I'm not going to lay here and 'rest up, Jul' while the lot of you kill me for your freak show."

She paused outside the wagon, taking in the clusters of people she could glimpse milling around in the front of the circus. Geppetto had been somewhat kind in closing the personal shows for the day, as well as the puppet state exhibits, so that Julia could be properly tended to. No matter; there was still plenty a crowd waiting for the big show, reporters and civilians alike ready to snap a picture of any inexplicable phenomena. Cigarette butts, peanut shells, and apple cores littered the ground, and there was a soft hum in the air.

But the crowds weren't what held Julia's attention. To the side of the circus entrance stood two men taking in the whole scene — the men who had been in the barley field, snooping around.

"Hey!" Julia jogged around the bystanders towards her targets. The older nudged the younger and darted his eyes back, away from the circus, towards town. They turned to walk away. This was no time for jogging—Julia sprinted, ignoring the frowns as she jostled past the last of the spectators.

The older of the barley men began to run, but the younger only jogged, Julia closing in on him. As she passed the circus entrance, he called out to her. "Stay back. Don't get closer; you can't come closer."

Julia was running out of air, but she couldn't give up when he was so close. Who were they, and could they help her? "Stop, wait," she gasped as her legs gave out. Both of them stopped, first the younger then the older much further away, but her legs wouldn't budge as she clasped her knees and panted. "Take me with you."

"You have to stay here," the one closest—only yards away—said. "You're meant to."

"No," she said. "Please, I'll...I'll die. Geppetto will kill me."

His brows furrowed. "You shouldn't have said that." A beat. "Trust me. Stay here. You will see us again." Then he was off running again.

"No, please." Julia quickly composed herself as she heard someone approach from behind.

"Trying to leave?" It was Phoebe. She patted Julia's shoulder, and Julia tensed.

"Trying to live."

"I never thought you to be one to give up." Geppetto had found Analiese behind Nick's tent. She squatted in the dirt, looking out at the barley and halfheartedly tracing patterns in the dirt then brushing them away. "I also never thought you to be one to care about what you're risking when it comes to sculpting others."

Analiese smirked. "It's not giving up; it's knowing my limitations."

She drew an 8 figure and rested her hand on top with a sigh. "I'm not going to kill *her* of all people."

Geppetto tsked. "No, of course not; you can't. We all know she lives for her biggest decision."

"Please, we have no idea how Phoebe's crap gifting works." Analiese added hooks on each end of the 8, creating glasses, before swiping it away. "But let me tell you, this is how my gifting works. One screwup and everything is wiped away forever. Can't take death back no matter how much sculpting I do."

"Funny thing," Geppetto gave a dry laugh, finding the situation very tedious. "You notice her safe spot, to get away from all troubles and rest, is the same as yours? So different the two of you." He waved his hand as he listed. "Different backgrounds and childhoods and social classes." He dropped his hands to his pockets. "And yet, you both hide by the barley field behind the tent of the person you find most trustworthy."

Analiese sighed wearily. "Get to your point, Geppetto."

"My point is that you've always thought you one-upped me, escaping the bounds of a contract that all the others have. Like you can hold something over my head with no repercussions. But, I'm afraid, I've always had something on you."

Analiese glared at the barley. "You've got nothing that bothers me."

"You've heard the Trencher rumors before, I suppose."

Analiese's finger froze in the dirt. Listening.

"A ghost, a soul, that haunts them. A loss in their past."

Analiese huffed. "They didn't lose anything."

"Precisely," Geppetto continued. "You see, I happen to know that ghost's body still roams the earth. I'd wager that Julia has never been told about this ghost, yes? And I'd wager as much that you're worried about what your sculpting *can* do to people because of what it *has* done. How close am I?"

Analiese stood and faced Geppetto. "You have no idea what you're talking about." But the words had a hollow ring to them. He could see right through her.

"On the contrary," Geppetto said, "you have a secret. A secret that for some reason you'd like kept. I won't pretend to understand, but I am more than willing to share it with the crew if you don't patch up Julia after the show."

Analiese pursed her lips.

"Think carefully about what's been said here."

21

 JUMP IN THE DRIVER'S SEAT before Fancy could hardly reach the car. I'm in a hurry, running away from the fact that I may be a "bad guy" in this story, that my brain isn't only holding my memories hostage, it may be holding Phoebe hostage, too. Fancy tosses me the keys, and I pull out of the lot.

"So," Fancy says, "first to the library to see if we can find any isolated cabins with creepy basements to your name."

I shake my head. "Not now." I'm not ready to find out I'm a psychopath. Maybe that's selfish to make Phoebe wait even longer in my hypothetical isolated cabin's creepy basement; but I figure either I'm not a psychopath and Phoebe isn't waiting, or I am a psychopath and making Phoebe wait is exactly what a psychopath would do.

"Then what's your genius plan to free Phoebe?"

"We need to find someone who was there. I'm not about to get tortured again, so preferably not your buddy RaeChaeline. We need to chase down the location of Nick or Analiese or Julia or...or a different, non-incriminating location of Phoebe. Someone who knows what actually went down. Preferably someone who remembers my role in the circus and who I am."

"And what are you gonna do when you find out you were never a part of the circus?"

I scowl. "I'll find someone."

Fancy slumps in her seat and runs her fingers through her hair. "Haven't you learned that's pointless by now?"

"Hey, I've been making progress haven't I?" I ignore the nagging thought that the only progress I made so far is finding out I'm the villain, and that's the progress I'm running from. "Besides, I've been to the library. It's gotten me this far, I may as well chase down this lead."

"Lead?" Fancy pauses a moment. "Wait a... Why'd you go without me, after I've been so supportive with your sketchy psychopath reveal?"

I roll my eyes. "Because you've *never* gone behind my back..."

"Where are we going, then?" Fancy begins to grip the door, then rubs her hand along it instead, as if she realizes her fear is showing and needs to shift that energy to something less conspicuous.

"I'm not leading you to your grave or anything, Fancy."

It's her turn to roll her eyes. "You could try."

Her head perks up as we turn off the main road into the spiffy suburb. It isn't "our" suburb, the one with the floundering dusty mansion. It's the other suburb. But she must have picked up on the concept, that we are on our way to some wealthy home. And wealthy homes pertaining to this circus tale are few and far between. She isn't so dense as to not figure it out.

"Stop the car," she says.

"No."

She grips the door handle. "This is a dead end, not a lead. Stop. The. Car."

"You don't know that," I insist.

"I do."

"You don't." I watch her hand, hoping she doesn't leap out of the car. But I don't slow down.

"Trust me," she says. I almost hear a plea in it.

I sigh. "It's already been a lead..."

"What?!" She's so taken aback her hand releases the door.

I smile. "So you trust me."

She huffs. "I certainly don't."

I park the car by the drive, completely aware it could be towed again. But at least this time Fancy would be stuck with me instead of the one sabotaging things.

I'm halfway out of the car when she says, "You'll want me to stay here. They won't want to see me or talk to me. Or you by association."

"You know them?"

Fancy side-eyes me. "I... I live in their house. How in the world is this a surprise to you?"

I shrug. She's quicker at putting things together than me, so really, I'm surprised that my surprise would be a surprise to her. And I wonder if in some roundabout way that might make me kinda clever like her. Kinda.

"You gotta come in. You might be able to get to them, and besides...I'm not about to let you leave me without a car here again." I pause, then add. "I won't tell them you're still in their house if that's the problem."

"It's not that." She harrumphs, but opens her car door. "This'll backfire, just you wait. You're not ready for this."

I shrug and walk toward the entry. The pristine Julia-not-Julia looms, and I can't help stopping in awe again at her piercing gaze. I turn to see Fancy's reaction, wondering if it's her first time but suspecting she must have been here before. The sculpture has the opposite effect on her, though. Fancy studies her feet and shrinks into herself as she hurries past. I jog to catch up to her, and bob my head at Julia-not-Julia in apologetic reverence as I race past.

This time with Fancy by my side, no matter how oddly she's behaving, I figure I could confidently march to the front door. If they let her live in their house, they must have some sort of rapport.

The door lurches open with more confidence than the presence within—Mr. Trencher. His gaze shifts from me to Fancy and back. "How dare you bring her here!? Who do you think you are?"

I look to Fancy, and she shrugs at me a "told ya so."

"You remember that investigative guy that was snooping around?" Fancy says.

I frown at her. How'd she know?

"Am I wrong? Isn't that your thing?" Fancy whispers.

Mr. Trencher's frown deepens. It's bad enough to see Fancy, let alone recall our tussle in the bushes, I guess.

"Hi again." I smile and pretend there's no qualms here, simply a neighborly chitchat. "I trust your morning is well, Mr. Trencher, sir. We're just popping by to check on you and the Mrs..."

I debate telling him what we've found thus far, give info to get info, but with the dead bodies and the escaped Nick and the incriminating evidence at Jasper's apartment... Yeah, not much I want to spread around, especially to someone so ready to be rid of me.

"I'm not about to let you into this house," Mr. Trencher says gruffly. "Not ever and certainly not now."

"If I may interject," Fancy says, "Mr. Trencher, I think you've seen how persistent...this investigator..." She just realizes she isn't sure which name I used with them in the past. Not the best save, but still, a save. I need to take notes. "...can be. And you know how persuasive I can be. You wouldn't want to turn us away; it wouldn't work for long anyhow, right?"

Mr. Trencher's frown couldn't deepen any further, but I'm sure he wishes it did. He opens the door wide. "In the sitting room only, and don't you dare disturb Mrs. Trencher."

"And you said it wouldn't help to bring you along," I whisper.

Fancy shrugs and speaks aloud for both me and Mr. Trencher to hear. "I have my ways, doesn't mean I like using them."

I take a seat and admire the bookshelves again.

Fancy isn't in the mood for relaxing, though. She stands inside the door and says, "I'll get to the point, Mr. Trencher. He's interested in the whereabouts of any of the circus folk."

I turn from the books to the conversation. "Not RaeChaeline, though. Any of the others: Nick, Phoebe, Analiese...Julia..."

Mr. Trencher gives a dry laugh. "You're kidding."

"So, why don't you help us out, and we'll be on our way."

Mr. Trencher looks back and forth between me and Fancy. I prop my legs up on the arm of the chair; didn't seem like he's about to kick me out so I may as well make myself at home. Plus, it feels like a power move.

"I haven't..." Mr. Trencher pauses. Either he is hiding something and trying to get out of revealing it, or he doesn't know anything and doesn't know how to convince us of that. "I haven't run into them, or Julia —who is not circus folk, for the record—since...everything... And I personally have no interest in encountering them when they *don't seem to want to be found*." His shoulders hunch and he ducks, peeking at Fancy like she might not believe him and might take it out on him in some way.

"How come?" I ask. "They could lead to Julia, right? That's what we all want."

Mr. Trencher shakes his head. "Too dangerous. Either Julia doesn't want to be found either, or there's nothing of her left to find. They ruined her, and ruined us, and I'm trying to live with that. Mainly I'm trying to live."

"You think they hurt her, or...worse?" I haven't yet explored the hypothesis that the circus folk are dangerous or to blame, but then again I was tortured by one. Maybe Jasper was trying to save Phoebe, and maybe the writing supported that. I'll have to re-read to determine if that's the case. But I cling to this new hope that maybe I'm not a bad guy, maybe I'm a hero—or, an attempted hero at least. I sit up straight in the seat, attempting to embody this new "good guy" side and see if it fit.

"I think they're dangerous," Mr. Trencher tentatively says, continuing to implore Fancy. "I think whether they mean well or not, they're capable of horrible things."

Fancy's eyebrows furrow, probably not too fond of his assessment of her pseudo-buddy RaeCh.

Mr. Trencher throws his arms up, newfound energy about his explanation. "The fire, I mean, that there is indication enough that it's not safe there. That all of them were in danger as they came together. Some are..." at this he looks almost tenderly at Fancy, like he knows her connection to RaeChaeline and that this could be a painful truth for her to accept. "Some are broken themselves, like my dear Julia. I accept that. But others, they do the breaking. And that's something Julia wasn't prepared for."

Fancy looks down at her hands and clasps them in front of her. It couldn't have been pleasant to hear him accuse RaeChaeline like that, but she is listening, attentive even.

"So," I jump in to switch course and ease the tension. "In your past interactions, you ever hear of a place they may run to, or hide evidence, or any direction to explore?"

Mr. Trencher laughs more readily than before. "Anywhere but here; you got the wrong tree. We hardly interacted with them or Julia. We know nothing, and we're not pursuing it so we'll continue to know nothing. I'm sorry I can't be of more help, investigator, but there's nothing here."

I am disappointed to hear it, and after how he opened up, I truly believe him. Maybe that is proof of the "good guy" in me, that I'm not jumping to cut off a finger to make him talk like RaeChaeline would.

I stand and extend my hand to shake his. "Thank you for your time, Mr. Trencher."

"With all due respect, I'm not gonna shake your hand after all this," he says.

"I admire that." I lower my hand. "I apologize for the intrusion." I exit the room, with Fancy and Mr. Trencher following, but waiting through the door is none other than Mrs. Trencher.

"My friend, you're back," she beams and clasps my hand between hers. She looks over my shoulder and gasps, jerks back, puts her hand to her cheek.

"It's okay, she's a friend, too," I assure as I look back at Fancy. Fancy is looking at the floor, hands raised, and I make note that ohh, that's how to take a non-threatening stance.

"Please," Mrs. Trencher whispers. "Please leave, Analiese."

22

Clue 15: Fancy is Analiese. Should I have seen that coming? Probably.

HE SHORT PIECE OF MY LIFE that I have memory of flashes before my eyes, replaying the moments with Fancy, trying to shift the story to it being moments with Analiese. All this time hiding under my nose, leading me... off her trail? Diverting my attention somewhere else? Or eliminating herself as a suspect so I could focus on the real culprit?

I do not know Analiese's relationship with Julia, or with Phoebe, or with Jasper. I don't know Analiese's character, other than her trickster ways as Fancy. I don't know her thoughts on the circus and if she would sabotage it all with a fire.

I do not know the person I know most in the world.

Fancy and I stare at each other—her face still isn't Analiese to me, it's Fancy's face. I try seeing her in a whole new light, her looking exposed and forlorn. The betrayal I feel is reflected back at me in her quizzical eyes. She opens her mouth, but no sound comes out. She pauses, then purses her lips instead.

She backs up, and when Mr. Trencher realizes she is about to walk into him, he runs sideways right into an entry table, and the floral arrangement crashes to the floor. Fancy turns at the racket, making her exit that much safer. Mr. Trencher pushes the clutter out of the way with his foot and stays to the side while Fancy walks past and out the door.

I don't know if I should follow her. I rode here with a person that no longer exists, and I'm not sure if I am supposed to leave with the replacement. I'm not sure if I should, nor if I want to.

"Why would you bring her here?" Mrs. Trencher spits out. "You're no friend of this house."

"I came to ask about your daughter," I try. "Julia. I'm trying to help find her."

"You've come for nothing," Mrs. Trencher responds.

Mr. Trencher murmurs, "She's nothing but a shell now."

"You mean the statue?" I ask. "The statue is Julia?"

"I mean Mrs. Trencher," he amends.

Mrs. Trencher's eyes light up, and she pushes past me out the door. "I told you before, it's not Julia. It's nothing like Julia!"

Mr. Trencher runs after her, but he is too late. She charges straight at the statue and slams into it. The statue stares forward resolutely, unaffected by the scene, and instead throws its piercing gaze at Fancy—Analiese, I mean—who stands by the car, waiting. I suppose for her travel companion? Perhaps?

Mr. Trencher wraps his arm around Mrs. Trencher, who is bound to be sore from the impact. Mrs. Trencher mumbles, I catch a "...have to listen," while Mr. Trencher soothes.

I see her eyes light up, and I know Mr. Trencher is in for a breakneck race again, but there isn't time to warn him. At the moment they are passing Fancy's car, Mrs. Trencher breaks free and jumps into the driver's seat before any of us can react.

The car begins to roll forward, and Fancy instinctively steps back. "Stop her!" Mr. Trencher implores, but what could any of us do? The car plows through the garden beds, leaving a horrendous dent in the pristine lawn. But it gets worse than that. She slams right into that huge sculpture, and Julia-not-Julia careens into the ground and splits into pieces.

Mr. Trencher runs to the car and helps Mrs. Trencher out. Her hair runs wild, but if she is injured her gleeful disposition doesn't show it.

"Now that we're past all that," she says, "would you like some tea, Mr. Trencher?"

Mr. Trencher scowls at Fancy—Analiese. "Why didn't you stop the car? Get it out of my yard, now."

And then him and Mrs. Trencher are safe in their home, and we are left outside with the shambles of a garden and a dented car.

I'm not about to let this Analiese character take off without me, so I am behind the wheel and detaching it from the yard while she grimaces at the newly horseshoe-style hood. She clambers into the passenger seat with a shrug—isn't like this was stellar transport to begin with—and we are off.

I am pretty sure I shouldn't be driving in what some would say is a volatile emotional state, but right now my feelings are as flat as could be. I assume it's from the shock—I don't know how to think or what to feel. My body needs to process before it can react. And thankfully Fancy gives me the silence I need, for once, and I wonder if that's the most Analiese side of her I've seen yet.

We make the drive in silence, and I pull into the circus lot hoping I am ready for a firm discussion to reestablish the new framework for this ... relationship.

"What are we doing here?" she says.

"You're gonna tell me everything that happened." My voice shakes, the first sign that I'm not as collected as I thought.

"I don't owe you anything," she responds.

"You owe me the truth!"

She opens the door and stomps away from the car, but I quickly follow.

"After everything we've been through, you have to tell me—" I grab her arm, and Fancy rips it away.

I am stupid and frantic, and I reach out again; she whirls around and covers my mouth. "Don't you touch me, don't you talk." I feel my jaw crack, and I grip my lips shut, but that doesn't stop my mouth from molding to her grip, my teeth melting into new shapes at her will. My eyes water and tears drip down.

The magic is real, I realize.

"Our entire relationship is built on deceit, half-truths, and unanswerable questions," she clips. "It goes both ways."

I grip my lips shut as I feel my chin disappearing into my neck and wonder what nightmare I've entered.

"I've let you sleep in my house, travel with my car. I've led you all over town and helped you find your own place, your own name, your own life, and then you *demand* I give even more without so much as an ounce of gratitude. Without a hint of interest in my own life, my own questions, my own story to pursue."

She takes a huffed breath, and the pause is enough for her to realize her hand's power. She lightens the grip. "Hold still, let me fix your face."

I don't know how to react; I am frozen in fear and confusion anyway. She grabs my face more like a sculptor this time, a soft and firm touch, massaging my skin and bones into the likeness of a human, and I think this must be what god is like.

She squints her eyes and frowns, adjusts my face some more, angles my chin. "Ugh, don't look in a mirror, you won't recognize yourself," she says. "I can fix you more, but it'll take that look of fear vanishing long enough for me to work on your relaxed face instead of... this..." She gestures at my face in disgust, and I have enough presence of mind to be insulted that she'd be disgusted when she's the one that did "this" to me.

I swallow, take a moment to appreciate that I am capable of that still, and choke out words. "Y-your enchanted, the circus, i-it's enchanted. It's real."

She rolls her eyes. "Next time, don't touch a lady without permission."

I am a little peeved she'd blame all that on me, but I'm not about to mention it now that I realize the power inside that stout frame.

She sighs. "The point is, Max, we're all con artists in our own way. Me, Geppetto, the Trenchers, you... everyone. Going through life saying and doing what needs to be done for ourselves, even at the expense of others. You should know that. I've seen it, and you've seen it. I've done it. And you have, too. And most people are just good enough con artists or just gullible enough marks that they con themselves into thinking they're the ones—the only ones—who are genuine."

"So, what then?" I ask. "What's your end game? What's got you 'traipsing' through my life if nothing is in it for you?"

Analiese smirks. "Sooner to get you out of my house, for one. But, I think we can come up with a sort of wager for what I'm really after."

"And what's that?" I worry that it's something I won't want to give, like chopping off my hand or turning myself inside out with her superpowers. Some voice of reason tells me that's nonsense, but a deeper voice tells me reason is no good anymore with what she's capable of. At this moment, I may be more open to a deal with the devil than a deal with Analiese, but he hasn't yet shown up with an offer.

"Nick," she says. "You fumbled that one, but not again."

"I help you get Nick?"

"Yes."

"And then you tell me about that night?"

Analiese frowns. "I never said that. We already established that I've helped you out of the goodness of my heart all this time, and you've offered nothing. Time for you to pay up."

I groan. "So where is this Nick, and how are we gonna ensure I don't get locked up like last time?"

We begin walking back to the car. Always off to somewhere, never getting anywhere.

"Ensuring isn't part of the deal," Analiese responds. "But maybe, out of the kindness of my heart, I'll fix your face to be a little less buffoon-ish."

I fake a smile. Then freeze. "Wait, are you insulting my 'normal' face, or is the face you made a totally botched one?"

She beams. "Find Nick, and maybe you'll find out."

Twenty-Eight

HIS PLACE SHE'D HOPED WAS FREEDOM had turned so quickly into a prison, as much as the doctor's office or the Trencher household. Leaving there had taken great courage that came in such a spurt Julia couldn't even be sure how it had come or gone.

Now courage was needed again, but she belonged here, she knew it. There were others, much like her, trying to cope with their abnormalities. People who she had more or less befriended. (Did it count as befriended yet? She wasn't certain, what with her shortage of experience in that area.)

Before she had left a building of strangers and scientists, always probing, always scrutinizing. Here she would leave not only a place, but a people, a camaraderie, a belonging. Family, perhaps.

She couldn't leave that. She had joined to save them, break the bonds that tied them. Nick to his fear. RaeChae to her anger. Phoebe to her naiveté. Analiese to—whatever her problem was.

But Julia couldn't let herself stay to die, either, for that would be just as much a failure. Her only choice was to escape, refuse Geppetto's demands for tonight, so she could live another day to save them all.

"Well, well, well. Julia dearest."

Lost in thought and with the sound muffled by the chatter of nearby crowds, Julia hadn't heard anyone approaching her hiding place behind Phoebe's tent. Of all the people it could have been, she'd never expected it to be him.

"Dr. Wise," she gasped.

"I've searched high and low for you. I must say, I've been concerned you were in a pile of pieces in some lonely gutter."

Julia put her hands to her hips and turned up her nose. "All the more convenient for you to pack me up and haul me off to return to your studies, right?"

Dr. Wise shook his head. "Nonsense, silly girl. I hear talk of a show dozens of people observed, all claiming a girl fell to bits. Some masterful illusion, and they're here again today to figure the trick. No one believes it, of course. No one, that is, except me."

Julia stepped around Dr. Wise toward the circus and crowds.

Dr. Wise grips her arm and she pauses. He squeezes hard, but with a polite smile as if they're still making friendly conversation. "I think to myself, falling to bits is precisely the sort of thing one Julia Trencher would do if I wasn't around. Was worried there wouldn't be a show, what with no one to stitch you up again. No 'King's horses and men' here, am I right?"

Dr. Wise laughed and jiggled his glasses. "I say, though, how are you standing before me in one piece right now? Thought I'd travel all this way to help out and here it seems I've been rendered obsolete."

Julia took advantage of the moment to jerk her arm out of his grasp. She glanced back toward the crowds. Two police officers walked the premises—either to maintain order in the crowds, or perhaps with the thought of investigating a piecemealed girl's suspected murder.

"Wouldn't you like to know," Julia said. She started in the direction of the officers, but Dr. Wise interrupted.

"Wait. I must say I'm concerned for your safety."

"Oh, are you?" Geppetto stepped out from around Phoebe's tent. "And who might you be to have concern for our Julia?"

Julia sidestepped until she brushed against Phoebe's tent. "I'm not a concern for either of you."

Phoebe came around her tent. She crossed her arms and frowned. "Julia's right. You both want her for your own gain."

Geppetto said, "You belong here, Julia. We accept you as you are, because we're like you. We see your ability as a gift. Not an anomaly to be fixed." He spat the word "fixed" like a curse. "A gift to be shared with the world. We see you."

"Preposterous." Dr. Wise walked to Julia's side conspiratorially and jabbed his finger at Geppetto. "You're exploiting her. I don't care if you're a con artist, kidnapper, or cult—you're sadistic, gaining money and popularity from her freak show. Julia, you can't believe this man."

"I don't," Julia said. "But I don't believe you, either. This isn't some tug-of-war; I'm not a rope."

"Let's not be rash, Julia," Dr. Wise said.

"Here's the plan," Julia's voice rang clear, decisive. "Dr. Wise, you will get me out of here."

Dr. Wise beamed, but Julia continued. "You won't be probing me with a needle or stethoscope or any medical object. You will only return me to my parents."

"Oh, perfect, they're waiting for you at my office as we speak."

"They didn't come?" Phoebe interrupted.

Dr. Wise shook his head and patted Julia on the shoulder. "I'm sorry to say they've been mostly unresponsive since they lost their daughter. Couldn't get them to focus on anything, even hope of her living. Tragic, really."

Phoebe bit her lip. "Stay, Julia."

"I'm not going to die here."

"No," Geppetto said. "Julia, I've spoken with Analiese. I believe she will help."

Julia put her hand to her forehead. "Coerced her to sign her life away, too? Seriously? No. I'm going home tonight. And I'll be back to end this."

Julia marched through the crowds with Dr. Wise trailing behind, prancing proud as a lion that just proved his mettle.

"Yes. Yes, you will, Julia." Geppetto called out. "You will return here tonight for the show and fall apart just as you did last night. You can't change that. It's on the dotted line."

Twenty-Nine

PPREHENSION WORMED THROUGH JULIA'S STOMACH as she approached Dr. Wise's office. She hadn't exactly thought through the repercussions of returning home, besides the fortuitous chance at living another day, of course.

Mr. and Mrs. Trencher would see her any moment—would they be relieved? Nervous? Miffed? How could she explain she wasn't staying? How could she tell them her home was not with those who provided and cared for her all this time? More practically, how would she return to the circus tomorrow and avoid falling apart again? Too many worries were jumbled together to adequately focus on any one.

She clenched her fists as she walked through the entryway with Dr. Wise. Here was the place she'd been poked, prodded, and studied—a human specimen. Julia tried to swallow the fist holding her throat. She looked around the lobby. Sterile and lonely as ever. Two nurses were rushing towards them. Julia pinched the tip of her nose. "Where are my parents?"

Dr. Wise patted her shoulder, then there was a prick on her arm. "I'm sorry," he said.

Julia backed away, but Dr. Wise blocked the doorway, his fist clenching an empty syringe. "She's had a mental break," he directed his words to the nurses. "We need to restrain her until we locate her parents and can return her to their care."

"No," Julia said. "No, I'm perfectly sane. I can—" but she already felt her mind spin, whatever he'd injected taking effect, and she grabbed for the nearest chair before sitting on the floor. "Let me go, I'm fine." She crawled away from the nurses, grasping her head with one hand. "Please." But her eyes wouldn't stay open a moment longer, and she dropped her head to rest.

White. Everything was white, too white. She'd take the lobby over this nothingness. White straps bound her arms to white walls while she sat on a white floor. Had no one discovered yet how inhumane this treatment was?

Julia tried to convince herself the white was comforting: structure, consistency, predictability. No worries in this room, a place she couldn't harm herself even if she wanted to. She was safe from Geppetto's scheme for her, safe from breaking to death. Humpty Dumpty would be grateful for such an offer, really.

"*Humpty Dumpty, tied to a wall...Humpty Dumpty, so he wouldn't fall...*" Julia murmured. "I really am losing it."

But the silence was so loud she had to finish. "*All the King's horses, All the circus men, needn't put me together again.*"

The door whirred open. "Julia, I truly am sorry for doing this." Dr. Wise commanded the white room with his dark shoes, dark suit, dark gaze. Even his white tufts of hair seemed dark in contrast with this whitest cell.

"Where are Mr. and Mrs. Trencher?" Julia crossed her legs and pressed against her white prison. It was hard to come across as demanding when bound at half the height of the captor.

"You must understand," Dr. Wise said, "you are ill, a danger to yourself. Crazed delusions of grandeur, at a circus, no less, coupled with a sense of daring that puts your life at risk. You must remember that your purpose is here, harnessing your ability to save millions to come back from death, just as you do. And if you exit this building and lose something vital..." Dr. Wise shook his head emphatically. "Who's to say you could ever come back from that. Until we know more, you are safest here."

"You have no right to hold me here!"

"I'm only keeping you safe until I find your parents."

Julia pulled against her restraints. "Where are they?"

"Not home; they've abandoned it. Perhaps your illness is hereditary, because if you haven't noticed, they aren't exactly on their rocker, either. Seeing ghosts around every corner. Their sanity seems bound to your predictability—something you sadly have little of."

"I don't know where they are. If they weren't home, they were at the doctor. Only two places we ever lived."

Dr. Wise squinted. "I wish I didn't believe you. Try to rest up. We'll bring you some dinner soon." And with that, he left her cell to its whiteness.

Julia slumped as much as the restraints would allow. She was trapped, with her only hope of rescue a missing and neurotic Mr. and Mrs. Trencher. How long until they were found? How long until Dr. Wise began his research, experimenting on her body again?

Even the circus couldn't save her—they thought she was gone of her own free will, happily munching on elaborate planned meals, sleeping on a fluffy mattress in a home larger than all their tents and wagons combined, and reunited with a family that would never sacrifice her body for renown.

Julia gave a very unbecoming snort. "Home sweet home."

Julia's arms pressed against the restraints that refused to budge. She squirmed and pressed her arms back towards the wall, only they wouldn't go back; they very decidedly wanted to escape her restraints. "Stop," she said. She gasped as her arms used more force against the bindings. Something had to give soon, and she just hoped her arms would stop pulling before the pain worsened.

The circus, she thought. *The contract. It must be time, and I have to go back.* She let out a yelp as her arms yanked. *Geppetto won't let me be.* She heard a tear, and was appalled to see her right bindings ripping against the persistent arm. Welts and burns covered her forearm, but she had no time to examine it. Her other arm demanded attention, pulling with more force as if indignant it was last to escape. The arm cracked and—no it was the arm, not the restraint—cracking and pulling apart in its urgency to leave, and Julia screamed as the end of her arm toppled to the floor.

"What's this racket?" a befuddled nurse entered the room, leaving the door wide. Julia took the opportunity and dodged past, grabbing her left arm from the floor quickly before she was dragged away from it, not sure if it was her or the contract compelling her out the door, down the street, and away from Dr. Wise. The nurse took little pursuit, only making it to the lobby before running to Dr. Wise's office. Julia wasn't concerned, partially because she had a head-start, but mostly because if she couldn't stop herself from moving then how could the whole of the medical team?

Her legs wearied, but pain was no matter to the contract, so she moved as quickly as ever. "I'm late. I'm late, I'm late, I'm late." Much like the bunny studying his watch, there was no intercepting Julia.

The circus came into focus and she rushed past the empty ticket booth, past the littered grounds and into the big top.

Spectators were packed together, but there was a walkway for her feet to propel on. Geppetto had his arms outstretched to introduce her. RaeChae scowled, but Nick looked apologetic, biting his lip and avoiding eye contact.

Her body rushed in front of them right on time to tear apart, and she let out a cry as each piece once again collapsed. Just before all feeling left, a breath of reassurance washed over her as Nick grasped her back.

Thirty

URE ENOUGH, ANALIESE PATCHED HER UP like before. No infection this time. Her and Phoebe must have been extra cautious about contaminants. Everything had turned out all right. *See, there was no reason to worry,* Julia tried to convince herself. Still, she couldn't help but feel violated. Her head throbbed, half in exhaustion and half in anger.

In place of her former dresses Julia had brought along, she now had her very own patchwork skirt and color block blouse made from the fabric much like Phoebe's. Julia felt more a part of the circus with her own new outfit. A meeting of her former and new life. It was a sense of belonging she was no longer certain she wanted.

Analiese said, "While I patched up the spoiled rich kid, Phoebe patched up the clothes that were, like me, getting tired of the strain your collapses bring on us."

Julia brushed her eyes, but the tears fell regardless. Puppet was too adequate a description for what she now was, with no life outside of the puppeteer's demands. There had to be a way to stop this nonsense before she lost even more of herself—before any puppet lost more.

Only one person could have that answer, hidden somewhere deep inside, if Julia could unlock it. And, like thunder after the rain, Julia's tears vanished as she stormed to Phoebe's tent.

Meanwhile, Phoebe peered out of the tent. The crowds were already vast waiting to enter the show; she couldn't see where they ended and the town limits began. So many people, here to watch her perform. *Tell us our secrets, give me hope.*

"Hope," she whispered. There was no hope, no future except the one she always saw. Every human was stuck in one place, one moment that forever altered them. *Can't you see?* She wanted to say. You are already made, sealed the deal, done—one brief moment in their history or future that would determine who they would be. Forever. And Phoebe didn't realize it quite yet, but one such moment was around the corner.

When Julia arrived, Phoebe was fiddling with her foam faux-crystal ball, and she turned to Julia. She gasped and covered her mouth. "Wait..."

Julia rushed to her.

"Wait, Julia. This is the most important decision you will make in life—for your good or for your destruction. Think it through some more."

Julia's mouth opened, ever so slightly. This was the moment, the actual moment. She shook her head. "I know. I need your help."

"You know?" Phoebe said.

"Well, at least, I hope so." Light steps outside interrupted them. Who knew how long it would take for her to get Phoebe alone to pick her brain again. But wait—this was her most important moment, Phoebe said—regardless of who was here.

The tent rustled, and Julia turned to see. It was the two men, the two sneaking men she'd been chasing. Only now, they weren't running; they approached with certainty. Julia glanced between the men and Phoebe.

"You!" Phoebe whispered. "Oh my...oh my..." Her eyes flitted back and forth between the two men, seeing memories anew and bracing with the impact of what she now knew again.

"It's time," the older man said. "It's time to break my father's hold for good."

23

ANALIESE'S PLAN TO FIND NICK is going straight into the belly of the beast. No, not the asylum beast, the torture chamber one. That's right. RaeChaeline, of course, and her connections would know of any Nick sightings. And for some reason, Analiese won't visit her buddy herself; she has to drag me along—ya know, for funsies.

We pull up to the torture chamber—I mean, clinic—and my stomach clenches, my hands throb. My body remembers. I feel oddly comforted by the thought that maybe my body could hold memories my mind can't. I wonder what other things my body remembers that I'll discover later. And that...it is the first time I look ahead with a semblance of hope. Which is new for me; at least, as far as I recall.

When Fancy's car door slams, I snap back to attention. I am here, the place my stomach and hands are telling me to avoid for their sake. I am about to go against their better judgment.

I follow Fancy, holding my head high to signal to my body that things are more okay than they actually are. It doesn't believe me.

RaeChaeline and the guy she calls Dr. Evil look up from the ginormous sheet of paper that covers his desk.

"What are you doing here," RaeChaeline says. It isn't a question.

"As you heard, Nick escaped," Fancy responds, cool as ever.

It dawns on me, the reason she was so chill all the time, like she has nothing to worry about. Because she has nothing to worry about; her super-powered curse would take care of any naysayer, even someone as knife-happy as RaeChae.

"Figured you lot would have a clue to his whereabouts with all your snooping," RaeChaeline quips.

"You're one to talk."

They both stare each other down, and I remember they aren't necessarily friendly just because they're from the same circus. They momentarily had a common cause in scaring me off their trail or getting info out of me or—something—that caused them to unite forces against me. But they aren't buddy buddy. They have a more volatile history, and *their* memories are just fine in that regard.

Dr. Evil ducks his head and leaves the room, not much for chitchat, apparently. Have I met someone even more secretive than the circus folks?

RaeChaeline turns to me. "Looks like you 'Fancied' something worse for your face than my knife."

I wince. Hooray. My face is worse for wear, apparently. "She can be as persuasive as you are, and without a knife, it turns out."

RaeChaeline smiles. "Surprise."

"We don't have to keep you long," Analiese continues. "Just any info you have on Nick."

RaeChaeline rolls her eyes. "It's quite simple, really. 'Fancy' could have figured this out ages ago if you took the time to know people instead of twisting everything inward."

"I'm not you." Analiese sniffs. "I may miss details, but I still care. Who's the one twisting everything inward now?"

"Oh, don't get me wrong; I admire the ability to set aside emotion to do what's needed. I'll admit, it's like a distorted reflection of my own strengths. You just miss the finer points of a person you could always save, use for later."

Analiese rolls her eyes. "Get on with it. Where is he?"

"Why should I help you?'

Analiese looks at me, gestures her head at RaeChae. Somehow she wants me to convince her. Great.

RaeChaeline laughs. "Tell me, boy. What do you need Nick for? I already gave you your past."

I swallow. Nod. "You want me to stop snooping. Fancy and I have a deal; you help me with it, I can get out of your hair."

RaeChaeline approaches, strokes her fingers through my curls and down to my beat-up hands. "We had a deal too. Seems it didn't mean much."

I lick my lips. "Neither of you have scared me off yet. Take a chance on teaming up." I don't tell her that they each absolutely terrify me; I just don't have much to lose anymore.

RaeChaeline smiles satisfactorily and turns back to Analiese. "Nick has still got some of his wits about him. He'd want to save the girl still, of course, but no hopes of that. He'd find the circus in crumbles, and when he found that, he'd land at the next best place—the next best person—that will take him."

RaeChaeline turns her gaze from Analiese to me. "And ironically, 'Fancy' here is using you to skirt past her lack of teamwork that could have helped her know the answer all along."

I squirm, remembering the pain she can cause. "I don't have the memories you all do, so you'll have to clue me in."

"There's this pl-" RaeChae starts.

"—the Trenchers, obviously," Analiese interrupts. Her and RaeChae exchange looks.

RaeChaeline nods and smiles. "Obviously."

It is here I catch up to what's been happening all along. I realize we're all running in circles, chasing each other's tails. From the circus to the old Trencher place to the new Trencher place to Jasper's place to RaeChae and back again. And there is only one way to stop running.

This is a trail we've been down before. Analiese and RaeChaeline, in cahoots, leading me along like a blind puppy. I'm mixing metaphors here, but the concept is clicking nonetheless. The simultaneous and disparate answers. That vulture's smile. Communicating in some silent code with each other beneath their words.

The Trenchers don't have Nick, or any answer I am looking for. At least, not the answer these two are hiding from me. I'll have to be one step ahead of them to find the location they haven't divulged, the location they've shared with each other with gazes that speak volumes.

It's time I am smarter than all of them, and I'm despondent to realize I'm still not. I comfort myself with the thought that maybe they don't notice my mood, maybe I am getting marginally better at hiding things, that maybe I am learning something from them.

Clue 16: Nick would go to some place—some person—but Fancy and RaeChae aren't saying where. Hiding something again.

Thirty-One

 OU KNOW HIM?" Julia jabbed her finger at the men who had entered. "Well Phebes, about time you did an introduction to these sneaks and cheats."

"This is Jasper." The older man gestured to the teenager hovering behind, nothing more than a shadow of the formidable presence speaking. "I'm the Forgettable. I've heard it described as a black fog."

Phoebe interjected. "The Forgettable is also the first and only Pinocchio."

"What?" Julia said.

The Forgettable shook his head. "No time for explanation. We must plan. You have a new outfit, which Phoebe says is indicative of your most significant decision. You just decided that to take down Geppetto you'd have to find the answer that Phoebe has in her head somewhere. Good news: she does—it's me. And I'm now found."

"Slow down," Julia said. "You can't barge into my most important decision without explaining exactly what I'm deciding."

The Forgettable rolled his eyes. "You're deciding to be freed. It so happens I know exactly where the contracts are kept. I also know that burning the contracts ends your tie to it."

"Burning them? Then no puppeteering?" Julia questioned.

The Forgettable laughed. "What exactly do you think 'first and only Pinocchio' means? I'm real as ever again."

Julia nodded. To have her choices back, her freedom, was everything she was fighting for. Except belonging. To be free meant no control over her limbs detaching, no say in when she fell apart. Analiese would refuse to help her and she'd be forced to endure Dr. Wise's consults again.

But she couldn't leave things the way they were—Nick, Phoebe, and RaeChae should be freed if nothing else. As for her fate, that could be decided when she held her contract before the fire.

"What's the plan?" Phoebe said.

Jasper handed two envelopes to the Forgettable, who waved them towards Phoebe. "These are exactly what you and Julia will do. You'll forget this whole meeting happened thanks to my presence, so you need these letters. I recommend writing in your own handwriting that these words can be trusted, so you know to follow through with them when you've lost your memory."

The Forgettable handed an envelope to each of them, and Jasper offered a pen. Phoebe refused the pen, but Julia sat her envelope on Phoebe's desk to scribble a note.

"Once we follow through on this," the Forgettable continued, "we should all be free. Geppetto can't own us forever."

Phoebe looked at Julia, then at Jasper. "It won't work. It could... it could kill somebody."

The Forgettable shrugged. "There's always that risk, but that is the risk of being *in* contract which is why it's time to get you all *out* of it."

Julia squinted. "What's in it for you? You're free already."

The Forgettable smiled, yet his eyes remained dull. "Let's just say it's a win-win. With this one act, I can complete my long-sought vengeance and also make restitution to an old friend I've wronged."

Ever focused on the prize, the Forgettable cleared his throat and pivoted back to the objective. "Quickly, I need to leave before someone sees me. Phoebe will distract Geppetto and Analiese, who will try to stop us. She remembers their names, so she can actually identify them. Julia, you need to enlist Nick and RaeChae to help. RaeChae is essential—she's Geppetto's blind spot; if she helps, he won't see it coming 'til we're free. If for one second he suspects, you all will be compelled by him and we lose."

"Are you wanting this, Julia? Even if it means..." Phoebe glanced at Jasper again.

"It's worth the risk, I think," Julia said. "For all of us."

Phoebe rubbed her palms on her skirt. "Okay, operation freedom: go now."

The Forgettable grabbed Julia's envelope off the desk and handed it to her again. "You all hit puppet state in a couple hours—it's now or never. Phebes, this'll work. It has to."

Thirty-Two

ULIA STUDIED THE ENVELOPE in her hand. *For freedom* it said, clearly in her flippant penmanship. She sat the envelope down and rubbed her forehead. What happened? She'd been ready to tell Phoebe they had to end their entrapment, and then, nothing. Phoebe stared at her, as confused as Julia, though this could be her usual amnesia.

"What's that?" Julia pointed at Phoebe's hand, clasping an envelope so tight it bent.

Phoebe started and looked at her hand. "I-I don't know." She ripped it open and pulled out a notecard. "'Phebes—I will free us all, I told you. Do this—this is how to be free.'"

"Who is it from?" Julia said.

"I don't know. What's yours?"

Julia slid her finger under the flap. Another notecard. "Do this: one—enlist strategic allies, Nick and RaeChae.' And it goes on from there."

Phoebe shot from her seat and towards the exit. "Let's go."

"Wait," Julia said. "Think about it. We don't even know what this is."

"It's a chance at freedom," Phoebe countered.

Julia looked down at the notecard again, the envelope peeking out from behind with her handwriting. "Worth a shot, maybe." She trailed out of the tent.

"I'm not enlisting allies," Phoebe said. "I'm distracting opponents. We'll meet up later, free hopefully."

"Deal."

But Phoebe hadn't stuck around to hear and was already entering the big top.

Julia read her notecard further. First to RaeChae. Julia jogged to RaeChae, who was tapping her foot outside her tent.

"RaeChae, we're getting out of here."

"What?" RaeChae laughed. "How did you miss this? We're stuck, Julia. You trapped us all."

Julia shook her head and pulled RaeChae into the tent. "We have a plan. Analiese and Geppetto will try to stop it, so I need your help."

"Seriously? What is it?"

"I need Nick to start a fire, and you are going to distract Analiese long enough for him to do it."

"The puppet prep."

Julia nodded. "My note says you can keep Analiese preoccupied with preparations in your, Nick, and Phoebe's tents."

RaeChae beamed. "You're slow. Around me, the mind chooses its reality. People don't see me, they see what they expect to see. Meaning if she ties me up in here, she'll be expecting Nick and Phoebe in their tents. I show up, bam, she sees Nick or Phoebe when it's really me."

"Really." Julia paused. "Okay, do your thing, then meet us back between the tents and wagons to burn the contracts."

Julia turned to leave, but RaeChae grabbed her arm. "Wait. Burn the contracts. What about Geppetto? We can't leave him stuck here."

"He's not stuck, RaeChae, we are."

RaeChae huffed. "No, we aren't leaving him."

Julia scratched her nose. She had to convince RaeChae, no matter the delusion about Geppetto, as if he was prisoner to the circus, too. "Look, you said yourself we can't free everyone if I'm trapped. We can't free Geppetto if we aren't free ourselves. This is one step in…"

RaeChae pressed her hand to Julia's lips. "Watch your mouth. Now we have to, you nitwit." She looked out of the tent, then whispered. "Okay, I'm in. Go get Nick to start the fire, I'll hold down the fort." RaeChae released Julia. "But our entire fate is riding on this now. One mistake on your part, 'hell hath no fury' and all that."

Thirty-Three

PHOEBE'S LIPS COPIED THE WORDS she scanned over and over. It'd be just her luck that she'd put the note away and then someone would walk past and take her memory with them. She finally slipped the envelope into her pocket and held her hand over it so she'd feel its presence if she forgot.

Phoebe ducked into the big top as Analiese was leaving. "Oh, I caught you," Phoebe scrambled for words.

Analiese scrutinized her. "Please, don't tell me you have something to say when you don't even remember me."

"I remember you," Phoebe said. "And Geppetto. Names I remember."

Phoebe nodded at Geppetto, who reassured her with a pat on the back.

"Enough," Geppetto said. "What is it, Phoebe? More memory trouble?"

Phoebe's brow furrowed. He knew she had a dark cloud smothering her, the moment of Julia's cut off as if a dream she'd awakened from, or perhaps fallen into. "I don't know about again," she dodged. "I wanted to talk to you, though. Both of you. About your most important moments."

"But you've already told us," Geppetto said.

Analiese edged closer.

"Yes." Phoebe swallowed her nerves. Analiese wasn't one to take

266

lies lightly, especially when it came to her future. "But there's a new one—inexplicably. It has to do with a secret."

"What secret?" Analiese said. "Whose?"

Geppetto's smile froze, and Phoebe hid her own smile by swiping her hair aside. Good, they both had a secret and they both knew it. "I can't tell. In the memory you're both dodging a confrontation with each other. Then, well, black fog. But I'm concerned. I don't want there to be any tension, not between the two who hold this circus together."

Geppetto shook his head with a harrumph. "Don't fret, dear Phoebe. Analiese and I have an understanding."

"I have nothing to say." Analiese pranced out of the tent to prep the puppets, right on schedule.

"Geppetto, I don't mean to cause trouble," Phoebe feigned remorse. "I just—we can't trust her. Maybe it's the black fog talking, the memory loss, the fear, but..."

Geppetto patted Phoebe's shoulder again. "You have little memories. Of course the few memories you hold will have great emotional weight in your judgment of others. But I have everything under control."

Phoebe walked over to a bench and sat with a huff, slouching her shoulders for effect. Tears seemed a little much, but she did appreciate a risky acting opportunity. She settled for a sniffle. "I don't want your trust to blind you and ruin all that we have here. You give us our space, but maybe that's not best in this situation."

"You've never really liked each other, but she's part of our family. I will handle this, you've no need to worry."

"Right," Phoebe said. "I mean, I won't even remember this conversation in a few minutes, so why bother? Maybe we've had this conversation five times already and you know you can appease me by walking away."

Geppetto crossed his arms, his countenance darkening. "You know it's not like that. You've got great intuition, now follow it. If I was stalling 'til you forgot, I'd walk out of the room without another word, problem solved. I never belittle you or mistreat your condition."

Phoebe nodded, but slowly, tentatively; she couldn't entirely agree, not yet.

"Tell you what," Geppetto offered, "what say you and I go see Analiese now? Talk this out."

"Oh, no." Phoebe stood and widened her eyes. "She packs a punch, and you said yourself we don't get on so well. You go. I will...I will trust your judgment if you talk it out with her. Please."

"Go get your tent ready, it's about that time." Geppetto sauntered off, and Phoebe crossed her fingers that this plan was really working.

She yanked the note out of her pocket, before she forgot it all: *Meet back by the wagons.*

"Meet back by the wagons." She chanted the words, her lifeline, her hope, she couldn't forget. "Meet back by the wagons. Meet back by—" but why was she meeting there? Right, for freedom. Somehow. "-the wagons. Meet back by the wagons." She pocketed the note, and muttered one last time under her breath as she ducked out of the big top.

Phoebe sidled around the large tent. A few people already roamed the circus, though no act was open. She couldn't forget. She had to focus, meet back by the wagons.

There went a teenage couple, in that awkward, bump-hands-together stage. *Don't take my memory,* she thought. *By the wagons.* She saw their decision, parking their car in the field and blushingly making way to the circus entrance. What a biggest moment to have—they must be soulmates or cirque folk or something. *The wagons,* she reminded as they passed. *Back by the wagons.*

"Where are you going?" Analiese and Geppetto were approaching.

"Your tent is that way, Phoebe," Geppetto said.

Phoebe looked behind her towards her tent. "Yes, I, I know," she said. "I uhh..." Phoebe rubbed her head, tried to jog her memory. Why was she not headed to her tent? "I'm meeting, there's the meeting."

"Meeting?" Analiese crossed her arms. "What's going on?"

"The wagons," Phoebe said. "Remember, I can't be the only one that remembers. 'Meet back by the wagons.'"

"How would you know that?" Geppetto said. "We just spoke and you were going to your tent."

"I don't know," Phoebe said. "It's ringing in my head like all the things I fight to remember. 'By the wagons. Meet back by the wagons.' I wouldn't make this up."

"Nick!" Analiese yelped. "He was—he was so weird, gave me the silent treatment. Something's going on, and whatever it is, Phoebe's in on it and doesn't even remember."

"Let's go," Geppetto said. "We don't want to miss this meeting."

24

KNOW I NEED TO BE A STEP AHEAD of Analiese and RaeChae, but I very quickly realize I don't know how. I could stay behind with RaeChae, and miss out on wherever Analiese is off to. I don't have a car to follow her, anyhow.

I briefly wonder if I could steal RaeChaeline's car, but dismiss that idea when I realize I don't know where I am going, and I can't steal it quickly enough to follow Analiese while also being subtle enough to secretly follow Analiese.

So, I hop in the car with Analiese. That whole despondent thing coming up again.

I tell myself I'll find a way, some way. I'll be ready when the moment arrives.

I'd like to say I scheme the whole drive there, but really I pout. I still am not quite to their level, but now I am just smart enough to know I'm not up to their level. Hooray.

Analiese pulls in to the Trenchers' drive. I marvel at the garden statue, not for the first time. Yes, the statue is upright again, but nothing like it was before. It has become a patchwork quilt of rock, smashed together into the semblance of a human, a semblance of what it once was. Yet the eyes, they have not changed one bit.

Mrs. Trencher sits under the statue in a delicate chair, proud of the wreckage. She must be *thrilled* to see the car again.

I don't know what we are doing here. Nick won't be here. It is all some charade, to check off our list and demonstrate that I've failed. A ruse to call the deal off.

As Analiese climbs out of the car, Mrs. Trencher waves. "Look," she cries. "It's her!"

I don't understand why she is so enthusiastic about Analiese. But Mrs. Trencher is quick to clarify. She points at the looming patchwork sculpture. "It looks like Julia now. It's Julia now!"

This is the moment. I could take the car. Analiese is further away than me. This time, I could leave her stranded. But, that wouldn't get me anywhere closer to answers. I'd have a car and no place to go. So, I wait.

Mrs. Trencher frowns at me, scrutinizes my face and touches the right side of her mouth. "She got to you too, huh." A great reminder that my face is no longer mine, but some stranger's face that Analiese has sculpted. A reminder of what's at stake if I don't find Nick before Analiese takes off without me.

And it occurs to me that Mrs. Trencher said "too," that whatever operation she'd had on her face could have been from damage done by Analiese. I wasn't sure if that was the right leap to make, but I made it nonetheless and worried I didn't have money to fix my face if Analiese wouldn't or couldn't.

As Analiese asks Mrs. Trencher if she's seen Nick, and as Mrs. Trencher squints and shakes her head, still beaming up at the statue like a lifeline... It hits me that there is someone else who wants answers from the circus folk. And that someone has a car.

RaeChaeline had said that Analiese was using me because she's no good at teamwork. And maybe RaeChaeline had given away the exact trait where I could stand a chance at one-upping them.

That I could work with someone instead of just "conning" them, as Analiese claimed. (Sure, it's conning someone by not conning another, but we're getting somewhere.)

Analiese continues her charade, and I continue mine. "Such a disappointment that Nick isn't here." "Yes, the reconstructed daughter statue is lovely." "We're sorry to disturb you."

And as Analiese turns back to the car, I say, "You go along, Fancy. I'll stay a bit with my friend and catch you back at your place."

Analiese cocks her head and looks at me the way her and RaeChae look at each other when they're talking without words. She thinks I have some grand plan up my sleeves, and I do, but she thinks she is in on it. And probably the only thing she is wondering is if she is okay with the plan I have or if it would sabotage *her* plans. But her poker face is impeccable—maybe she froze it with her magic powers?—so she didn't give that bit away.

I hope it was her magic that gave the poker face, because I want my own poker face right now. I smile nonchalantly, and she forces a smile back. "See you later then, I guess."

She drives off, I wave, perfectly pleasant scene besides the odd sculpture that watches over it all. The instant she turns the corner out of sight, I spin around to Mrs. Trencher. "No time, Mrs. Trencher. She's hiding something."

"Of course she is." She says it so matter-of-factly, like what else would I expect from Fancy/Analiese, and...fair.

"Is the car here? We need to follow."

She leaps out of her seat and heads to the front door. "Let me fetch Mr. Trencher."

Thirty-Four

ICK HAD BEEN ALL BUSINESS up until this point, gathering fuel, lighting the fire, directing the smoke away from circus suspicion, and bombarding Julia with questions to ascertain every detail of the entire plan would succeed. He was still rather skeptical about the elusive author of the note that devised the scheme and vanished, from their presence as well as their memory. Now he was giddy, clapping his hands and beaming. "Now we wait."

He patted Julia's back, as if they had accomplished some gigantic feat, though really it was a meager fire and Julia certainly had nothing to do with it. Still, it was nice to see him happy. Hopeful. Julia wanted that for him.

"Freedom," she murmured. "Yes, well, we don't have long before our bodies are dragged to the tents for puppet state, so if anything will come of this harebrained scheme, it's happening now."

"We'd done our part, at least." Nick sniffled and stared off toward the circus.

The fire licked at the barley they'd scrounged up, hinting at the promise of swallowing the contracts whole. Julia scanned their surroundings. From the side of the barley field, the two men who snuck around were approaching. Maybe they were the meeting. "Dagnabit." Julia was no longer certain of the plan—how could they be working in tandem with these sneaks?

"Huh?" Nick looked past Julia at the others. "Oh, think it's them?"

"Maybe."

"Cheer up." Nick started towards the men. Julia trailed behind. As she neared them, a memory popped in her head. The Forgettable. And his sidekick. Their plan and the notecards and losing their memory. Maybe this could work.

Next she remembered running into them even earlier—the Forgettable showing up in Phoebe's tent while Analiese gave Julia the grand tour, to confirm Julia's identity so he'd know when to appear again for the most important decision. Phoebe couldn't chance remembering that moment for Geppetto to get it out of her, so had found the Forgettable and convinced him to show up.

With that memory came yet another, of chasing them in the barley field; the Forgettable told her to trust him, to go back to the circus, that he was going to free them all. So many memories he took with him every time he walked away. How Phoebe coped with every person being like that for her, Julia couldn't imagine.

The sidekick was pulling out papers—the contracts—from a knapsack. Their plan was working. Everything was falling into place. As soon as RaeChae and Phoebe arrived, they could be free.

"Stop!" As if the thought had summoned her, RaeChae jogged around Nick's tent. "Problem. They're coming."

The words came like a punch in the gut. Julia clenched her teeth, biting back the profanity that bubbled up.

The Forgettable didn't look the least bit fazed. "No matter," he reassured. "The papers are practically burned. As long as Phebes gets here, we'll be good."

RaeChae scowled. "Didn't realize we were in cahoots with you and Jasper for the plan. Should've known, 'cept well, of course I forgot."

The Forgettable snatched the contracts from Jasper and rifled through them. He offered one to Julia, then Nick. He pushed one at RaeChae. "RaeChaeline. Phebes invited me."

"You're kidding." RaeChae jutted her chin up and crossed her arms without accepting. "Pathetic, going back to scum like you."

"Couldn't agree more." Geppetto and Analiese came around the tents with Phoebe in tow. Geppetto's eyebrows and mustache furrowed into a matching set as he took in the scene. His mouth twitched when his eyes landed on RaeCh. Phoebe gasped as she saw the newcomers, and she looked at Julia for reassurance.

The Forgettable pushed past Geppetto, holding out a contract for Phoebe. She tentatively reached for it, but Analiese bumped between.

"Uh uh," she said. "One step closer and I'll sculpt you 'til your feet can't run off, your tongue can't spout lies, and your hands can't hold empty promises."

"Please, she doesn't even know."

RaeChae leaned in and whispered to Julia, "I got this." She pushed through the group to join Analiese and addressed the Forgettable. "She does know. She doesn't *remember*. She doesn't need memories to feel. You weren't even here to know how it affected her. Now get your grubby paws off our contracts so we can burn them and leave you in the dust."

Analiese snatched Phoebe's contract while the Forgettable was distracted. Before Analiese could think, though, RaeChae made a grab for the paper. Jasper and the Forgettable stepped back as Analiese reached for RaeChae's arm. Julia gasped, and Nick held her back, sensing the urge to leap into the thick of it.

"Analiese, don't." RaeChae grunted. "You don't want to."

Analiese squeezed RaeChae's hand.

Bones snapped and popped, coaxing a moan from RaeChae who still refused to release the contract. "We need this, Gep—"

Analiese grasped the contract and pushed RaeChae to the ground, ripping the contract in two—one piece with Analiese, one piece in RaeChae's deformed hand. Analiese clambered on top of RaeChae, shoving her hands at her face.

"Nooo," RaeChae muffled through Analiese's hand as it distorted her face. Analiese again grabbed for the other half, which ripped a few times before finally giving way to her.

RaeChae stumbled to her feet, clutching her hand. Her face was misshapen—mouth pressed in against her neck, nose twisted and eyes bulging, shooting fire at Analiese's triumphant prance.

Julia covered her mouth in horror. The Forgettable's mouth twisted in distaste, a small homage to what had been done on RaeChae's face. Whereas before people couldn't take their eyes off RaeChae due to her timeless beauty, now they wouldn't be able to look away because of her grotesque deformity. Julia wasn't sure how her pride was going to handle that.

Analiese ignored the gawks caused by her destruction. She handed Phoebe's contract pieces to Geppetto. One contract remained in the Forgettable's hand—Julia ran through the list of performers and realized it was RaeChae's. She still hadn't accepted it from him.

The Forgettable took RaeChaeline's contract and tossed it in the fire. "You don't own us, old man. That's one puppet, gone forever. Give it up. We won't stop until Phoebe is free, too."

"I call bull," Geppetto said. "Face it: the only thing you are known for is giving up."

Julia squirmed.

"Not this time." The Forgettable stepped toward Geppetto, but

Analiese stood in the way. Julia wondered if she could finagle her way in, but she wasn't ready for a sculpted deformity. The Forgettable cocked his head—reexamining his approach, no doubt.

"Gep, you know me," he tried. "Don't do this. Not to your son."

Geppetto laughed. "I am simply maintaining status quo. *You* are the lot trying to ruin me, ruin us."

"I would not try to ruin you," the Forgettable said. "I'm trying to tell you I'm your son and I want you back."

"No, I would remember my son—you're tricking me, just like he did, just like they all do."

The man named "Sullivan" must have heard the ruckus and came around the tents behind Geppetto and Analiese. Julia shook her head. *Don't be stupid*, she thought. This wasn't his fight. Julia glanced to Nick, who still held his hand in front of her. He was raising his eyebrows, approving of Sullivan's carelessness.

Julia leaned slightly against Nick's hand, ready to burst forward. She had to step in, keep him from RaeChae's damage. Sullivan was right behind Geppetto now. Julia ran forward. Nick responded, but too late.

"No!" Julia shoved her contract in her skirt's waistband while Analiese prepared herself, but Sullivan grabbed Analiese first. He screamed as Analiese collapsed on him. Julia's only shot was now. She used her momentum to crash into Geppetto, who was taken off guard by Analiese's preoccupation. Geppetto took only a moment to catch up to his situation, then shoved Julia away. Her fury kept her strong, though. Analiese was already finished with Sullivan and turning her attention to Julia.

Julia leaped again, her last chance at saving Phoebe. She grabbed Geppetto's arm that reached out to defend the contract and bit down. Analiese froze for a moment, shocked at the bestial instinct, but only for a moment. She jumped into the fray and ripped at Julia's hair, yanking her away. Julia's arm flailed out, but missed the contract.

"Go!" RaeChae yelled. "Anyone!"

Julia struggled with Analiese, who held her hair tightly but didn't sculpt her. "You're not worth the trouble, brat."

RaeChae and Nick simultaneously rushed Geppetto. He stepped over to the fire, and they adjusted their trajectory, slowing so as not to hit the flames. Analiese pushed Julia to the ground and went after RaeChae, but it was too late. Nick was within arms' reach of the contract.

Geppetto didn't wait to lose—he dropped the paper into the fire. "Wouldn't have you think you beat me so easily."

The flames ate at the paper, and Julia wondered at Geppetto's intent. He did not want them free—why would he burn Phoebe's contract after all that effort to stop them?

The Forgettable voiced Julia's thoughts. "What's your game, old man?"

"Simple," Geppetto said. "Burning the contracts won't work."

Julia tensed. It couldn't be true. She walked over by Nick and stared at the flames. So close, leaping out for the paper in her hand.

"Now, if you hand me the remaining contracts," Geppetto said, "we can forget this ever happened. I'll write Phoebe and RaeChaeline up a new one in no time. All's good as new."

The Forgettable shook his head. "No. You're bluffing. You forget it worked on me."

"It didn't work on you," Geppetto countered. "I couldn't remember you to command anything. A mistake I won't make again now."

Nick tapped Julia's shoulder. He held his crumpled contract over the fire. Julia tilted her head. "No," she whispered.

RaeChae was watching them wide-eyed, either from Nick's act or Analiese's destruction. "You've always been a good bluffer, Gep," RaeChae said. "You gotta trust me."

Nick nodded his head and dumped it in. Julia's heart sped. This had to work now. Julia was the only one left. She pulled the crumpled contract from her skirt.

"Julia, don't," Geppetto said. "Think about this."

"Come on, Jul'," Nick said. "It's okay."

Julia held the contract over the fire. What could it hurt? Either she was free after, or she was still trapped.

"If I must," Geppetto said, "no Pinocchio can escape, and it's time to prove it. Forgettable lad, your contract has never been null and void. It's simple—when Julia drops her contract into the fire, you will be dead. That's all there is to it."

Julia yanked her hand from over the fire. She couldn't be responsible for a death, even if Geppetto was bluffing to keep her under his commands. Nick touched her shoulder.

"Now I know you're bluffing," the Forgettable said. "You wouldn't kill your own son, no matter how estranged."

"My own son would never sabotage my life's work." Geppetto growled. "Clearly, you are an imposter."

"Do it," the Forgettable said. "Julia, don't fall for his tricks. Burn the contract."

"No," she said. "I can't take that risk. Not with your life."

The Forgettable rushed Julia. Analiese, for once not caring what happened, stood back and smirked at the dilemma.

"Burn the contract," the Forgettable repeated.

"I can't."

RaeChae wrapped her arms around Julia's waist, the deformities clenching her ribcage and taking her breath. "Drop it, Julia. We need this now—you can't drag me this far and leave me hanging."

"RaeChae," Nick cautioned.

"I-I can't," Julia said. "He might...die..."

"I don't give one wit what happens to that imbecile. Burn the contract."

The Forgettable pushed Nick to the side and grabbed Julia's arm. "Just like this." He dangled the arm over the fire and pried her fingers.

Julia clenched strong, but RaeChae's force was occupying her energy. She felt her feet give out as she lost her breath, and the Forgettable finally opened her fist. RaeChae released her and she collapsed to the ground, gasping for air.

The fire lapped at her contract and she knew. She was free. She had to be. Hope pressed into her and gave her breath back. She sat up and held her head. It was over.

Julia looked up at the performers around her. Nick was crouched, watching her. RaeChae and the Forgettable glared at each other, as if not wanting to admit the teamwork they exhibited. Jasper watched the scene with arms folded, guarding his thoughts as well as his frame.

Then, the Forgettable dropped to the ground. Julia, seated only inches from his collapsed frame, stared into his blank, wide eyes. "You didn't," she murmured.

Julia reached out and touched his face. Cold, already so cold. This was no natural death.

"No!" Jasper called. He rushed to Julia's side, touching the Forgettable's face, his arms, his chest. But it was long over—there was no life in that body. "You can't," he said. "You can't do this to me. Not to him." Jasper looked up at Geppetto, tears streaming down his face. "Why, you...you can't..."

"Let this be a lesson," Geppetto said. "You can't escape your word. You are under contract."

The Forgettable was dead. Jasper imagined a different story than the one we're telling, perhaps one more like his life when the Forgettable lived. He imagined he couldn't actually leave the body to make some sort of ceremonial arrangement—he'd be forgotten, of course. He imagined the police questioning, but then forgetting everything as the coroner took the body away. And then the coroner forgetting he had a body as soon as he left work, until he arrived the next day.

No, much too confusing. A hassle. The problematic magic of the alive Forgettable would mean Jasper having to stay and bury him somehow without leaving once. Somehow. He wondered about a shovel. About how deep he'd have to bury him in this field to never be discovered. He would need the body, this body that holds all his memories, until he could get home. Just a little longer.

Except, the Forgettable was dead. This story is no longer under the rules of the alive Forgettable. The memories aren't held in this body anymore. They weren't held anywhere anymore. Jasper clenched his fists and looked into the distance. He knew what would come next: the darkness. And he had to be faster than it, had to get ahead of it, to where his memories were stored that the Forgettable couldn't take away.

So, Jasper ran, fast, leaving his unlikely roommate behind. The Forgettable was about to be both Gone & Forgotten.

Geppetto gave a grim laugh. "Didn't take long to scare him off, it seems. Analiese, get the body away from the crowds. We'll take care of it later. The rest of you, we have a show to put on here soon. I will cancel the pre-show, and you will each behave, stay in your tent, and think carefully about how you will support this circus in the future."

Geppetto scrutinized Sullivan, who still stood wide-eyed amongst the group. "You man…" He saw the name tag. "Ah, yes, Sullivan. Get back to work. Julia, you will wait in the big top. Next idiot that leaves their tent will know exactly what it's like to fall to pieces, and that's the end of *that*."

Then, on a more personal note, Geppetto looked sadly at RaeCh. "RaeChaeline, I'd like to think you wouldn't double-cross me."

RaeChaeline frowned and turned up her nose, but didn't say a word.

It was a cloudy evening, perhaps from the smoke billowing through the crowd more so than any fault of the sky. The gloom settled over the fields, suffocating everyone, perhaps as a memorial of the breath it had already taken today.

They should have never lit the fire. To think that burning a piece of paper would change anything? Ridiculous. The problem was more—well—problematic than that. The whining, the begging, a duel over silly scraps of paper—it got them nowhere. Nowhere but dead, that is.

Thirty-Five

ICK MANEUVERED THROUGH THE CROWDS, looking for a sign of Julia as he rushed to his tent. Why hadn't they listened? They should have listened. They shouldn't have tried to free themselves.

No. Of course they should have. They'd failed, but they couldn't give up. Julia was captive now. She shouldn't be captive.

The crowds—so many people, rushing through, rushing to the tents. Here to gawk, stare, laugh at the freaks, laugh at Julia. So wrong. It had to stop, it all had to stop.

But Julia was nowhere to be seen.

Downcast. That's what it was. The hope deflated her features as...as...well, darkness filled his mind; he didn't know why hope was gone. It didn't work, though, and she had given up. He was sure of it. She had shuffled off, head drooped, and he couldn't have that.

But he was back at his tent. His body had dragged him here, that cursed contract, and now he had a choice—stay and live this cursed life with Julia or leave to save them all somehow, only to die.

"Fall to pieces." That's what Geppetto had said, and if he fell to pieces, then there would be no being put back together for him. May as well be Humpty Dumpty.

Nick stroked the walls of his tent, his prison. Soon Julia would have her own prison. Nothing but a show-monkey, trapped with the rest of them.

The details had faded to black, but he knew they'd failed. Yet he couldn't leave it like that. He had to convince Julia there was another way, some other way.

The lanterns flickered; he was sure the flames were mocking him but he couldn't say how. He picked up the nearest lantern. That flame—something about the flame, but it was so black.

Stop! He thought. *Focus.* Julia was hopeless. He had to give her hope, or convince her to hope, if not for the rest of them then at least for herself.

He would find her. He would find another way. With her. Nick blew out the lantern—was that hope in the darkness, or hope dying?—and stepped out of his tent, hoping Geppetto's words didn't hold power for once, that he wouldn't fall to pieces as he'd said.

Thirty-Six

NALIESE HAD MOVED THE BODY a little, but rushed here before properly disposing of it. She had someone to save first, and that came with a sacrifice.

"It's very simple," Analiese said—threatened, really—storming into the big top the instant Julia had arrived. Julia didn't even have time to react before Analiese gripped her throat, in stark contrast from the light touches she usually preferred, to demonstrate how unnecessary force was with her skillset.

"You've got my cirque-mates wrapped around your little finger," Analiese continued, "and one of them will be killed into tiny pieces from Geppetto's curse as they try to keep the sparks of revolution flying. That is, if you aren't out of this tent this instant."

She shoved Julia out of the tent and Julia stumbled to the ground, coughing. She coughed until her tongue fell out, followed by her teeth, forming a grotesque little pile.

She saw Mr. and Mrs. Trencher in the distance as her eyes left their sockets; entering the circus based on a curious flyer and note on their doorstep, here to see what's become of their daughter. But they wouldn't see her now, and she would no longer see them.

Her fingers detached, her ankles, until every piece was crumbling at once and Julia came to a rest. Analiese stood over her, triumphant. She gingerly stepped over the pile of pieces and the puddle of blood, and pranced away into the night.

Thirty-Seven

NALIESE GRABBED NICK the instant he stepped out of the tent. She'd been waiting for him. Her grip was tight on his shoulder and he dared not move, knowing it would only end in bones breaking.

"Nick," she soothed, crooning in his ear. "What were you thinking, leaving your tent? You know you're the only idiot to try. Now Geppetto's words must come true and you will fall to little bitty chunks, like a crumbly bread, or hmm, crumbly pie maybe." She smirked. "Pies are more yummy."

Nick swallowed. Head games. She could keep up with the best of them, keep up with Geppetto, probably even one-up ol' Gep. "A price to be paid I s'pose."

Analiese squeezed tighter, watching his shoulder ooze and flatten, not to bone yet, just to reestablish power. "A price for what? You're not free when you're dead, Nick. But who, that bratty rich girl, Julia? Trying to save her, be a hero? In case you haven't noticed, she isn't crying out, 'Nick, save me!' She's not asking for your help. And you see that fidgety guy, Sylas, running around saving her?"

Nick winced. That uppity guy vying for her affections. A sore subject.

Analiese relaxed her grip and pivoted to face him. "That lover boy, he's not trapped. He's never been trapped here, and as soon as you free Julia, she'll waltz away with her fidgets pal to love him all over the place and leave you here to rot in your teeny tiny pie pieces." Analiese massaged his shoulder. She leaned in and placed a light kiss on his cheek, so close, near touching his lips. "You ready to rot for her, Nick? Do you want to be alone forever while she has her happily ever after without you?"

Analiese pulled away ever so slightly to look him in the eye. He felt her warm breath touch his nose, his cheeks. Warmth, security. Julia could have that without him. Julia could leave him behind.

His eyes glistened, and he blinked. "You drive a hard bargain."

"You can never be alone again. If you choose your side right." Analiese smirked. "Or I could be eating pie to celebrate Humpty's marriage to Paranoid SocioFreak."

Nick shoved Analiese. "Stop," he whined, sauntering back into his tent. "Satisfied? I chill here and you call off Gep's curse."

Analiese followed Nick into his tent. "I already called off Gep's curse." She eyed him up and down and exaggeratedly batted her lashes. "And now we're stuck in here waiting. Whatever will we do?"

"Whatever..." he repeated shakily.

She bit her lip and nodded. "Precisely."

Thirty-Eight

RAECHAELINE DUG INTO THE POUCH at the bottom of her storage, the pouch she hadn't touched in ages, to the item that had started it all. A copy of the very first contract, the one she had signed with Geppetto on that fateful night. "It's the only way," she had said, and it had led them here. To this moment. What she wouldn't do to change that night, or any number of previous choices she'd made that led them to it.

Yet here she was now, with no choice but to move forward. She perused the document she'd created so long before, the document she'd signed her life away on, and she finally found what she was looking for. The one word that could free them all.

She rushed out of the tent; never mind the consequences, it was her only choice. She was too late, though. She only made it in time to see Julia broken and lifeless, Analiese towering in triumph, the shortsighted witch. Analiese traipsed off to Nick's tent, practically bouncing with glee.

RaeChae approached the pile of blood and guts and skin, but there was nothing she could do. Analiese was the one who'd pieced her together last time.

RaeChae crouched over the pieces of flesh. The crowds would arrive any minute; there wasn't much time. Wait. That was it. The solution. The crowds that couldn't be allowed to see this.

"Phoebe," she said, then called louder. "Phoebe! Come quick!"

Phoebe ran out of her tent, looking around with confusion. When she saw RaeChae, she ran over, eyes wide as saucers. RaeChaeline knew she was probably seeing her dripping in blood. She'd have to handle that.

"Phoebe, quick," RaeChae said. "Carry all of this into the tent. Before people see. Can you sew it together?"

Phoebe looked at the pile of a person. Julia.

"Phoebe, listen. Can you sew it?"

"Her," Phoebe said. "Can I sew her?"

"Yes, her. Try, but first take her in the tent where no one will see and start a panic. I'll talk to Gep and get him to release us from our puppet state before it's too late."

RaeChaeline ran off before she could even see if Phoebe was doing as she'd been asked. In the grand scheme of things, it didn't matter. She hadn't been working with Julia from the start, so why should she rely on her now? What mattered was convincing Geppetto.

25

RS. TRENCHER MOVES MORE QUICKLY than decorum would dictate, yet, as I'm sure you can imagine, by the time we get Mr. Trencher moving and hit the road, Analiese has disappeared. So much for my grand plan.

I hate to disappoint the Trenchers quite yet, not without a bit more of an attempt, so I head toward Dr. Evil's lair, however fruitless it seems.

We park a few houses down. I am thankful, at least, that the car fits into this neighborhood so we are more inconspicuous. And as luck would have it, while we sit there waiting for RaeChaeline and Analiese to return with Nick in tow from whatever location they have been to, we find that we've actually caught up. Analiese and RaeChaeline's cars both pull out of Dr. Evil's estate.

Analiese's putters past while Mr. Trencher shoves our heads down out of line of sight from the windows, and RaeChaeline's car follows by without so much as a rattle. While Mr. Trencher holds me down, I move the car from Park and prepare to step on the gas; they aren't getting away this time.

As we follow along, Analiese veers off toward "her" Trencher place, and RaeChaeline continues forward, toward the circus lot. I decide RaeChaeline's circus visit would be more likely to include a Nick sighting, so I follow her and hope I am correct. Mr. and Mrs. Trencher don't complain...perhaps they've worn out their investigation of Analiese and are ready to move on to other options.

She doesn't pull in to the circus lot. She pulls to the side before she gets that far. She exits the vehicle and approaches a rundown diner. Dinah's.

I find the closest parking spot I can while the Trenchers holler at me to hurry. They leap out of the car before I can park, and I race behind them. We all stumble out of breath into the beat-up place, probably looking quite a sight. RaeChaeline is talking to the waitress, and lo and behold, Nick is crouched in a seat at the bar. Just my luck.

The waitress looks at me in shock. I know I've burst into the diner quite dramatically, but she looks at me like I've done something. She gulps, and I gulp, too. RaeChaeline or Analiese's gaze dims in comparison to this one. She knows something; she sees something.

She races up to me, grabs my arm and begins to pull me out of the building. Forgetting her shift, forgetting the customers. "I know where Julia is," she says. "Hurry."

Thirty-Nine

I T STARTED INNOCENTLY ENOUGH. A small campfire to render oaths to ashes. But a fire was never meant to begin in a barley field. Too hungry, it lapped up its contents and found more around it. And as the circus performers began to turn the crowd away, the fire gulped up the field and took the first tent.

Sullivan was the one who noticed first. The man who could never make an impact; at least, that's what he worried. When he learned that his contract to work at the circus included a pretty hefty non-disclosure agreement, he thought nothing of it. No one noticed what he said, anyway.

And once he'd been there long enough to witness the other acts, he decided he was like them. No one noticed, of course; he was just one of the crew. Ordinary, others would think, and sometimes he wondered if that meant the whole world had the same fate as he.

Four seconds. He'd counted it over and over throughout his life, wishing he had counted wrong every time before. Four seconds before his imprints on the world were erased as if they never happened. A four second delay where he could dream of his life having some amount of meaning before it reverted on itself. He wasn't invisible; just close enough.

He'd try to make an impact on the world, the smallest thing; even picking up a piece of trash would prove in vain because it'd quickly be replaced in only...well... four seconds.

He was forgettable, because he never took up any space, neither convenient to have around nor an inconvenience. Just there. But he always tried to change that four second glitch. After all, he'd overheard the performers claiming no one knows for sure how these oddities work.

And so, when the fire crept up to the tent, there was no chance of him putting it out. He could douse the flames for four seconds before they'd return as if they'd always been there. His only hope was for his life. He could dump water, he could call out, and it still would make no difference. He could save no one else. He'd seen the proof in too many four second intervals to count. So, he ran.

But sometimes hope is a flame that won't go out, no matter the proof, no matter the trying. He'd seen it play out so many times. He would count:

One: Hope. He would take whatever action in eager possibility. He would hope that for once he could make some small, minute impact on the world. Not some grand claim to fame, mind you, simply proof he existed and maybe even mattered.

Two: Reaction. Someone or something would respond. It was sticking. It was working. The world would know he was here, or at least, some individual would be relatively aware of his presence.

Three: Dread. Of what comes next. Because he knows what comes next. The dread chases the hope away, a silly childish fantasy. And then...

Four: Reset. The past three seconds exist, but Sullivan's part in them is erased, as if it never was. As if we're still at second one in terms of his piece of the story. And since he's reset to the first second, well, there's hope.

And so, in this moment, there was no reason for Sullivan to hope. There was only reason to run.

But hope doesn't listen to reason. Hope is ready at any time for second one.

Sullivan ran, but he didn't run for his life. He ran to the ticket booth.

One: He began distributing tickets faster than people could pay, whisking them through the line, toward the fire, even shoving a couple to the ground.

Two: His efforts worked. The crowd looked about in confusion. Were they supposed to get in without paying? What's with the shoving, and are those people on the ground okay? Am I safe? Do I need to get away from this volatile jerk? What's with the cacophony up the line?

Three: Dread. He looked back at the tent that was alight, deceivingly peaceful as ever, the flames still yet to explode. It wasn't enough time; four seconds is never enough time. He should have known. How could he never remember second three would come for him?

Four: Reset. As the chaos was calming and the crowd began to move forward, as the man at the ticket booth reached to pull him aside and give him a talking to, as the tickets vanished from the hands they'd been passed into and the people on the ground returned to standing in a blink... Those few seconds were all it took. The fire erupted into a blaze, covering the tent for all eyes to see.

Sullivan shuffled off, a sly smile on his face. They were warned. They were four seconds further away from the danger, and he hoped that was enough. For the first time, his brief seconds had meant something. He had meant something. And now he ran to save his life that now had worth assigned to it.

He glanced back once, just long enough to see the fire race down the line of barley, creating a wall of flame. Screams erupted, and the blessed stampede followed.

Forty

PUT HIM ON THE DEFENSIVE, RaeCh thought. *So he'll never suspect. Defensive.*

While the fire found its first tent to devour, RaeChaeline entered Geppetto's wagon without hesitation, without knocking.

"How—" he started to say, but RaeCh got ahead of it.

"What were you thinking?" She jabbed her finger at his chest. "You're going to bring this circus to ruin with your heat-of-the-moment decisions."

It was Geppetto's turn to interrupt. "Of all the stories of traitors throughout history, I would never have expected you."

"I had things under *control*!" RaeCh yelled. It needed to sound passionate, the injustice and fear of it all. It had to be convincing. "The contracts do nothing. Of course, but you had to barge in and blow my cover, and now you're about to have the cops pounding down our door."

Geppetto laughed. "The cops," he said. "They wouldn't have the gall to involve the cops. No one will believe in this 'magic' we're entrapped in."

Good. He'd forgotten not to trust her.

"Gep. Naive Gep. You actually believed that no one would exit their tent."

"What?" Geppetto's eyes widened. "What's happened?"

RaeCh said, "I'm here because I knew I'd be intact. Because I knew that your little threat wouldn't stop her."

"Her? Julia? Please tell me it's Julia..."

"It's Julia," RaeCh reassured. "But the crowds will be here any minute."

"No," Geppetto said. "We can't let them see. They can't see our finale yet."

RaeChaeline rolled her eyes, though she doubted Geppetto would see. Too caught up in his dreaming. "It's worse than that. They won't see her intact the second before. They won't know it's a trick, they'll call the cops for a brutal slaughter, Gep. We'll be locked up before we can prove that she's fine."

His eyes widened, the danger they were in finally dawning on him. Here was her moment.

"Gep... We have to move her body from public view, and we have to put her together."

"Yes, but we'll never have time with the puppet state about to begin. We'd have to... we'd have to cut things short. Yet the show must..."

"The show must go on. Yes, but the grand show, not the individual tents."

Geppetto paused, considering, then nodded. "You're right. We have to let the tents go, only for tonight..."

"...or we risk the entire show disappearing, never to be seen again."

"Yes, you're right, as always," Geppetto agreed quickly, their kinship returning in an instant, the way they bounced ideas off of each other for a successful business from the start.

He thought for a moment. "We'll spin it as...a rebranding. Yes.

Everything part of the grand show, all the acts together at once, a—a—kaleidoscope of wonder rather than drip by drip."

He paused, thought a moment longer. "It'd be nice to have more time for a rebranding, but desperate times and all."

"Perfect," RaeCh said. "Your genius at work." As if it was his idea all along, not her own implanted into his thoughts.

"Let it be done. No puppeteering 'til the grand show. You and Analiese take care of the body and keep the others in their place. I'll start plans for tonight."

"Consider it done."

"And RaeCh...you still have my heart."

"And you have mine." RaeCh opened the door and stepped out. Now, to get rid of the crowds and control the narrative.

Lucky for RaeChaeline, the crowds were already handled. A wall of flames raced across the barley, and the crowd screamed.

RaeChaeline was the picture of calm as she yelled, "Gep, quick!" He opened the door and bumped her head as she called out, already warned by the panic of the people.

"Get Julia," he said. "We need her."

"I'll handle it. You get out of here."

Geppetto shook his head. "I'm getting that other body. The fire will be a good cover." With that, he was off. He didn't see RaeChaeline turn away from Julia's body, away from Phoebe and even Analiese and Nick, and follow Geppetto. It was time to break the curse.

Forty-One

ICK JUMPED UP when the pandemonium broke out. "Something's wrong."

Analiese sighed. "They must have found the body."

Nick gave Analiese a quizzical look. "Body? What body?"

Analiese patted the ground. "Sweet, naive Nick," she soothed. "Someone had to step out of their tent in time to save you. Someone had to trigger the curse, someone who could recover from it."

Nick glowered. "What did you do?"

"Julia sacrificed herself. For you and the rest of us." Analiese combed her fingers through her hair nonchalantly. "She'll be put together in no time, I'm sure, but there is the matter of her body lying in a pile for the world to discover and all that. A little bit of a fiasco, I imagine."

Without a word, Nick stormed out of the tent. He should have known. But then he saw it wasn't body parts eliciting the riot. It was the fire, eating up everything in sight. The wall had engulfed RaeChaeline's tent and was towering towards his. His gaze followed it back to its place of origin, the fire where they burned the contracts. It was only the wind tugging the opposite direction that gave him a fighting chance. The little curls of flame dancing amongst the grass were inches from touching the fabric. He was next.

He ripped the cloth entrance. "Analiese, hurry!"

She smiled coyly and sidled toward him. "If you insist."

Then the flames hit. They hungrily climbed the tent as Nick grabbed her and pulled.

Analiese turned and gasped. "Run."

The flames lapped at them just as they exited.

"Julia!" he yelled.

"Nick, get out of here."

"Where's Julia? She'll need help."

Analiese grabbed his hand and twisted. This wasn't her usual slow, excruciating, sadistic forming. She was in a hurry, given the circumstances. There was a crack and a snap, not even heard above the ruckus.

Nick cried out and jumped back. "What are you doing?"

Analiese jumped on him and he collapsed to the ground. "You have to trust me," she said as she grabbed his hand and wrenched it back. He screamed.

She climbed off of him. "Get up," she said, "you have to run."

Nick struggled without the use of his hands, and she reached out and pulled him to his feet. "What was that for?"

"You're of no use to Julia now. Run."

Nick's eyes went wide. "How dare you! I have to help..."

A large crack boomed through the air, and the tent caved in. Analiese and Nick ducked and covered their faces from the too-close flames.

"You have to live," Analiese coughed out. "I'll get Julia as soon as I can stop worrying about you. The faster you leave, the faster she's saved."

Nick paused. "Then the others, I can help the..."

"The others are already running like we should be. Catch up to them."

He could have argued, but there's no arguing with Analiese. And she was right; he was no use to Julia, and long behind the others now.

"Save her," he said, and he stumbled off toward the crowd.

Forty-Two

NALIESE RAN TOWARD THE BIG TOP amidst the smoke, partially from memory and partially from the wall of flame ahead that she assumed was the big top alight. A figure stooped over Julia's body.

Analiese cursed. No one was supposed to still be here. As Analiese approached, the figure took shape.

"Phoebe!" Analiese yelled over the roar. "What are you doing? We have to go."

Phoebe held her skirt like a makeshift bag, holding a pile of Julia's body parts as she scooped more in. "I can't leave her," Phoebe said. "Not like this."

Analiese grabbed her arms, causing some of Julia to fall back to the ground. "Get a grip. Do you want to die here with her?"

Phoebe was as stubborn as Analiese, though, nearly as calculating and much less self-serving. "If you're interested in my life, help me carry her." She returned to scooping up the pieces of Julia.

Analiese looked around at the flames heading straight their way. She remembered what Geppetto had said, that she was concerned about what harm she could do because of the harm she had done. And she wasn't ready to add a corpse to that list. Especially not this corpse. Not her.

They wouldn't make it out, not hauling an extra body along.

But she had a better chance of saving Julia with the extra help. And if she could convince Phoebe to save her life, maybe they could save Julia together before saving each other.

Analiese dropped to the ground and began scooping up an arm here, an ear there. She dropped the ear in Phoebe's skirt and pulled out half a leg and a foot. "Phoebe, put the tiny pieces in your skirt. I got the larger ones."

Analiese grabbed the head last—earless, noseless, eyeless, a sight to behold, though she simply chose not to look. "Let's go."

The fire blocked their exit through the parking lot. Their only choice was the field ahead. Phoebe trotted, ever so careful with her bag of human. Analiese, on the other hand, ran recklessly ahead.

A ditch between the circus and field lay in wait. Simply a drop where the dirt went from packed in to loose for sowing. Analiese stumbled at the edge, dropping almost every piece she carried into the ditch. Phoebe climbed down more cautiously.

"Hurry," Phoebe said, grabbing the foot that Analiese had meant to take off her hands.

Analiese looked back at the fire, felt the loose dirt beneath her hands. They didn't have time to escape with their lives and Julia's body.

"Stop." Analiese began digging. "Put her here."

Phoebe scrunched her nose. "We can't leave her."

"Either we don't and we all die, or we do and we all stand a chance of surviving."

Phoebe paused only a moment—that was all she had. Then she dropped the contents of her skirt into the hole Analiese was digging. She ran and picked up the pieces Analiese had dropped. An arm here, a heavy torso there. When they'd piled up all the parts they could see, Phoebe began to pile dirt on top.

Analiese glanced at the pile. "Stop!" She searched the ditch.

Phoebe paused, but only for a moment before continuing. They didn't have time for discussion. "What?"

"The head," Analiese said. She looked around again, then climbed out of the ditch towards the flames mere feet away.

Phoebe looked at the pile she was burying. Sure enough, no head. Analiese jumped into the ditch a moment before the fire took hold of the drop-off. She carried the head like a football and placed it in the pile before burying it.

"It has a cut," Phoebe noticed.

"From dropping it, I presume. Hopefully just a surface injury." The heat was upon them now, a furnace a yard away.

"Run!" Analiese jumped up and grabbed Phoebe's arm and pulled. Phoebe kept adding dirt to the pile though.

"Not yet," Phoebe said. "She's not safe yet."

"We have to go," Analiese said.

Then with the fire mere inches away, Phoebe agreed, but not before being singed by the flames.

Analiese dragged a reluctant Phoebe through the field, whether in shock from the burns or simply concerned for Julia's wellbeing, Analiese wasn't sure.

Analiese wasn't heartless, either. She hoped the dirt fully covered the body. She hoped it was enough. She hoped she hadn't abandoned her sister, Julia, to be burnt to a crisp. But she had to be pragmatic and save the person she still had with her.

Her and Phoebe raced away from the flames. The ditch full of dirt and little in the way of fuel slowed its fury, but only for a moment. Only enough for them to escape with battle wounds.

Analiese led Phoebe down the road toward the gathering of witnesses, all the people who had escaped. Nick was in a straitjacket, mumbling and being escorted who knows where. *People are so quick to write us off as lunatics*, she thought. But maybe it'd keep him quiet long enough for her to disappear.

Medical vehicles had arrived, so Analiese headed that direction. Phoebe followed without a word, numb and in shock. The medical staff treated Phoebe for second degree burns, the worst of the injuries they'd seen so far that night, though they anticipated more casualties as the night progressed.

Analiese escaped with only mild burns—because she cowered before Phoebe did, some might say, though she tried to instead tell herself it was because she saved Phoebe's life. At any rate, Analiese refused to be consoled by the medical staff on hand.

Both her and Phoebe had streaks of blood covering them and their clothes, but Analiese reassured them it wasn't theirs. The staff didn't think to ask who it belonged to, and of course Analiese didn't elaborate. She would let them assume it must be someone else they were already treating.

Then, she saw familiar faces from a lifetime ago, faces she wasn't sure she wanted to see again. Certainly not now. Mr. and Mrs. Trencher. She'd never been given the luxury of calling them mom and dad. They were searching the crowd for the daughter they wouldn't find, while the daughter they didn't want to remember was suddenly in their way. The menace, the curse that they'd abandoned before she could even walk, proving today to be all they feared. And she couldn't face that.

Analiese pushed through the crowd as fast as she could. Her hands moved from shoving people out of her way to forming her skin. Pressing in here, pushing and pulling there, a gentle touch and a firm grasp in turn. She twisted her hair up high, stretching until a tight bun crowned her head. She pursed her lips tightly until only the seeable portion of the lips existed. Then only a mild nudge to the nose and a scrape of her fingernail along her cheek for a dimple to form, one that would stay permanently, more like a scar than a beauty mark. (Or are those one and the same? She would ponder and hope in the days to follow.)

Having transformed her identity in mere seconds, *Goodbye, Julia*, Analiese thought as she turned down a sparsely populated side street, never to be seen again... (Or, so she hoped until Jasper—I mean, Max—came knocking.)

She left the scene of the inferno without a word, as if she was unscathed. Phoebe wouldn't remember this night to tell about the body she buried or the person who came up with the scheme in the first place. No one would believe a word Nick said. RaeChaeline and Geppetto were nowhere to be seen. Analiese could move on with little repercussions and fewer companions.

26

Clue 17: Waitress at Dinah's Fine Dining seems to know where Julia is. And Nick is at the diner, too.

DON'T UNDERSTAND WHAT IS HAPPENING. I don't understand why this Dinah lady is pulling me out of the restaurant so quickly for Julia, like she couldn't have told the Trenchers or anyone else all this time. For some reason she was waiting for me.

When RaeChaeline rushes to follow, pushes past the Trenchers who are close behind, she says, "What do you mean, you know where Julia is? You can't know."

"I do," the waitress says.

"Phoebe, wait," RaeChaeline says. "The car is right here. Let's go get her."

Phoebe, as it turns out, stops and walks back to the car RaeChaeline stands in front of, and we all pile in. Me, the Trenchers, Phoebe of course, RaeChaeline, and Nick, who's been meandering behind as well. Sure, there's another car available, but who has time for that? Six people in a car that was not made for six people, and we couldn't care less. The mystery is about to be solved!

As we drive, I don't have time to process the good news, that I apparently haven't kidnapped Phoebe. That she's been living—

maybe not her best life, but a life—right under our noses this whole time. And that maybe RaeChaeline has known about it, too.

Phoebe leads RaeChaeline back to the circus lot and we all pile out. Phoebe rushes into the burnt field, and it's then I know that we aren't here to get Julia; we are here to get her body.

Phoebe leads us through the lot, her eyes frantically searching, I assume reliving the memories of that night. We race past the wagons watching with their secrets, about to be uncovered, I think, and somehow wonder if the wagons would or could retaliate for it. Or perhaps they are grateful to get this off their chest. We go past princesses and wolves and pumpkins, beckoning us further in to find the tale's ending. Fairy tales aren't always happy ever after.

Phoebe sees a ditch and runs to it, drops to the ground, and begins clawing at the dirt with her hands. RaeChaeline drops to the ground at her side and helps. The Trenchers and Nick look on, frozen in shock and grief and terror of what must come next. I guess I must freeze, too, for a moment, because I see them digging while I'm not. But a moment later, my legs work again, and I drop to help.

Phoebe cries out, a painful wail. She's found the first piece; at first, it looks like she's holding up a muddy stump, a small log from the bonfire, perhaps. But of course. It's human. A limb.

She lays it down gingerly and covers her mouth as tears pour down her face. The Trenchers cover their mouths, too, and Mrs. Trencher collapses to the ground by our side. Nick grasps her shoulder, either to comfort or to keep himself from collapsing as well.

RaeChaeline keeps digging, never letting the emotion hit her long enough to stop the work that must be done, and she pulls out the head. A hand. An ear. She keeps piling the pieces up, and my stomach recoils when I realize this is worse than whatever fate came to Ferguson. This body had been chopped to smithereens.

I turn to vomit into the ditch, away from the people both assembled and dismantled. I guess that's my natural reaction to dead bodies in fields.

I don't know what part I've had in this. But I have to make it right to the Trenchers. I have to find every piece of their daughter to return to whatever gravesite she belongs in. Certainly not here. We dig more of the trench, into the clay and far to either side, until we can find no trace of disturbance. The grave was shallow and unpacked, and the adrenaline keeps us moving. Phoebe digs longer than all of us; we have to pull her away.

We pile back into the car, grimy, covered in snot and vomit and blisters and mud and...well, with a corpse. And the adrenaline wears off quickly as RaeChaeline pulls in to Dr. Evil's.

"W-where are we burying her?" I ask.

"No!" Mr. Trencher responds. "W-we have to go to Dr. Wise. He can help."

RaeChaeline opens his car door and pats him on the back. "Analiese can help," she says. "It's always been Analiese."

Forty-Three

T HE FLAMES TOWERED ON ONE SIDE, the lifeless stretch of field to the other, as RaeChaeline followed Geppetto down the alley. Any moment the wind could change course, bring the deadly flames with it, but Gep was too busy dreaming to notice.

That's what RaeCh was for. Always the practical one, simultaneously killing and feeding his buzz with the tedious steps necessary to make the dreams reality.

No one knew better than them that dreams require sacrifice. They'd sacrificed their lives before, each of them.

The problem being, she wasn't sure Geppetto would be ready to sacrifice again—not now, not in this way. If he knew what she was here for, he wouldn't let it happen. There would be no convincing or swaying, not for this. She would have to explain herself, yes, but only once it was too late for him to stop her.

So, she followed behind. As long as he didn't hear her, she would remain invisible, and the crackle of the flames and the screams of the crowd ensured the sound of her presence was masked.

Geppetto reached the origin of the chaos, the makeshift fire pit. On the other side of the alley, somewhere in the field, was the body Analiese had left behind. Near the abandoned drive, but also not too far from the road. Too close to the firetruck and ambulance rushing past, lighting their faces in a brief moment of terror. But they sped on, toward the true emergency, the tower of flames near the crowd. Not the two lonesome souls sandwiched within murder.

Geppetto looked around, confirming his surroundings as he searched for the body. And there were no vehicles, not yet, but of course, he saw his follower in the distance. RaeCh.

"What are you doing?!" Geppetto yelled over the flames. "You're supposed to get Julia or all hope is lost."

RaeCh approached. "Leave the body, Gep. The answer isn't here."

"We had a plan."

"There's only one way…"

"Well, then, what is it? If you're so certain, what is it?" He marched up to her, frazzled, on edge. Too many threats to his dreams, too many sacrifices about to all come to nothing.

"Please," RaeCh said, backing up, closer to the flames. "Trust me. I'm still for you, I'm always for you." And she pulled out the knife.

"Wha—"

"I thought it through." RaeCh backed toward the flames and lifted the knife to her chest. "You know me, I'm not impulsive."

"Don't." He rushed toward her. "Let's talk this through." The flames licked at her, just out of reach. His arm was outstretched toward her, but she was just out of reach—fifteen feet, then ten, then five…

"The contract calls for sacrifice."

He was on her, grabbing her wrist, pulling it away from her, pleading. The flames towered over them ready to devour, and he was right here.

"It calls for death, Gep." Her wrist stopped fighting him, flung into him, the knife stabbing his stomach. "It calls for *your* death, Gep." A tear trailed down her cheek.

His eyes bulged, his mouth gasped.

RaeCh gasped, too. Did the betrayal sting as much as the blade? "I'm so sorry," she whispered. She pulled the knife out of his chest, and he collapsed. She knelt at his side.

"Rae—" he sputtered. "Wh—"

"I'm going to make your dreams come true," she said. "I promise."

His stare froze, his body quieted, settled. He could finally rest easy, while RaeCh handled things. At least, that's the version she comforted herself with. She couldn't dwell on the fact she drained the life from her companion's body. The one she'd been through everything with and for. He was gone, at her hands, and she was now alone. The weight of his dreams rested on her shoulders, but more than that, the burden of living rested on her shoulders.

She gripped his arm and pulled, pushed her weight under his shoulders and lifted. She wrapped her arms under his and began to drag him away from the flames. A car approached on the road, and she ducked. It turned into the drive, much too close. It stopped. A figure opened the door, stepped out, and waved at the wall of flames.

"Looks like quite the tussle," the voice said. "Gep always tried too hard, didn't he?"

Dr. Evil.

RaeChaeline stood and approached him. "He always dreamed of a better world."

Dr. Evil laughed. "A better world for him, maybe. The world is just dandy. But this fire puts a damper on things; it'll be fun to see how he gets out of this one."

Blood rushed to RaeChaeline's face. "He's not getting out of this one." She bent over and lifted Geppetto's hand.

Dr. Evil pursed his lips. "Oh my. That is quite disappointing."

"I thought you might think so."

"We can't have that," he said. "Get him in the car. Now."

RaeChaeline smiled. It felt forced, but she should appreciate this moment. Things were going exactly as planned.

27

E WAIT FOR ANALIESE. She never comes.

The waiting room of the clinic has a different feel now. A mixture of hope and despair. No longer just a place I was sneaking into and being tortured. Somehow, all that is past with the recognition of a body in pieces.

Nick rocks back and forth, mumbling a prayer. The Trenchers rest their heads on each other, resigned.

I now know who I am, and where everyone is except Analiese. I even kind of partially understand what happened. And now we're back to Fancy's question: "What are you gonna do when you find out you were never a part of the circus?" And I don't know. I don't think any of us know what to do after what happened, and that's why we're here. (And also, that's why Analiese isn't here, right?)

Dr. Evil approaches and speaks to RaeChaeline quietly. She responds, "He doesn't remember anything. It's the same darkness."

He says something else I can't hear, then approaches me. "You don't remember who you are...?"

"Nope."

"Ever since... well..."

"Since the circus vanished. It's some curse or prophecy or something."

"Oh?"

I'm not sure what I am supposed to say (or not say) to this guy. I mean, RaeChaeline calls him Dr. Evil, and she's bad enough. So, I pick the words I say carefully, bordering between lies and truth.

"I've found the circus and Julia and fragments of a past life. Not much, but it should have been enough, you'd think. And my mind doesn't remember. Nothing comes back, only darkness. And that's all well and good, but not even a spark of light, not a tug at the heart, nothing that says I should feel something about what I've found. Just...blank. And if I don't feel something, if my mind and my heart don't remember it, then maybe I'm caught up in the wrong story."

Dr. Evil's eyes spark halfway through my speech, a speech I almost convinced myself was fully truth. "Your mind and your heart..." he mutters. His hand shoots up and waves at RaeChaeline.

"We've been going about this wrong, RaeChaeline. We don't need to fire the neurons in his brain."

I jump up from my seat and nearly high-tail it to the door, but he grabs me.

"Not you, rascal. Gep. The solution is right under our noses."

"What is it?" RaeChaeline says, more hope in her voice than I've ever heard, as far back as I remember.

"We need to use the neurons already firing in his heart."

RaeChaeline looks quizzically at him, hope waning quickly. "What do you mean? Everything's wasted."

Dr. Evil releases his grip on me and walks toward the hall, toward Geppetto, likely to do mad scientist things on him. But he changes his mind and walks back to RaeChae.

"Of course, he's past saving there, too; it's been too long. But!"

"Tell me."

Dr. Evil lifts his finger knowingly. "Gep may have transferred his neurons to someone else."

RaeChae shakes her head. "Ferguson is dead, too; worse off than Gep."

"Not kin, silly! What sort of medical student are you, thinking I mean kin?!"

RaeChaeline huffs, clearly not used to this treatment.

Dr. Evil continues his mad ramblings. "He's given his heart away. He truly loved someone, and we can only hope my meddling didn't get in the way."

"Stop," RaeChaeline says. "It's not the woman he loved. He gave *me* his heart. If what you're saying is true, I have the power to bring him back."

"Yes," Dr. Evil says, "I believe so. It all adds up." He ponders a moment, then adds, "But not just him, you know. You could bring everyone back. When Gep gave you his heart...Gep also gave you his power."

RaeChaeline's eyes widen, and she steps back. She looks around the room, at all the hopeful and weary gathered.

She opens her lips, pauses for the right words: "Analiese will return to fix Julia when Gep walks out of this building. Until then, none of you will find me." And she runs out the door.

We chase after her car, but she is gone. I say "we" generally, but Dr. Evil knows better. He stays put. Mr. and Mrs. Trencher more walk briskly than chase. The rest of us jog, not quite certain what we are running from or to. Except Nick, who sprints like his life depends on that car.

True to her word, no one could find her.

And this comes back around to what was said in a different piece of this story. The question of if there ever is an end to a story. We are all mid-story, touching snippets of other stories. And I suppose it's fitting for me—Max, Jasper, whoever I am—the person with no clear beginning, to pose that question in my journal, my piece of the tale. One story's ending is also the beginning of another, perhaps, which means maybe I have a chance at a beginning now, too? It's too philosophical for me to be sure, but I can hope.

What I do know is, this isn't a book with tidy closure, certainly not yet. It's only a setup, a snippet, of all the other stories we're in the midst of.

And so, while we balk in the drive, back in the clinic, through the door, down a hall, and into the last room on the right, a corpse's eyes open.

THE END

The Story Continues...

AECHAELINE ISN'T ONE TO LEAVE a mess behind. She'd handled—hopefully—Julia and Gep's resurrection earlier. But there was still one other body needing her words.

It would be more tricky, only knowing his false name and his connection to Max, nothing else. As she drove, she rehearsed carefully in her mind what words might help—Max's roommate...? No. The man known as Ferguson...? No. No idea if people knew him as that. The man whose ID said Ferguson E. Tibble. That. Super specific.

Then, she opened her mouth, forming the words with her tongue silently to practice. She only needed to tie the sentence to herself in some way now. She whispered in hope, "As I approach his body, the man whose ID said Ferguson E. Tibble will rise..." As she turned onto the road past the barley field though, her words twisted, as they're wont to do.

Ferguson's body did rise, but not on its own. Police lights flashed and crime scene tape fluttered in the breeze. A stretcher was raised, with his still very much dead body on it, and placed in a van. Her stomach clenched, and she gritted her teeth. She drove past without slowing.

RaeCh didn't know where she was going, or what it would help. Once again, the gift Gep had bestowed on her was too much to bear, too much to grapple with. It was enough to resurrect him—hopefully—to give them a second chance. But it also doubled the chances of their destruction. So she ran, much like Analiese, knowing it prevented nothing, knowing she was simultaneously helpless and powerful beyond imagination…

…

Return to the world of Unfixed, where dead bodies don't always stay dead. The Circus of Strange Marvels is under new ownership, an investigation is under way, and doctors both wise and evil have their own schemes.

Travel through months following the circus inferno and decades into its past, discovering new characters that have been creeping about far longer than you, dear reader.

Ladies and gents, distinguished guests, you've only just witnessed the setup. The real show is about to begin…

…

*Buy now at **AmyLSauder.com/Picked-Up-Pieces***

~Couldn't do it without you~

To Dr. Barr's Uncanny Literature class, with the final project of writing our own uncanny fiction and a research paper on it. Julia wouldn't exist without the great stories, discussions, and feedback from you all.

To Chrissy, somehow determined that Julia's story was not done after she died a second time in her short story, and telling me I need to finish it. This story wouldn't exist without you. (And don't worry, I know this isn't the end and I still need to "finish it.")

To all the early readers, the first fangirls and fanguys, who held on to the snippets for…let's not talk about how many years…and fell in love with it and kindly pestered me with encouragement, motivated me to continue, and bore with me in my lengthy timeline as I wove this intricate tale. You the real MVPs: Yasmeen, Kim, Megan, Paul, Jenn, Monica, Laura, Amber, Hope, Abigail… Did I miss anyone? It's been too long to keep track (but ssh, don't talk about how long it's been…) That enchanted circus book I keep talking about is finally here, and you had a part to play in that!

Many a #WritersSlumberIt with Megan, writing morning with Jenn, and writing days with Kim and the King's Pen kept this book trucking along. Let's have many more, mmk?

To the King's Pen writer's group and EC writing buddies, who walked me through realizing that I want to be a writer and who helped me identify my writer's voice. And who read all my cliché and boring drafts of writing, providing honest feedback so I could become a debatably-competent writer.

To Her Majesty's English Tearoom writers, who keep me moving on this whole writing-as-a-business thing even when I just wanna hide at my computer.

To the love of my life, the best support of my writerly dreams, who surprises me with Cirque du Soleil tickets, book-themed birthday cakes, & tshirts with my book on it; who drives hours without sleep for a booklaunch, and allows me way too many circus trinkets around the house, and watches for Little Free Libraries on every drive. And besides all that, loves and supports me outside of my identity as a writer. I'd get sappy and say "You'll always have my heart," but considering how that turns out in this particular book, instead I'll say I'm so glad we met mid-story.

To the magnificent stories already out there, all the tales that faithfully inspire me in making my own stories. Specifically inspirational to this story: The Great Gatsby, The Legend of Sleepy Hollow, Princess Bride, Sandman, the Map of Time series, Heroes, and the Inkheart trilogy.

To my readers, all of you who believe in this more than I do.

~We did it!~

Author's Note:

Circus continues to inspire through its many forms in both history and imagination. I hope this story gives even a taste of that awe to you readers.

While researching, I visited Baraboo, Wisconsin and its Circus Museum. It is there in the wagons exhibit that I encountered the fairy tale wagon that inspired each performer's residence in Unfixed. I encourage you to visit and feel that sense of magnificence approaching these larger than life wagons.

As of publication, more on this wagon's history can be found at www.circuswagons.org/tableaus/fairy-tales-tableau-75

~Liked it? Or didn't?~

The book world needs you!

...

Lend the superpowers of an honest review on Goodreads, Amazon, your social media, wherever. Your reviews help readers choose a book they'll enjoy, and help authors find their readers. It's a win-win-win-win-win-win... You get the picture.

...

~Be the reviewer~

~the world needs today~

~The party ain't over!~

Tag your fanfiction, fanart, & headcanon:

#UnfixedWorld

...

Send it my way:
Website: AmyLSauder.com
Facebook: /AmyLSauder
Twitter: @AmyLSauder
Instagram: @AmyLSauderCreations

About the Author

Amy L. Sauder is a creative and a writer of introspective psychological stories, including the quirky mystery "I Know You Like a Murder." She lives on the edge of an enchanted wood with her husband Josh and her mannequin Delilah.